A very real ~~...~~ *red*
on the shor ~~...~~

Ben Powell, the ~~...~~ Carlie had hoped to avoid.

She stifled a gasp. Dressed in his crisp military uniform, Ben wasn't a man to fear. Just as certainly, he wasn't a man to love. But he was definitely as cruelly handsome as the images she'd tried not to conjure up in her mind over the past ten years.

His sensual lips were compressed into a firm, uncompromising line. Honed by a decade in the army, he was angular and stern. Not a trace of the youthful features—features she'd held dear in her heart—remained.

Where was the laughing, loving boy she'd once hoped to marry? This man stood ramrod-straight, his uniform starched, his cap square on his head.

And he glared at Carlie with undisguised hatred....

Dear Reader,

Well, it's that loving time of year again! Yes, it's February—and St. Valentine's Day is just around the corner. But every day is for lovers at Silhouette **Special Edition,** and we hope you enjoy this month's six novels dedicated to romance.

The February selection of our THAT SPECIAL WOMAN! promotion is *Sally Jane Got Married* by Celeste Hamilton. You met Sally Jane in Celeste's last Silhouette Special Edition novel, *Child of Dreams*. Well, Sally Jane is back, and a wedding is on her mind! Don't miss this warm, tender tale.

This month also brings more of your favorite authors: Lisa Jackson presents us with *He's My Soldier Boy,* the fourth tale in her MAVERICKS series, Tracy Sinclair has a sparkling tale of love in *Marry Me Kate,* and February also offers *When Stars Collide* by Patricia Coughlin, *Denver's Lady* by Jennifer Mikels and *With Baby in Mind* by Arlene James. A February bevy of beautiful stories!

At Silhouette **Special Edition,** we're dedicated to publishing the types of romances that you dream about—stories that delight as well as bring a tear to the eye. That's what Silhouette **Special Edition** is all about—special books by special authors for special readers.

I hope you enjoy this book, and all of the stories to come.

Sincerely,

Tara Gavin
Senior Editor

Please address questions and book requests to:
Reader Service
U.S.: P.O. Box 1325, Buffalo, NY 14269
Canadian: P.O. Box 1050, Niagara Falls, Ont. L2E 7G7

LISA JACKSON

HE'S MY SOLDIER BOY

SPECIAL EDITION®

Published by Silhouette Books

America's Publisher of Contemporary Romance

To my family:
Mark, Matthew and Michael

 SILHOUETTE BOOKS

ISBN 0-373-09866-9

HE'S MY SOLDIER BOY

Copyright © 1994 by Susan Crose

LISA JACKSON

was raised in Molalla, Oregon, and now lives with her husband, Mark, and her two sons in a suburb of Portland, Oregon. Lisa and her sister, Natalie Bishop, who is also a Silhouette author, live within earshot of each other.

The Legend of Whitefire Lake

*It is said that when the God of the Sun creeps
above the mountains and aims his flaming arrow to
the sea, sparks and embers drop into the lake,
causing the mists to rise like white fire on the water.*

*The man who drinks of this water before the mists
are driven away by the sun will inherit much wealth
and happiness and will be destined never to leave
the hills surrounding the lake. But the man must sip
the magic water and drink only until his thirst is
quenched. For if he takes more of the sacred water
than he needs, the God of the Sun will be angry and
the man will be cursed. He will lose his wealth and
that which he loves most on earth will be stolen
from him.*

PROLOGUE

Whitefire Lake, California

The Present

Prologue

Carlie Surrett!

That woman had been the bane of Ben Powell's existence for over eleven years and he'd thought...no, he'd *vowed* he would never lay eyes on her again.

"Yeah, and you're a damned fool," he said to himself as he brushed off the snow that had collected around his collar. Still cursing his luck, he yanked open the door of his secondhand pickup and reached inside. A six-pack of beer was on the worn seat, and he slipped one of the long-necks from the carton. With a frown, he opened the bottle by placing the edge of the cap on a rusted fender and snapping down hard—a trick he'd learned ages ago when he'd first enlisted. The cap spun off into a snowbank and foam spewed over the lip of the bottle to run down his fingers as he lifted the beer to his mouth and took a satisfying pull.

Why couldn't he get Carlie out of his mind?

Muttering oaths under his breath, he kicked the door shut and stared at the rubble that had been his sister Nadine's lakeside cabin. Once charming, the cottage was now only twisted black metal, charred beams and a sagging soot-covered chimney. Ash and debris. Nothing worth saving.

Nadine had asked him to rebuild it. His eyes narrowed on the snow drifting on the cold pile of ash. Did she really want to give him a job or was her offer merely a handout to her only surviving brother, a man who had to start over in this shabby little town? After her wedding today, Nadine would be able to build a damned palace on this side of the lake. She could hire a bevy of architects, builders, and yes-men who would bow and fawn over the new Mrs. Hayden Garreth Monroe IV.

Damn! He should be pleased, he told himself. Nadine had struggled for years. But was marrying Monroe, that class-A bastard born with a silver spoon wedged firmly between his teeth, the break she deserved? Why not just sell her soul to the devil?

And why invite Carlie to the ceremony?

"Son of a bitch." Angry at himself and the world in general, Ben picked his way over the frozen path to the dock. His knee hurt like hell, compliments of embedded shrapnel from that skirmish in the Middle East, and his pride had been bruised and battered over the course of the past decade, starting over a decade ago in this very town. With Carlie Surrett. Beautiful, seductive, treacherous Carlie. She'd managed to destroy Ben's brother as well as rip Ben's world apart in the bargain.

And now he'd have to face her again. All because of his sister and her insistence that it was time to let bygones be bygones. "Thanks a lot, Nadine."

Through the snow swirling to the ground, he shot a glance across the angry gray waters of Whitefire Lake where lights glowed warmly from the windows of Monroe Manor—Hayden's mansion on the lake. Smoke curled lazily from the chimney and twinkling Christmas lights, still glowing though the holiday season was long over, glimmered in the gloomy day. *I hope you know what you're doing, Nadine,* he thought anxiously. She was the only person left in the world that he really cared about. He'd never forgiven their mother for turning her back on the family when the going got tough, and his father...well, the old man had never gotten over Kevin's death...which brought Ben's thoughts back to Carlie again. Always Carlie. He scowled darkly, then took another long swallow from his bottle.

A north wind, raw as January, blew across the choppy surface of the water and sliced through his dress uniform.

Today was the big day—the day of reckoning, or rejoicing, of ignoring decade-old feuds and, in Ben's opinion, of doom. He should be on his way to the wedding, but he couldn't stomach all the small talk, gossip and curious stares his presence was bound to inspire. No, he'd wait until the last minute, then stand in the back and watch his sister make one of the biggest mistakes of her life.

He glanced at his watch. The ceremony was scheduled to start in less than an hour. His guts twisted just thinking about the fact that he'd probably see Carlie there. He'd been furious when Nadine had told him that Carlie was on the guest list.

"Are you out of your mind?" Ben had demanded of his sister. "It's bad enough you're going to marry Monroe—" He'd caught the mutinous set of his sister's jaw and held up a hand in surrender. "Sorry, Nadine, but I never did like the guy and you know it as well as I do. I'm not gonna stand here and tell you that all of a sudden I think he's a wonderful choice—"

"Enough, Ben," she'd warned.

He'd plowed on. "But if that isn't bad enough, you invite *Carlie Surrett?*"

"It's time to bury hatchets, Ben. All of them."

"You've really lost it, Nadine. First marrying Monroe, that's... Well, it's damned unbelievable. But inviting Carlie..."

"Just behave yourself," Nadine had said, her green eyes glittering with an impish light that meant she was scheming again.

"You don't have to worry about me. I'm the model of civility."

"Yeah, right. And I'm the pope. Save that one for someone who'll believe it."

She'd turned the conversation back to rebuilding the cabin. The topic of her wedding had been effectively closed and she was going to have her way come hell or high water. Ben, like it or not, would have to abide by her whimsical, *I'm-the-bride-and-I'll-do-as-I-damned-well-please* wishes.

So he was stuck. "Hell," he ground out. He didn't want to think about Carlie. Not now. Not ever. He'd planned on avoiding her the rest of his life. That woman was trouble. No two ways about it. Beautiful, headstrong, kick-you-in-the-gut trouble.

Telling himself that she probably had more sense than to show up at Nadine's wedding, he finished his beer. Certainly she wouldn't want to cause all the old speculation again. Or would she? Carlie Surrett had been a woman drawn to the spotlight, a woman the camera loved, a woman whose brush with celebrity, though fleeting, had been real.

Frowning, he slipped a small pair of binoculars from his pocket and held them to his eyes. Monroe Manor loomed larger than before. With snow clinging to the eaves, the three-storied Cape Cod looked like something from Currier and Ives.

Charming, he thought with a sardonic sneer. Well, he hoped his mule-headed sister knew what she was getting into by saying "I do" to the likes of Monroe.

Give it up, Powell! He's marrying her and she's happy. As for seeing Carlie again, you can handle it. Couldn't be much worse than what you went through in the action you saw in the Middle East. Or could it?

Ben allowed himself a grim smile. He'd willingly return to combat rather than stare into Carlie's erotic blue eyes ever again.

Through the magnification of the binoculars, his gaze skimmed the banks of the lake, past frozen, empty docks, ancient sequoia trees, stumps and rocks to land on the shoreline by the old church camp. He saw a movement, a flash of deep blue and he adjusted the glasses.

His heart nearly stopped. His muscles tightened as she came into focus: a long-legged, beautiful woman staring across the water. Her black hair was braided loosely and coiled around the back of her head, but a few strands whipped across a face that was branded in his memory forever. She looked as if she could grace the cover of a fashion magazine in her long black coat, thrown open to reveal a gauzy blue dress that skimmed her ankles and offered a view of her elegant throat.

His fingers tightened over the binoculars as she turned, staring straight at him, her cornflower blue eyes as warm as a June day, her cheeks pink from the cold, her full lips glossy and turned pensively down at the corners. Drawing in a frozen breath, Ben waited for a wave of disgust to sweep through his blood, but instead of revulsion he felt a pang of regret for all the could-have-beens that would never be.

"Fool," he ground out, though he kept the field glasses to his eyes.

Model slender, she stood in heels, her long coat billowing in the breeze. She shivered and tightened the belt as snow melted against her cheeks and turned to jewellike drops in her ebony hair.

"Great." He forced the binoculars from his eyes. No doubt about it. From her getup it was obvious that she was going to the wedding. So much for hoping she had the brains or common decency to decline.

So, whether he liked it or not, he'd have to face her within the hour in front of a hundred guests. His stomach knotted at the thought of his father and how the old man would react to seeing Carlie Surrett, the woman who, in George Powell's rather prejudiced estimation, had brought nothing but agony and disgrace to the family, the woman he blamed for the death of his first-born son.

There would be a scene and Nadine's wedding would be ruined. "Damn," Ben swore at the world in general. He knew what had to be done. It meant facing her alone. Dealing with the infamous Ms. Surrett would be best ac-

complished without a crowd of wedding guests peering over
his shoulder and whispering behind his back.

It wasn't that he wanted to see her alone, he half convinced himself; he had no choice.

Jaw set, he stalked back to his battle-scarred pickup and
climbed inside. Throwing the rig into reverse, he told himself that he was just going to talk to her and set her straight
on a few things before they squared off at the wedding.

He owed it to his father. He owed it to Kevin. And most
importantly, he owed it to himself.

Crazy. That's what she was. *Certifiably nuts!* Showing
up at Nadine Powell Warne's wedding to Hayden Monroe
would be more than asking for trouble; she'd be begging for
it!

Carlie shivered, rubbing her arms as she followed the
snow-encrusted path that rimmed the rocky banks of the
lake. Snowflakes caught in her lashes and her braid was
loosening. She should just go to the wedding and get it over
with or turn tail and run. Instead, she was out here, in the
middle of nowhere, second-guessing herself.

This was all Rachelle's fault. Her best friend had insisted that Carlie put the past to rest and accept Nadine's
olive branch to bridge the gap between the two families. But
it wasn't Nadine who worried Carlie. Nadine was happy,
content with her life, ready to forgive and forget; that much
was evident by the fact that she was marrying Hayden
Monroe, a sworn enemy of the Powell family.

But Ben was a different matter. A different matter en-
tirely. Carlie's heart squeezed a little when she thought of
him, but she closed her mind to such traitorous thoughts.
She'd see him today, try and be pleasant and that would be
the end of it.

An icy blast of wind ripped through the thick wool of her
coat and she shivered. The sounds of muffled traffic on the
road winding around the perimeter of the lake reached her
ears, and for a second she thought she heard the sound of
a truck's engine much closer than it should have been, as if
someone else had seen the open gates to the old church

camp and pulled into the long-abandoned property. Silly. She was alone.

Her satin heels slid on the icy ground and she decided she should turn around, climb into her worn-out Jeep Cherokee and drive to Nadine's wedding where she belonged.

Ha! What a joke! *Where she belonged!* That was the problem. She didn't *know* where she belonged. It certainly wasn't in the town of Gold Creek, California, where she'd been born and raised, and it didn't take a genius to realize that she didn't really belong at Nadine's wedding where she'd have to see Ben again.

Her heart tripped a little and she bit down on her lip as she shoved aside a frozen cobweb dangling from a low-hanging pine branch. In her mind, she'd played the scene of meeting him again over and over again, silly fantasies of a love long dead. If it had ever existed at all.

A thorn caught on the sleeve of her coat as she walked along a curtain of cedar and spruce trees rimming the shore. She paused, extracting the barb.

On the day of Rachelle's wedding the lake had been blue and serene, the mirrorlike surface reflecting the mountains that spired above the timberline. But this afternoon, with the winter wind ripping through the ridge of peaks to the north, the gray water was whipped to an angry froth, whitecaps rising and falling above murky depths. Tiny particles of ice had begun to form in the water that lapped along the rocky banks and the low-lying clouds were a thick mist, the same mist that was a part of the old Native American legend.

The sight of the chilly water brought back memories. Some happy, others painful, all tracing back to her youth. It had been on these very shores where Carlie had first been kissed, where she'd tasted her first sip of wine, where she'd given away her virginity... She'd been young, naive, believing that she could someday change the world, trusting in true love and never once thinking that tragedy, shame and scandal could touch her.

Fool! Drawing in a cold breath, she remembered running away from the small town of Gold Creek with its narrow minds and wagging tongues. The comfort and security of her home had crumbled, turned to hostility and pain, and all the joy she'd felt growing up in this small community had disappeared. So she'd left and put time and distance between herself and the pain, tried to forget that she'd ever heard of the Powell brothers.

She'd run as fast and far as possible, to the bright lights and dazzle of Manhattan—to the noise, the bustle, the glitter—always hoping that she would leave the heartache and humiliation of this small Californian town behind her. Unfortunately the past had always been nipping at her heels. Dogging her. In New York. In Paris. In Alaska. The dark shadow of Kevin's death clung to her tenaciously, never far away, never to be lost, always clutching at her subconscious.

An icy blast of wind cut like a knife, and she shivered. If she'd learned anything in the past ten years it was that she could depend upon no one but herself and that she'd damned well better hold her head high.

A twig snapped. Carlie spun, quickly searching the undergrowth. Probably just an animal, but she couldn't stop the goose bumps from rising on her arms. She stared into the thickets of brush and trees, but saw no one. Skeletal berry vines clawed along the ground; oak trees, naked in winter, reached gnarled branches up to the steely sky; and overhead, a hawk circled in the falling snow, but no one appeared from the shadows of the trees.

Just your imagination, she told herself. *Just because you're back at Whitefire Lake and caught up in memories you should have buried a long time ago.* She turned, intent on hurrying back to the open area of the campground where she'd parked the Jeep. Her gaze landed squarely on the one man she had hoped to avoid.

Ben Powell.

A very real ghost of the past appeared on the shores of the lake. It was fitting, she supposed, and ironic. She tried not to gasp and managed what she hoped would appear a confident smile.

Dressed in his crisp military uniform, Ben Powell wasn't a man to fear, just as certainly as he wasn't a man to love. But he was definitely as hard and cruelly handsome as the pictures she'd tried not to conjure up in her mind for a long, long time.

His sensual lips were compressed into a firm, uncompromising line, and his face, honed by years in the army, was angular and stern; not a single trace of his boyish features—the features she'd held dear in her heart—remained. Eyes, beneath flat dark brows, snapped with unrestrained hostility, and Carlie wondered how in the world she'd ever thought she'd been in love with him. Where was the kindness, the humor that had been such an integral part of the boy she'd once secretly hoped to marry?

He stood ramrod straight, his dress uniform starched, his cap square on his head, and he glared at her with undisguised hatred.

"All dressed up and no place to go?" he asked, his voice as sharp as the bite of the wind.

So much for pleasantries.

"I could say the same about you." Her gaze drifted from his shoulders to his spit-and-polished shoes.

His chest was still broad, his waist trim, his hips as lean as ever. He hadn't even had the decency to start to bald. His hair was as thick and coffee brown as it had been all those years ago and his eyes, hazel, shot with silver, could cut right to her soul.

"I don't suppose you came here to escort me to the wedding?" she asked, deciding to give as much as she got.

He snorted.

"I didn't think so." She rolled back the cuff of her coat and glanced at her watch. "We probably should get going. We're already late."

"I can't believe you were invited."

Echoes from the past rippled through her mind as an old memory surfaced and she thought of the first night she'd been with him. She swallowed hard and kept her mind on the present. She didn't think for a minute that Nadine wouldn't have told him her name was on the guest list. No

doubt Ben's sister had warned him. So what was his game?
"Believe it, Ben. I don't show up where I'm not wanted."

"That's not the way I remember it."

She felt the color drain from her face, but she inched her
chin up a notch, refusing to give him an inkling that she
remembered with crystal clarity the party she'd crashed,
just to be with him. "Look, you don't have to pretend to
like me—"

"I won't."

"Good. Then we're even," she lied, her pride ruling her
tongue.

His lips tightened at the corners.

"Now all we have to do is endure your sister's wedding.
We don't have to speak, touch or so much as look at each
other. Then, after the reception, you can go your way and
I'll go mine."

He rubbed the back of his neck and seemed to wrestle
with something on his mind. "I just didn't happen to show
up here," he said, "I was at Nadine's dock and I saw you
through field glasses." The stubborn set of his jaw didn't
alter. "You're right, I knew you were invited to the wedding, but I thought I should warn you."

"About what?"

He stared at her long enough that she was certain he'd
studied every pore on her face.

"My dad won't appreciate your being there."

"Your dad didn't invite me."

"You're not wanted, Carlie."

That stung, but she wasn't a virgin in the pain department. "Not by you maybe, but—"

"Not by me ever."

The old wounds opened, but she wouldn't give Ben the
satisfaction of knowing he still had the ability to hurt her.
She shook her head and sighed. "I was hoping that it
wouldn't be like this between us."

"It couldn't be any different."

"Why?"

"Because Kevin's dead, damn it. Don't you remember?"

"Every day of my life." She swallowed back that old, painful lump that filled her throat when she thought of Ben's older brother. "But—" she forced the words over her suddenly thick tongue "—nothing I can say or do will bring him back. We have to let it rest. Both of us."

He looked as if he planned to disagree. Shadows darkened his clear eyes and he quickly glanced away, past her, to the mountains rising in the distance. Seconds drummed by, punctuated by the silence that stretched between them. A tic throbbed near his temple and his jaw was clenched so hard, she wondered if his teeth were being ground into his gums. "I don't think we should talk about this," he said at length, but his voice was less harsh; the accusations in his eyes had faded.

"The way I remember it, you don't think we should talk about anything!"

"Fair enough."

"Good. Because we—or at least *I*—have a wedding to attend." The brisk air crackled between them and he didn't reply. Again, the silence was deafening and it was all she could do to stand her ground under his hard, uncompromising gaze. "Are you always this rude," she asked impulsively, "or did the army teach you how to be a jerk?"

"You just seem to bring out the best in me."

"I don't remember handing you an invitation to bulldoze your way over here and insult me. This time, Ben, you're doing the crashing." She turned, intent on leaving him, but he moved quickly, reaching out, his hand clamping firmly over her elbow. He spun her back to face him with such force that his cap fell into the snow. For a breathless second she remembered him as he had been: impetuous, young, bold, sought after by most of the girls who had attended Tyler High. And she, Carlie Surrett, had been flattered that she'd caught his attention—even if she'd had to chase him a little to get it.

His gaze settled on her mouth. The breeze seemed to die and they were alone. Two people, man and woman, lost in a swirl of snowflakes and icy air. In the span of a heartbeat she thought he might kiss her, and her lips felt suddenly dry. How could she even let one single memory of the love they once shared into her heart? It had all been so long ago.

"I'm surprised you're back," he said roughly, his eyes narrowing, his warm breath fogging in the cool air. "I heard you were married."

Her spine stiffened slightly. "For a while."

"Didn't last?" He raised a dubious black eyebrow. "I can't imagine why."

"Irreconcilable differences," she said, ignoring the little bit of pain that still remained when she thought about her short-lived marriage. "I believed in monogamy. He thought it was a drag."

Ben's skepticism was etched on his face, but she told herself she didn't care. What Ben Powell thought of her didn't matter. Squaring her shoulders, she was determined to change the subject. "What about you, Ben? What're you doing back in Gold Creek? Unless things have changed, there's no army base for hundreds of miles."

"I'm through with the military."

She eyed the buttons of his uniform, the medals decorating his chest. "Doesn't look that way."

"The wedding was news to me when I got back to town. Didn't have anything to wear. The trunk with my tux hasn't arrived yet."

So he still had a sense of humor—cynical though it was. And his eyes, angry and smoldering, were staring at her with an intensity that caused the chilly air to be trapped in her lungs.

She had to remind herself that she wasn't going to fall for his sex appeal again. Not now. Not ever. Quickly she yanked her arm from his. "We'll be late."

"You shouldn't go, Carlie. Not after what happened."

She felt like dying. All the old pain and shame ripped fresh holes in her heart.

"My old man, if he sees you..." Ben's brows drew together.

"He'll get over it," she said, though she didn't know if she was up to facing the censure and accusations in George

Powell's eyes. "This is Nadine's day. If we're smart, none of us will do anything to spoil it."

Backing up, she nearly stumbled, then turned and strode briskly back to her vehicle. She could feel him watching her as she climbed into the Cherokee, twisted on the ignition and pumped the gas. The engine turned over and in a plume of blue exhaust, she drove away from the little campground by the lake, away from the ghosts of the old legend and away from Ben Powell, a man she'd loved with all of her naive heart and a man who had all but destroyed her.

Had it really been eleven years? A decade of carrying around a load of guilt she should have unstrapped long ago? She switched on the defroster, clearing the suddenly misty windshield.

"Forget him," she told herself angrily. He was wrong for her then, even more wrong for her now. Not that she wanted him—or any man for that matter. It had taken awhile, but she'd grown up to be her own independent woman.

She wiped at the fog the old defroster couldn't make disappear. Her fingers came away from the windshield wet and cold. Forgetting Ben Powell was easier said than done. She'd already spent so many years trying and had obviously failed. Why else would she care what he thought of her?

Gritting her teeth, she took a corner a little too fast, the Jeep's tires skidded and spun and she slid into the oncoming lane. From years of practice negotiating the icy roads in Alaska, she turned into the slide and guided the Cherokee back to the right-hand lane. Her heart was pounding, her hands tight around the steering wheel and she couldn't help remembering Ben and how much she'd once loved him.

It had been summer when she'd crashed that party, a warm July night filled with the sound of crickets and thick with the scent of honeysuckle. She'd been young and reckless and anxious to experience all that life had to offer.

Because of Ben Powell. Ben with his irreverent smile, his intense hazel eyes and his promises.... Dear God, why couldn't she forget him? Why did just the sight of him inspire memories that she'd kept locked away in a dark corner of her heart and promised herself that she'd never open?

As an old Fleetwood Mac song about the chains of love filled the interior of her vehicle she hummed along.

Despite all Carlie's vows to herself, her mind circled backward in time to the hot summer nights that had changed the course of her life forever....

BOOK ONE

Whitefire Lake, California

Eleven Years Earlier

Chapter One

"Maybe we should turn back." Carlie gnawed nervously on the inside of her lip, but continued to paddle forward. She didn't usually second-guess herself, and she'd always been adventurous, but this time she questioned her own wisdom as she dipped her oar into the water and glanced over her shoulder to her friend, Brenda, paddling steadily at the stern of the small rowboat.

Dusk gathered lazily over the lake. Water skippers and dragonflies skimmed the clear surface and mosquitoes droned in the early-evening air.

"Turn back now? Are you crazy?" Brenda asked, clucking her tongue in disappointment. With springy red curls, freckles and eyes the color of chocolate, Brenda was new to Gold Creek, but she and Carlie were fast becoming friends. "This was your idea, remember?"

"Can't I change my mind?"

"Not now." Brenda shoved her oar into the water and threw her shoulders into her stroke. The small boat skimmed closer to their destination, an abandoned log cabin on the south side of the lake.

The Bait and Fish, lights glowing warmly from the windows, slid by. Flickering neon signs announcing favorite brands of beer stood in stark relief against the weathered old boards. In the distance, near the north shore, speedboats dragged water-skiers. Carlie recognized Brian Fitzpatrick at the helm of a racing silver craft that rimmed the shoreline and left a thick rippling wake over which an experienced skier, probably Brian's younger sister, Toni, was balanced on one ski.

"What a life," Brenda said dreamily as she glanced at the sleek speedboat.

"You'd want to be a Fitzpatrick?" Carlie shook her head. "With all their troubles?"

"They've got *soooo* much money."

"And *soooo* many troubles. Haven't you heard about the root of all evil?"

"So, let me sin a little."

Carlie laughed, enjoying the breath of a breeze that fanned her face and lifted her hair off her shoulders. Though the sun had set in a blaze of gold and pink behind the mountains, the July air was hot and sticky.

Their destination loomed ahead, a thicket of pines surrounding an ancient cabin with rotting, weather-beaten shingles for a roof and rough log walls. No one knew who owned the property, but the single acre was referred to as the "old Daniels' place" by most of the people in town. Jed Daniels built the cabin for his bride just before the turn of the century, and successive generations of Daniels' kin had used the place as a summer cottage. Eventually the Daniels family was spread too far and thin to keep up the house, but if the place had ever been sold, no one in town talked of it.

Carlie eased the rowboat to the old dock of weathered pilings and broken boards. Though the house was dark, music and laughter drifted through the broken, boarded-up windows, and she recognized an old song by the Rolling Stones.

She bit her lower lip and worried it over her teeth. What was it about her that was always seeking out adventure or "looking for trouble," as her father had so often said?

"She's just curious, nothing wrong with that." Her mother, Thelma, had quickly defended her only child on more than one occasion. "She's got a quick mind and she gets bored easily."

"Dreamin', that's what she's doin'. Thinkin' she can become some hot-damn New York model. Where I come from that's called being too big fer yer britches," Weldon Surrett had stated as he'd sat at the kitchen table smoking a cigarette.

"Where you come from, a six-pack of beer and a deck of cards were considered big-time," her mother teased gently, then adjusted the skirt of her uniform and kissed her husband on the cheek. "See you after my shift." Thelma had always been defensive of Carlie. Sometimes she went too far and was overprotective. Carlie blamed it on the fact that her mother couldn't have any more children. A hysterectomy one year after Carlie's birth had denied Thelma the large family she'd always wanted. Consequently, Thelma had poured all her motherly affection, concern and love onto her only child. If it weren't for the fact that Thelma's job at the Rexall Drug Store in town kept her busy, she would surely have suffocated Carlie with all her good intentions long ago.

"This is the place?" Brenda asked skeptically as she eyed the dilapidated cabin.

"Uh-huh."

"You sure you heard right?"

"Positive."

"And Ben Powell will be here?" Brenda lifted a doubtful eyebrow.

"I heard him talking to his brother," Carlie said as the boat rocked softly against the dock. She'd run into Ben and Kevin at the new video store that had opened up near the supermarket. The boys had been arguing about which movie to rent when Kevin had looked up and caught her staring at them. Carlie felt a little jab of guilt when she re-

membered the spark of interest in Kevin's eyes when he'd
caught her gaze.

Kevin was older than Ben and had spent a year away at
college before Kevin's grades had slipped and the money
had run out for his education. Now he was working at
Monroe Sawmill and was unhappy with his life. He and
Carlie had dated several times, but then she'd stopped seeing him. Kevin was seven years older than she, and was
much too serious and possessive. By the third date, Carlie
had known that their relationship was doomed. He began
calling twice a day, demanding to know where she'd been,
jealous of her friends and the time she'd spent away from
him. After three lousy dates!

She'd never really broken up with him because they'd
never really gone together; she'd just stopped going out
with him. He spent a lot of his time at the Buckeye Restaurant and Lounge, drinking beer and watching sports on
television through a smoky haze as he relived his own days
of glory as one of the best basketball players to ever graduate from Tyler High School.

Carlie shuddered, thinking of Kevin. Too many times
he'd wanted to touch her, kiss her, get her alone. They
hadn't had one thing in common and she probably didn't
have much more with Kevin's younger brother, Ben.

So what was she doing here? Crashing a party because of
Ben Powell, Kevin's younger brother? *Boy, Carlie, you are
looking for trouble!*

She tied the boat to one of the sturdier pilings, walked
carefully across the bleached boards and hiked along a
weed-choked path to the broad front porch, where an old
rocking chair swayed slightly with the breeze. The sound of
voices grew louder, some from inside the house, others
from around back, but a heavy chain and padlock on the
front door suggested they find another entrance.

"I'm starting to have second thoughts about this,"
Brenda admitted. "It's kind of creepy, you know. Aren't
there laws about criminal trespass and breaking and enter-
ing?"

"I thought you didn't want to turn back!" Carlie, too, was torn. She remembered another party, less than a year before, when a group of kids were gathered at the Fitzpatrick house on the other side of the lake. Things got out of hand and Roy Fitzpatrick, the golden boy of Gold Creek, heir to the Fitzpatrick fortune, had been killed.

Jackson Moore was suspected and arrested for the crime, but Carlie's best friend, Rachelle Tremont, had given Jackson the alibi he needed to avoid being indicted. Jackson had walked away from jail a free man, but he'd left town, leaving Rachelle with a soiled reputation and a broken heart.

The aftermath of the party had been devastating, but now, even remembering the hell the Fitzpatricks and Tremonts had gone through, Carlie still couldn't turn around. The lure of seeing Ben was greater than her fear of being caught breaking some kind of minor law. She walked off the porch and took an overgrown trail of flagstones toward the back.

Why she was so attracted to Ben, she didn't know. He should be the one boy in town to avoid, considering the fact that he was Kevin's younger brother. But everything about Ben appealed to her—his rugged good looks, his easy, slightly cynical smile, his open irreverence for all things monetary.

Shorter and more compact than Kevin, Ben wasn't quite six feet, but he was more muscular and his hazel gaze seemed to burn right into her soul. So here she was, acting like a sneak thief, sticking her nose where it didn't belong and stepping around the corner to... *nearly run right into him.*

She gasped and Brenda, walking behind her bumped against her backside.

Ben didn't seem the least surprised. Stripped to the waist, wearing faded Levi's with split knees, he stopped dead in his tracks. A bottle of beer dangled from his fingers and a slow, lazy smile spread across his beard-darkened jaw. "Carlie, right? Carlie Surrett?"

She nodded, her throat dry, her heart hammering.

"And I'm Brenda." Her friend stepped out of Carlie's shadow to introduce herself.

Ben seemed amused. His lips twisted upward a little and an intense spark of interest lighted his hazel eyes. Never, not for one second, did his gaze waver from hers.

Carlie swallowed hard and shoved a handful of hair over her shoulder. She suddenly felt awkward and wondered why she'd been so stupid as to come party crashing.

"Kevin isn't here," Ben said, taking a long pull from the beer. Carlie watched in fascination as he swallowed. Sweat trickled down his neck and his Adam's apple moved slowly.

"I didn't come looking for Kevin."

One dark brow shot up. "Who then?"

"Nobody," she lied and heard Brenda's sharp intake of breath. "I just, um, heard there was a party."

He leaned a palm against the rough sides of the building and moved his fingertips restlessly along one hand-hewn log. She noticed his tanned arms, the muscles of his shoulders, the veins bulging beneath his skin. "So this is what you do . . . crash parties?"

"I didn't know it was engraved invitation only."

He smiled at that. "We were just trying to keep it small. Avoid a fiasco like what happened at the Fitzpatrick place."

"No one knows we're here."

"No one?"

Brenda shook her head.

"You can trust us," Carlie said, wondering why she felt like baiting him.

"Can I?" His eyes narrowed a fraction. "Kevin seems to think you're his girl."

She felt the hackles on the back of her neck rise. "Kevin's wrong."

He took another swig from his beer. "So why he'd get the wrong information?"

"Look, I don't think it's a good idea to discuss—"

"Kevin got too serious," Brenda cut in. "Besides, he's too old for her." With a shrug she walked past Ben and Carlie. "I'll let you two work this out."

"There's nothing to work out," Carlie protested. Heat climbed up her neck and she was suddenly aware that coming here was a big mistake. "Look, maybe Brenda and I should take off."

"You just got here."

"I know, but—" She waved in the air.

"You weren't invited."

"Right."

"It doesn't matter." His gaze held hers and her mouth turned to cotton. The sounds of the night, deep croaks from hidden bullfrogs and the soft chirp of a thousand crickets, were suddenly muted. The fragrance of wild roses soon to go to seed, filtered over the acrid odor of burning wood and exhaust.

"Let's go check out the action. That's why you're here, aren't you?"

"Brenda and I were just taking a turn in the boat. We heard the music...." It was a little bit of a lie, but she couldn't admit the reason she'd shown up here was because of him.

"You want a beer?" His gaze was neutral, and yet she felt as if he were challenging her.

"I guess."

With a shrug, he turned and walked barefooted along the dusty path. Nervously, Carlie followed him to what had once been a backyard. Gravel had been strewn near a dilapidated garage, and several cars, pickups and motorcycles had been parked in the rutted lane. A stack of bleached cordwood partially covered with blackberry vines, seemed to prop up a sagging wall of the garage. Kids sat on bumpers of cars, on the drooping back porch or wandered into the house through an open door. A rusted lock was sprung and lay with an equally neglected chain that had slid to the floorboards.

"Who owns this place?" she asked.

"One of the guys here—" Ben took the time to point to a pimply-faced boy of about nineteen who was trying to build a fire in an old barbecue pit "—lives in Coleville and claims his uncle is the Daniels' heir who ended up with the cabin. He says the uncle is trying to sell it.''

"And he doesn't care if your friend has a party?"

Ben slanted her a sly grin. "What do you think?"

"That the uncle doesn't have a clue."

"Smart girl."

Ben introduced her to some of the guests, most of whom were a little older than she was—kids who worked in the mill or the logging company or the Dari-Maid, some with full-time jobs, others who were spending their summer back in Gold Creek until they returned to college in the fall. She knew some of them of course, but there were a lot that she'd never seen before.

Brenda had already grabbed a beer and was trying to make conversation with Patty Osgood, the reverend's daughter. Patty was a couple of years older than Carlie, but already had enough of a reputation to turn her father's hair white, should the good reverend stumble upon the truth.

Patty sat on the edge of a stump, her long, tanned legs stretched out from shorts that barely covered her rear end and a white blouse knotted beneath her breasts. Her flat abdomen and a flirty glimpse of the hollow between her breasts left little to the imagination.

Patty wasn't a really bad girl, but she liked to flaunt the gorgeous body the good Lord had seen fit to bestow upon her—and hang the consequences. She'd dated a lot of boys in town, but now her eyes were on Ben.

"Well, well, well . . ." Erik Patton said when Carlie and Ben moved in his direction. Erik dragged on his cigarette and shot smoke out of the side of his mouth. "I didn't think you'd ever show your face at a beer bash again." Leisurely, he plucked a flake of tobacco from his tongue and eyed his friend, Scott McDonald. Both boys had been friends of Roy Fitzpatrick and believed Jackson Moore had killed Roy last fall. Most of the citizens of Gold Creek agreed, though Jackson had never been indicted. Only a few people in town believed in Jackson's innocence. Carlie belonged to that small minority and it obviously bothered

Erik, who had given her a ride to the Fitzpatrick summer home on that fateful night.

Goose bumps rose on her arms. "I was just—"

"Save it, Surrett," Erik said through a cloud of smoke. "We were all there. We know what happened."

"Jackson didn't—"

"Oh, sure he managed to get Rachelle to claim they'd been together all night, but we all know that's a pile of crap. She just made up the story to give him an alibi."

"She wouldn't!"

"Sure she would." Erik let out a sigh of disgust. "She made it with him and she didn't even know him, did she? Face it, she's a slut."

"Shut up!" Ben ordered, but not before Carlie could lunge at Erik.

"Don't you ever—"

Ben grabbed her arm. "That's enough," he said with quiet authority aimed in Erik's direction. "Maybe you want to apologize."

"I just call 'em as I see 'em."

"Then you're blind!" Carlie said.

Eyes slitting as if he were sizing up the enemy, Erik glared at Ben but had the good sense to back down a little. "Forget it. Forget I said anything."

"That's more like it." Ben's gaze could have cut through lead and the smell of a fight filled the air.

Carlie could hardly breathe and she noticed that all conversation had died and a dozen pairs of eyes were trained on the two boys who were squaring off. She wanted to die a thousand deaths. "Leave Carlie alone, Patton," Ben said loudly enough so that everyone got the message. "She's with me."

Erik flicked his cigarette into the gravel and ground the smoldering butt with the toe of his boot. "Your loss, man."

Ben's smile was crooked but self-assured. "I don't think so."

Carlie felt Ben's fingers tighten over her arm and her heart pumped a little faster.

Scott spit into the scrub oaks, his eyes dark with disgust. "You can have her," he muttered.

Embarrassment rushed up Carlie's neck as she remembered the pickup ride to the Fitzpatricks' lakeside cabin. She and Rachelle had ridden in the cab of Erik's truck and Carlie, because of lack of space, had been forced to sit on Scott's lap. She'd giggled and flirted with him, unaware that what was to happen that night would put her at odds with almost everyone in town—including Erik Patton and Scott McDonald.

She'd been naive then, younger and foolish and the thought that she'd actually been that close to Scott made her skin crawl.

She should have learned her lesson.

So what was she doing here hoping to catch Ben Powell's attention? Didn't she have enough trouble with Kevin?

The fingers clamped around her forearm didn't move and her skin tingled slightly. "You certainly know how to create a scene," he said quietly.

"Maybe I should leave."

With a lift of his shoulder, he let go of her arm. The warmth of his fingertips left soft impressions on her arm. "Up to you." His silver-tinged gaze touched hers and her throat caught for a second.

"We'll stay... for a while," she said, as the night closed around them and the fire cast golden shadows over the angles of his face. Someone had a portable radio, fiddled with the dial and the strong notes of "Night Moves" by Bob Seger wafted through the air.

"Good." Ben stuck close to her the rest of the evening, but he never touched her again and any little flame of interest in his eyes was quickly doused when he talked to her.

She listened to music, nursed a beer, talked to some of the kids and always knew exactly where Ben was, whom he was talking to and what he was doing. It was silly really, but she couldn't help the attraction she felt for him.

"He's interested," Brenda told her when it was near midnight and the party was breaking up.

"I don't think so."

"Definitely interested," her friend maintained. "He watched you when he didn't think you were looking."

"Really?" Carlie whispered just as Ben left a small group of his friends and approached the girls.

"Need a ride?" Ben slipped his arms through a faded denim shirt. He didn't bother with the buttons.

"We've got the rowboat," Carlie said, managing to hide her disappointment.

"It'll fit in the back of my truck." His gaze touched hers for just a heartbeat. "It's no trouble."

"I don't think—"

"We'd love a ride," Brenda cut in as she glanced at her watch. "There's no way we can row back to my house by curfew."

"But—"

Ben wasn't listening to any arguments. He followed them to the back of the house, waded into the thigh-deep water, dragged the rowboat to shore, then swung the small craft over his head. Lake water drizzled down his neck and the back of his shirt, but he didn't seem to notice.

"I don't think this is a good idea," Carlie whispered to her friend.

"You wanted to be with him, didn't you?" When Carlie didn't answer, Brenda gave her a nudge. "Go for it."

Ben shoved the rowboat into the back of his father's truck and told himself he was an idiot. Why borrow trouble? Why take Carlie home?

Because you can't help yourself!

He now understood his brother's fascination with Carlie Surrett. Reed-slender, with thick black hair that fell to the middle of her back, high cheekbones, lips that always looked moist and eyes that sparked with a misty blue-green intelligence turned his insides to jelly. No wonder Kevin had been so hot for her. But it was over. Kevin had said so himself.

Ben might have felt guilty taking Carlie home a couple of weeks ago, but Kevin had sworn just the other night that he was over Carlie Surrett. They'd been down at the Silver

Horseshoe, the local watering hole, tossing back a few beers after Kevin's shift at the mill.

"She's too much trouble, that one," Kevin had said, signaling the waitress for another round. "So I broke up with her and I found someone else."

"I thought you were in love with her. She's all you could talk about for... what... two or three weeks."

Kevin snorted. "We only went out a few times." He fished into his front pocket of his jeans for change and avoided his brother's intense stare. "'Sides, you and I know there's no such thing as love. All a big lie. Made up by women with their stupid ideas that they get from books and movies."

"You believe that?" Ben had known that Kevin had turned cynical over the years after losing his chance to play basketball in college, but he hadn't believed his older brother could be so hard-nosed and jaded. A few weeks ago, Kevin had been on cloud nine, talking about Carlie Surrett as if he intended to marry her. And now he thought love was just an illusion.

"Look at Mom and Dad," Kevin said, as if their parents' ill-fated union was proof of his opinion.

Ben scowled and picked at the label of his bottle. His parents, Donna and George Powell, after fighting for years had separated and were now divorced. The battles had started long ago and had always been about money—the kind of money the Monroes and Fitzpatricks had and the rest of the town didn't. For as long as Ben could remember, his family had been one of the many "have nots" and this point only became crushingly clear when his father had lost all the family's savings on some lamebrained investment scheme concocted by H. G. Monroe, owner of the sawmill for which George and Kevin worked, and one rich, mean son of a bitch.

"So who's the girl?" he asked his brother rather than think about the past. "The one who's replaced Carlie Surrett?"

Kevin's lips turned down. "No one replaced Carlie," he said defensively as a buxom waitress, wearing a skirt that barely covered her rear, left two more bottles on the glossy mahogany bar. In one swift motion, she emptied the ashtray and quickly picked up the crumpled bills Kevin cast in her direction. "Keep the change," he said with a smile that invited trouble.

"Thanks, sugar."

"No problem."

The waitress moved through the smoke to a table in the corner. Kevin took a long swallow from his bottle. As if they'd never been interrupted, he said, "I'm seein' a girl named Tracy. Tracy Niday from Coleville. Ever hear of her?"

Ben shook his head and Kevin seemed relieved.

"Is she nice?"

"Nice? Humph. I'm not lookin' for nice." Kevin's eyes darkened a shade. "But she's . . . simple. Doesn't have big dreams of goin' to New York, becoming a model or some such bull. She's just happy that I take her out and show her a good time."

"And Carlie wasn't?"

"No way. No how." Kevin scowled and reached into the pocket of his flannel shirt for his pack of cigarettes. "Carlie has big plans—thinks she's gonna be some hot-damn model or somethin'. Didn't want to be tied down to Gold Creek and . . . oh, hell, she was a load of trouble. I'm better off without her." He lit up and shot a plume of smoke out of the corner of his mouth. "If you ask me, she was all screwed up over that Roy Fitzpatrick murder. Her and that friend of hers—Rachelle Tremont—are both more trouble than they're worth."

And that had been the end of the conversation about Kevin's love life. Ben hadn't believed that his brother was truly over Carlie and so he'd questioned her when he'd first found her climbing out of the boat at the dock. But her story had been close enough to Kevin's to convince Ben that they weren't seeing each other anymore.

He watched as she wiped her hands on the front of her shorts. "Hop in," he said, opening the driver's side of the pickup and wondering why he felt a twinge of relief knowing that Kevin wasn't interested in Carlie any longer. He and Kevin had never dated the same girls—there seemed to be an unwritten law between them when it came to going out and heretofore maintaining their silent code hadn't been a problem. Kevin was a few years older than Ben, and no conflicts had arisen. Until Carlie. Until now.

Carlie was the youngest girl Kevin had ever taken out, and, without a doubt, the most gorgeous. He noticed the shape of her buttocks and the nip of her waist as she slid onto the old seat of the truck. He didn't question that she could become a successful model and he didn't blame her for wanting to taste more of the world than Gold Creek, California had to offer.

He wanted to get out of town himself.

He rammed the truck into gear. "Where to?" he asked the girls.

"My place," Brenda said quickly. "It's a little ways from the old church camp."

"Just point me in the right direction." Ben shoved the Ford into first and the truck bounced along the rutted lane. Near a dilapidated mailbox, he turned south on the county road that rimmed the lake. Carlie reached for the radio, but Ben shook his head. "Hasn't worked for a few months now," he said, his fingers brushing her bare leg as he shifted into third. His fingers skimmed her thigh and he felt a tightening in his gut.

Carlie felt the touch of his fingers, and her skin tingled. She pretended to stare out the dusty windshield, but she watched him from the corner of her eye. He squinted slightly as he drove and the planes of his face seemed more rugged in the dark cab. He was dark and sexy and dangerous.

The porch light was burning at Brenda's old farmhouse. Ben unloaded the rowboat, and, following Brenda's instructions, propped the boat against the side of a concrete-block shed. "Thanks for the ride," Brenda sang out as she ran up the cement walk. "I'll talk to you tomorrow, Carlie!" She dashed up the steps and disappeared into the house as Ben climbed behind the wheel.

"Now where?" he asked, glancing in her direction and noting that she'd moved to the far side of the cab, as if she didn't want to chance touching him.

"I live in town. The Lakeview Apartments on Cedar Street—one block off Pine."

"I've been there." He slashed her a smile that was white in the darkness and caused her heart to flip.

"Then you know there's no lake and no view." She relaxed against the worn cushions and rolled down the window. Fresh air blew into the cab, ruffling her hair and caressing her cheeks.

A train was passing on the old railroad trestle that spanned the highway into town as the lights of Gold Creek came into view. They passed the Dari-Maid and turned at the corner of Pine and Main by the Rexall Drug Store, the store where her mother had worked for as long as Carlie could remember.

Though she was nervous just being alone with him, she hoped he didn't notice. Her palms were sweaty, her throat dry and her heart knocked loudly as the night seemed to close around them.

He took the corner a little too fast and the truck's tires squealed as he pulled into the parking lot near her parents' apartment complex. Built in the thirties, the Lakeview was comprised of three six-plex townhouses. On the exterior, the bottom floors were faced in brick while the upper story was white clapboard. Black shutters adorned paned windows and though the apartments weren't very big, they still held a certain charm that her mother loved. "Just like home," Thelma, who had been raised in Brooklyn, New York, had told her daughter on more than one occasion. "You can't find quality building like this anymore."

As the pickup idled, Carlie reached for the door handle.

"You don't have to go in," he said, drumming his fingers on the steering wheel.

Her fingers froze in midair. "It's late."

"Not that late." He turned off the ignition and the ensuing silence was suddenly deafening. She could hear her own heartbeat and the hum of the security lamps that shed a blue light over the pockmarked asphalt of the parking lot.

"I've got to work in the morning."

"So do I."

She turned to face him and barely dared breathe. Lounging against the driver's side door, Ben was openly staring at her and his eyebrows were drawn together as if he were trying to piece together some complicated, mystical puzzle. He fingered his keys. Silence was thick in the truck. She swallowed hard.

He reached across the cab, lifted a lock of her long black hair and let it drop again. "Why did you show up at the cabin tonight?"

"I told you—"

"I know what you said, but I was wondering if there was another reason."

"No."

"You're sure that it's over between you and my brother?"

Her heart was beating so loudly, she was embarrassed. "It never really got started, Ben. It just didn't work," she said honestly.

"Why?"

"I liked Kevin ... I still do, but he wanted to get more serious than I did...." Before she realized what he was doing, his fingers slid beneath her hair, found the back of her neck and drew her face to his.

"So what are you? Just a party girl?" he asked, his breath fanning her lips.

Oh, God, she could hardly breathe.

"No, but—"

His lips found hers in a kiss that was hot and wet and promised so much more. His mouth moved easily and Carlie couldn't help the little groan of pleasure that escaped her. Somewhere in the back of her mind she knew that kissing him was asking for more trouble than she could ever hope to handle, but she couldn't stop herself and she didn't protest as his arms surrounded her, pulling her close against him. His chest was rock hard and bare where his shirt didn't quite close and his mouth moved easily over hers.

She felt as if she were melting inside when he finally let go of her.

Her heart was thundering as he slid back to his side of the truck and ran an unsteady hand through his hair. "Damn!" His breathing was loud and he cast her a glance that could cut through metal. "You—"

"I what?" she asked, bristling a little. After all, he'd kissed her. Not the other way around.

"You're . . . well, you're just not what I expected. Son of a—"

"Gun?" She tried to break the tension building in the cab.

"Close enough." His fingers still shook a little as he placed them over the steering wheel. So he had been as affected as she. That little bit of knowledge helped because she was surprised at her own reaction. She'd kissed her share of boys during high school and some of the kisses had been pleasant, but she'd never felt so downright shaken to her toes.

"I'd better get going." He reached for the keys still dangling in the ignition.

"You want to come in . . . for a soda, or some coffee or something?" Lord, that sounded so immature. They'd just been at a beer bash and shared a kiss that was as deep as the night and she was offering him coffee like a middle-aged woman in a commercial on television.

Hesitating, he glanced in her direction, appeared to wrestle with a silent decision, then pocketed his keys. "I don't think this is a good idea."

"Probably not." Relieved, she laughed and climbed out of the truck.

Now what? she wondered as she waited for him to round the fender and walk to the front door. Her fingers fumbled a little as she pushed the key into the lock and turned softly. The door opened silently and her cat, in a streak of gray, bolted inside.

"Get locked out, did you, Shadow?" Carlie said, thankful for the distraction. "That's what happens when you don't come in when you're called." With the cat at her heels, Carlie walked quickly and quietly down the hall to the kitchen where she snapped on the light. Shadow sprang to the counter and perched on the windowsill.

"You've got a friend," Ben observed.

"Most of the time, but she's a little fickle."

"Like you?" he asked and she felt heat flood up her neck. Of course he'd think she was as flighty as the stupid cat. There was no telling what Kevin had told his brother.

"I'm a lot of things," she said, opening the refrigerator door and pulling out a carton of milk. She sniffed the edge to be sure the contents weren't sour, then poured some into a saucer and placed the dish in the corner by the back door. "But definitely not fickle." The cat hopped off the sill, trotted over to the saucer, wrinkled her nose, then began to lap greedily.

"No?" Ben twisted a kitchen chair around and straddled the back.

"We've got cola, or lemonade or I can make coffee."

"The soda's fine."

She poured two glasses, rattled ice out of a tray and plopped a couple of cubes into each glass. "I just want to know that we're not together because of Kevin," Ben suddenly tossed out.

"What? That's crazy!" She nearly dropped the glasses. Was he serious?

"Some girls would date a guy's brother to get back at him."

"I don't want to get back at anyone!"

"And some would try and make him jealous."

"Do you really believe that?" she asked, dumbfounded.

His eyes turned sober. "I don't want to."

"Good, because I'm tired of talking about your brother, okay? I told you that I was never really serious about him. Either you believe me or you don't."

"I just want things straight."

"Me, too."

He stared at her a long minute, then took the glass from her outstretched hand and lifted it a bit. "Cheers."

"Here's mud in your eye."

"Better than a foot in the mouth, I guess." He smiled then, a long slow smile that touched a corner of her heart, before he placed the glass to his lips.

Carlie's heart did a stupid little somersault and she knew that she'd misjudged her reaction to him. She'd hoped that after meeting him, her fascination for him would fade, but instead, the more she was with him, the more intrigued she was and try as she might, she couldn't forget that single, long kiss.

"I heard you plan to leave town," he said. She guessed his information had come from Kevin. "That you've got big plans to model. L.A. or New York. Right?"

She felt heat flood her face. "It's a dream," she admitted. "I worked on the school paper, taking pictures. And so after I graduated, I took a job in Coleville at a studio, just doing grunt work—filing, typing, developing negatives—that sort of thing. And then the owner of the studio—his name is Rory—asked me to pose for him. So I did."

Clouds gathered in his eyes. "So the rest is history?"

She lifted a shoulder. "Hardly."

"No contract with the Ford Agency?"

"Not yet." She relaxed a little. He was teasing her and the twinkle in his hazel eyes wasn't malicious—just interested.

"I don't blame you for wanting to get out," he admitted, then drained his drink.

"You don't?" She didn't believe him. Kevin had acted as if Gold Creek was the end-all and be-all. She'd suspected that he hadn't always believed it, but that once he'd lost his basketball scholarship and his dreams in the process, he'd forced himself to settle for a job in the mill and now was rationalizing . . . or pouring himself into a bottle. Though she'd never voiced her opinion, she thought Kevin spent too many nights on the third stool of the Silver Horseshoe Saloon holding up the bar and watching sports on television. He'd even given up on city-league basketball with friends. She expected his brother to feel the same.

"Sure. I don't plan to hang out here any longer than necessary."

"What're you going to do?"

"See as much of the world as I can. Maybe join the army. My dad thinks I should enlist first and let the military pay for my schooling when I get out."

"You want to go into the army?" she repeated.

"Why not?" He slanted her an uneven grin. "You know, join the army, see the world."

"I don't know. It sounds so...rigid and well, kind of like prison."

"It'll be a challenge."

"You have a thing for guns, or something?"

"I have a thing for adventure." His eyes glimmered a fraction as his teeth crunched down on the ice cube. All at once she could imagine him creeping through some foreign jungle, rifle slung over his back, searching out the enemy. There was a part of Ben Powell that seemed dangerous and forbidden—a part of him that longed to walk on the edge.

"It's peace time, remember?" she said, feeling more than a little nervous. She hated guns. Hated war. Hated the military.

"There's always action somewhere."

"And you want to be there."

"Beats sitting around this Podunk town and ending up hoping that the mills don't shut down and praying that some jerk like H. G. Monroe III keeps on handing out paychecks that barely cover your bills." He frowned darkly and his jaw grew hard. "I don't plan on working at the Bait and Fish for the rest of my life and I'm sure as hell not going to sign up with the Monroes or the Fitzpatricks."

"But you would with the army." Carlie didn't bother hiding her sarcasm. Her father had worked at Fitzpatrick Logging for nearly thirty years. He was a foreman and made decent money. Time after time Weldon Surrett had told his only daughter that Thomas Fitzpatrick had given him a job when there was no work, he'd kept the logging company running in bad times and good, he'd spotted Weldon as a dedicated worker and promoted him. Carlie was convinced her father would lay down his life for Thomas Fitzpatrick, even though she didn't completely trust the man.

When Roy, Thomas's eldest son, had been killed last fall, her father had cried and forced his small family to attend the funeral. It had been painful that rainy day and the fact that Carlie had sided with Rachelle in defending Jackson Moore had caused friction in the family as well as friction at Weldon's job.

Almost everyone in town believed that Jackson Moore had killed his rival. Everyone but Rachelle and her friend, Carlie. It had been an argument that simmered around the apartment for weeks after Jackson Moore left town.

She took a sip of her drink. "I, um, think Thomas Fitzpatrick isn't all bad," she said, though, truthfully, the few times she'd met him, she'd been uncomfortable. Thomas, tall and patrician, had looked at her intently each time and his smile had seemed to have a hidden meaning that chilled her blood.

"I'd hate to see what you consider 'all bad.'"

She wiped a drop of dew from the side of her glass. "Look, years ago, Fitzpatrick gave my father a chance and he's kept him on, even when Dad was out with back surgery. Dad never missed a paycheck."

Ben's jaw tightened into a harsh line. "Yep. Fitzpatrick. Helluva guy. He and Monroe. Peas in the same dirty pod." He scooted back his chair, handed her his glass and shoved his hands into the front pockets of his jeans. "I guess I'd better shove off. Big day at the Bait and Fish tomorrow."

"You don't have to leave," she said, hating the fact that they'd come very near an argument.

"It's late." With a bitter smile he strode to the front door and she followed. "Thanks for the drink."

She thought he might kiss her again and he stared at her for a heartbeat that caused her throat to catch. His gaze lingered on hers a second longer than necessary. "Good night, Carlie," he whispered, his voice rough.

She leaned forward, expecting to be taken into his arms, but he opened the door and disappeared, leaving her feeling empty inside.

Disappointment curled in her stomach as she watched him through the narrow window. The pickup bounced out of parking lot and disappeared into the night. Touching the tip of her finger to her lips, she closed her eyes and wondered if she'd ever see him again.

"I heard you were with Carlie." Kevin lifted his head from beneath the hood of his Corvette long enough to stare his brother hard in the eye. "At the lake the other night. Some of the guys said you met her at the Daniels' place and wound up taking her home."

"Does it bother you?" Ben asked, wishing he hadn't stopped by Kevin's rented house unannounced. His brother was checking out his one prized possession—a six-year-old Corvette with engine problems. Keeping the car running cost Kevin nearly every dime he earned at the sawmill. Glossy black and sleek, the car seemed to hug the asphalt of the driveway.

"Bother me?" Kevin slammed down the hood and leaned a hip against a low-slung fender. "'Course it bothers me. She's trouble, man. I told you that before."

"You also said that you were through with her, that you were going with someone else . . . a girl from Coleville."

"Tracy," Kevin agreed, wiping his hands on a greasy rag. "I am."

"So it doesn't matter—"

"Like hell!" Kevin said, bending a little so that the tip of his nose nearly touched Ben's. "That little bitch gave me nothing but grief. Nothing! If you're smart, you'll stay away from her!" He opened the car door, slid inside and started the Corvette with a roar from the powerful engine. Blue smoke jetted from the exhaust as the sports car idled for a second, backfired and died. "Great," Kevin ground out. "Now what?"

Ben ignored his brother's question. "You've still got a thing for her."

Kevin stiffened, but his mouth twisted into an ugly little smile as he glared up at Ben through the open window. "No way. I'm through with her. Used goods."

Ben's fists clenched and he gnashed his back teeth together to keep from uttering a hot retort. He hadn't come over to Kevin's to pick a fight with him. No, he'd just stopped by to clear his conscience and make certain that Kevin didn't still hold a torch for Carlie because, for the past three days, ever since taking her home from the lake, Ben had thought of little else than her easy smile, glossy black hair and blue eyes. During the day, when he was supposed to be stocking the shelves or selling fishing tackle, thoughts of her had invaded his mind. And the nights were worse—he'd already lost three nights' sleep, tossing and turning, remembering the feel of her body against his when he'd kissed her.

Muttering under his breath, Kevin climbed out of the car, checked under the hood one more time and, in exasperation, tossed the dirty rag into a box of tools. He reached into the pocket of his shirt for his cigarettes and his face creased into a frown. "Probably needs a whole new engine." Then, as if he remembered why his brother had stopped by, he added, "Look, if you want Carlie Surrett, I'm not standin' in your way. She's all yours. She doesn't mean a thing to me."

"You're sure?"

Kevin flicked a lighter to the end of his cigarette, then let out a long stream of smoke. "It's your funeral."

Ben wasn't convinced that Kevin didn't still harbor a few unsettled feelings, but it didn't really matter. Ben had laid all his cards on the table. "So how'd you find out that I was with her at the lake?"

Kevin snorted. Smoke curled from his nostrils. "This is Gold Creek, remember? Bad news travels fast."

Chapter Two

Ben didn't call. Not the next day, nor the day after. Carlie began to believe that she'd imagined the passion in his kiss.

"Face it," she told her reflection as she stared into the oval mirror mounted over her bureau. "It wasn't a big deal to him." She brushed her long hair until it crackled, then braided the blue-black strands into a single plait that fell down the middle of her back. Shadow was curled on the window seat in her room, washing her face and obviously unconcerned about Carlie's love life.

"I shouldn't care, you know," she said with a glance at the gray tabby. Shadow did her best to ignore Carlie and continued preening. In disgust, Carlie tossed her brush onto the bureau. "You make a lousy sister, you know," she said, wishing she had someone in whom to confide. She considered Brenda, but shoved that idea quickly aside. Brenda was too gregarious; she didn't know how to keep a secret. But she could always confide in Rachelle.

Or she could just forget Ben. He obviously wasn't interested in her and she wasn't the type to go chasing after boys. Or she hadn't been until she'd become interested in the younger Powell brother.

Grabbing her purse, she headed for work. Upon her mother's urging, she snatched an apple from the fruit basket on the table, and walked outside. The morning air was already hot, the dew melted away. She left the windows of her car rolled down and turned the radio up as she drove the few miles to Coleville and her summer job. What she'd do come September, she hadn't really considered.

She didn't have enough money to go away to school, and she'd applied at a local junior college, but she wasn't convinced that academics was in her future.

Neither is Ben Powell, she told herself firmly as her mind strayed to him. Why had she met him this summer, when she was already confused about the rest of her life? She didn't need to be so distracted by a boy who hardly knew she existed.

Disgusted that she couldn't put him out of her mind, she spent the next five hours in the photography studio concentrating on her work. She developed negatives, helped frame some of Rory's, her boss's, most recent shots and generally tidied up the studio. Rory didn't seem to believe in the connection between cleanliness and God.

"I have to be creative," he'd told her when she mentioned the general mess. "I can't be bothered with trivial things." He was joking, of course, but Carlie had taken it upon herself to pick up the clutter around the studio, clean the kitchen and bathroom, and vacuum the carpets. She couldn't bear to work in a pigsty.

Rory didn't seem to notice. However, he was adamant that she model for him when he was doing an advertising shoot for local merchants or creating his own portfolio.

Rory had told her time and time again that she was wasting her time on the wrong end of a camera.

"Thousands of girls would die for what you've got," he said as he set up the studio for a shoot. Mrs. Murdock was coming in with her two-year-old son and her border collie.

"The camera loves you. Look at these—" He waved pictures he'd taken of Carlie, showing off her high cheekbones and blue-green eyes. "The face of an angel with just the hint of the devil in those eyes of yours. I'm telling you, Madison Avenue would eat these up."

"I like to take pictures, not pose," she'd replied, though the idea of modeling held more than a little appeal.

"So spend a few years in front of the lens. Make some bucks, give it your best shot before you grow old and fat, or God forbid, fall in love." Rory was a tall man, thirty-five or so, with a dishwater-blond ponytail that was starting to thin and streak with gray. His face was perpetually unshaven and he never wore a tie. "Now, do we have any Christmas props? These pictures are a Christmas gift for Mrs. Murdock's husband, even though Christmas is what—seven months away?"

"Five," Carlie said. "I'll check the upstairs." She climbed the rickety staircase and opened a door. The attic was sweltering and dusty. She dug through some boxes and came up with several sprigs of fake holly, some red candles that had already melted a little and a stuffed animal that looked like a reindeer. She even uncovered a rolled backdrop of a snow-encrusted forest.

Carrying the box downstairs, she blew her bangs from her eyes. "There's not much," she admitted as the front bell chimed and Mrs. Murdock strolled into the reception area. She held a perfectly behaved border collie on a leash and her dynamo of a two-year-old son was wearing a white shirt, red-and-green plaid vest and black velvet shorts. Red knee socks and black shoes completed the outfit.

She offered Carlie a tired smile. "I know this won't be easy," she admitted as she licked her fingers and tried to smooth a wrinkle in her son's hair. He jerked his head away with a loud protest. "Jason's in the middle of the 'terrible twos,' but my husband would love a picture of him with Waldo." At the moment Jason was tugging hard on Waldo's leash and the dog was sitting patiently.

Carlie led the entourage back to the studio where Rory was adjusting the light.

Mrs. Murdock's prediction was an understatement.

Jason pulled at his bow tie, cried, pitched a fit and generally mauled the dog, but both the collie and Rory were incredibly calm. By the end of the shoot nearly two hours later, Carlie's patience was frayed, Mrs. Murdock had lost her smile and Rory wasn't convinced any of the shots he'd taken would be satisfactory. "Keep your fingers crossed," Rory suggested as they locked up for the night. "I'd hate to go through that all over again."

The thought was depressing. "I'm sure at least one of the shots will turn out," she said, hoping to sound encouraging.

"If today was December twentieth, I would worry. As it is, we still have a lot of time for retakes."

Carlie groaned inwardly at the thought. She drove home in her hot little car and felt positively wilted. Sweat collected at the base of her neck and dotted her forehead, and her clothes, a black skirt and white blouse, were wrinkled and grimy.

Wheeling into the parking lot, she nearly stood on the brakes. Ben's truck was parked in the shade of a larch tree and he was leaning against the fender, arms crossed over his chest, as if he had nothing better to do.

He glanced up when he saw her and shifted a match from one side of his mouth to the other. His lips twitched in what one might consider a smile.

She cut the engine and climbed out.

"Thought I might find you here," he said, taking the match from his mouth and breaking it between two fingers.

"Have you been waiting long?"

Shaking his head he glanced at his watch. "A few minutes."

She couldn't stop the wild beating of her heart. He looked much the same as the last time. Again he wore faded blue Levi's, but this time a white T-shirt stretched across his chest. His gaze was lazy when it touched hers. "I wondered if you wanted to go for a drive. Up to the lake or something."

"I thought you'd forgotten all about me."

Again the sexy smile. "Forget you?" He let out a silent laugh. "Is that possible?"

"It's been a while since I heard from you."

"I've been busy." He leaned one hip against the truck's fender and waited. "So what do you say?"

"Just let me grab my suit."

The apartment was empty and Ben waited downstairs while Carlie dashed into her room, stripped out of her work clothes and threw on a one-piece sea-green swimsuit. She couldn't believe that he was actually waiting for her. Her heart pounded as she stepped into a pair of shorts and a sleeveless blouse with long tails that she tied under her breasts. She ran a brush over her hair, touched up her lipstick and was back downstairs in less than ten minutes. She felt breathless and flushed as she wrote her parents a quick note and let Shadow inside.

Once they were in the parking lot, he unlocked the truck and held open the passenger door for her. She climbed into the sun-baked interior and wondered why, after hearing nothing from him for the past few days, he'd decided to pick up where they'd left off. Or had he?

With a roar the old truck started and Ben eased the Ford into traffic.

"Did something happen?" she finally asked.

His brows fastened together as he squinted through the windshield. Frowning, he reached across her, into the glove compartment and extracted a pair of sunglasses. "Happen?" he asked, sliding the shades onto the bridge of his nose.

"Well, I just figured that you didn't want to see me again."

"You figured wrong," he said with a trace of agitation. He stopped for a red light, rolled down the window and rested his elbow on the ledge. "Besides, I thought I should make sure that I wasn't stepping on Kevin's toes."

She nearly dropped through the seat. "What's he got to do with this?"

"Nothing. But I wanted to double-check."

"Double-check? This is my life—" she began, but held her tongue. It didn't matter anyway. Obviously Kevin understood how she felt and Ben was here with her now. Still, the thought galled her.

As they drove through the outskirts of town, Ben fiddled with the dial for the radio and found a station that mixed old songs with newer recordings.

"I thought that didn't work."

"Fixed it." He sent her a quick glance as they approached the sawmill. Ben's expression changed and his jaw grew hard as the truck sped along the chain-link fence surrounding the yard. Thousands of board-feet of lumber were sorted according to grade in huge stacks and a mountain of logs waited to be milled. Trucks, many bearing the logo of Fitzpatrick Logging, roared in and out of the yard and men in hard hats waved to the drivers.

Cranes hovered over huge piles of logs and forklifts carried planed lumber from sheds. The shift was changing and men sauntered in and out of the gate. They laughed and smoked, shouted to friends and brushed the sawdust from their shirts and jeans.

Kevin's sleek Corvette was parked in the lot between the dusty pickups and station wagons.

"So why don't you work at the mill?" she asked, sensing him tense as they sped past the activity at the sawmill.

"Don't you think two Powells bowing down and paying homage to H.G. III is enough?"

"It's a good job."

"I prefer the hours at the Bait and Fish."

She slid a glance in his direction and noticed the way his hands gripped the steering wheel—as if he were going to rip it from its column.

"You don't like the Monroes much, do you?"

"I try not to think about them."

She lifted a brow and he caught the movement.

"Okay. It's like this. I just don't appreciate the way Monroe does business. He lives in a mansion in some ritzy neighborhood in San Francisco, sent his son to private schools, flies into Gold Creek in a company helicopter once, maybe twice a week, does some rah-rahing and claps a few men on the back, then speeds back to his country club for eighteen holes of golf before he plants himself in the clubhouse. Like some damned visiting royalty.''

''He's rich.''

''So that gives him the right to use the sweat of people's backs to pay for his yacht harbored in the marina?''

''That's the way it works.''

''At least Fitzpatrick has the guts to stick around Gold Creek,'' Ben said as he shifted down and turned onto an abandoned logging road that curved away from the lake and switch-backed through the forested hills.

''I thought we were going swimming at the lake.''

''We are.''

''Unless my sense of direction is way off, we should be driving toward the setting sun instead of away from it.''

He laughed then and the anger that had been radiating from him since they passed the sawmill faded. He touched her lightly on the back of her hand with strong, callused fingers. ''Trust me.''

Her heart flipped over and she knew she'd trust him with her very life.

They drove slowly, past fir and maple trees that allowed only a little of the fading sunlight through a thick canopy of branches overhead. Dry weeds brushed the belly of the truck as it labored up the steep grade. The radio began to fade and Ben snapped it off as the forest gave way to bare hills that had been stripped of old-growth timber. The scarred land looked as if it had been shaved by a godlike barber who took huge cuts at the remaining stands of old growth. Where the land had been logged, nature was taking over. A fine layer of grass and brush, dotted with a few scrub trees, began to reclaim the rocks and soil between the rotting stumps. Farther on there was evidence of reforestation, small fir and pine trees planted by man and machines to replenish the forest and provide the next crop of timber for another generation of loggers and sawmill men.

''The lifeblood of Gold Creek,'' Ben observed wryly.

It was the truth, whether he meant to be sarcastic or not. For generations, Gold Creek had depended upon its rich stands of timber. Though the town had been optimistically named during the gold rush when a few miners had discovered glittering bits of the precious metal in the streambed of the brook that flowed into Whitefire Lake, timber was the real gold in the area. The fortunes of men like the Monroes and the Fitzpatricks had been founded and grown on the wealth of the forest.

Ben drove until the road gave out and he parked in a rutted, overgrown lot that had once been used as a base for the machinery that winched the trees up the hillside and a parking lot for logging trucks that had hauled the precious timber back to Monroe's mill.

He grabbed a backpack and slung it over his shoulder. "Come on," he said and she climbed out of his pickup. They left the truck and followed a path that was flanked by berry vines and brush. Eventually the forest resumed and Carlie struggled against the sharp incline. She was breathing hard as they passed through shaded stands of trees that had never been touched by a chainsaw. Birds flitted through the trees, while squirrels scolded from hidden branches. The earth smelled cool, and far in the distance she heard the sound of water tumbling over rocks.

"Where's the river?" she asked.

"No river. Gold Creek."

"Clear up here?"

"Has to start somewhere." They continued to climb and Carlie's legs began to ache. "You know, I'm not really dressed for mountain climbing," she said as the back of her heels began to rub in her tennis shoes.

"It's just a little farther." He grabbed her hand and helped her through the woods. She tried not to concentrate on the feel of his fingers twining with hers.

"What is?"

"A place I heard about at the store."

"You're not taking me fishing, are you?" she teased, but he didn't answer, and the warmth of his hand over hers was as secure as a promise. They hiked for another twenty minutes before the forest began to thin. The trees eventually gave way to an alpine meadow, complete with a profusion of wildflowers blooming between thin blades of sun-bleached grass. Butterflies fluttered in the dying sunlight and bees droned lazily.

Still holding her hand, Ben led her through the knee-high grass to the head of a spring where clear water spilled into a small ravine and washed along the rocks as it tumbled downhill.

"Gold Creek," he said.

"I thought the creek started at Whitefire Lake."

"Technically it does," he agreed, "and if you look on a map there's probably another name for this particular brook, but since all this water rushes down to the lake and runs out to feed Gold Creek, I'd say this is where it all starts." Leaning down, he ran his fingers through the water.

"Why'd you bring me up here?"

His hand stopped beneath the clear, shimmering surface. Straightening, he let the water drip from his hands and touched the line of her jaw. His fingers were cool and wet, his eyes dark with the coming dusk. "I wanted to be alone with you," he admitted with the hint of a smile. "No Brenda. No Kevin. No parents. Just you and me."

"Why?" She hardly dared breathe. Her chest was so tight, she thought it might burst.

"I thought we got started on the wrong foot the other night."

She swallowed against a knot in her throat. "I was starting to believe that we didn't really get started."

"Silly girl," he whispered. He shifted and the fingers that had traced her jaw moved around her neck, pulling her gently to him as his lips found hers in a kiss that was filled with wonder and youth and the promise of tomorrow.

Carlie's knees felt weak and she didn't protest when the weight of his body pushed them both to the soft bed of dry grass near the water.

She wound her arms around his neck and opened her mouth to the gentle pressure of his tongue. A curling warmth started somewhere deep in her abdomen and spread outward, racing through her bloodstream, causing her skin to tingle. He flicked the tip of his tongue against the ridges along the roof of her mouth, touching her teeth and delving farther.

Was this wrong? she wondered, but didn't care. Nothing that felt this right should be forbidden.

Groaning, he flung one leg between hers and kissed her harder, pressing hot lips against hers anxiously.

"Carlie," he whispered when he lifted his head and stared down into her eyes. "Is this what you want?"

"I just want to be with you," she said, not thinking about the words, just anxious to assure him that she cared. She touched his cheek with her fingers, then ran them along the back of his neck and drew his head down to hers.

Her lips were wet and eager as they kissed again and she didn't stop him when his fingers found the knot at her blouse and untied the cotton fabric.

Somewhere in the back of her mind she knew that she should tell him no—that she should cool things off before she lost control, but she couldn't. Her blouse parted and his hand surrounded her breast. Through the shiny fabric of her suit, he touched her, kneading the soft mound, causing her nipple to tighten.

Stop him. Stop him now a voice in the back of her mind cried, but she ignored the alarm and kissed him with more fever than before. She felt the cool air touch her shoulder, knew that he was lowering the strap of her swimsuit and before she could say a word, his hot lips had pressed a kiss to the top of her breast.

A low moan escaped her throat as he tugged and the suit fell away, baring the breast to the last rays of sunlight. "So beautiful," he whispered gently, his breath hot as he took the nipple between his lips and tugged.

"Ben," she whispered, her voice rising on the breeze.

"Don't tell me to stop."

"I can't," she murmured, closing her eyes to the feel of his callused hands kneading her flesh, the warmth of his mouth drawing hard on her nipple. Her hips raised anxiously from the nest of dried grass and desire ran hot and thick through her veins when one of his hands moved lower to cup one of her buttocks.

Somewhere, far away, a train whistle blasted, echoing up the mountainside.

Ben tensed, abruptly pulled away, looked down into her eyes, and with a stream of oaths rolled away from her to lie spread-eagled on the grass. He flung an arm over his eyes and said, "Get dressed."

His harsh words were like a slap. Feeling like a fool, Carlie adjusted the strap of her suit and rebuttoned her blouse. "Is . . . is something wrong?"

Sighing loudly, he shoved his hair out of his eyes and stared up at the dusky sky. "I didn't plan to bring you up here and seduce you." His brows drew together in a serious line of vexation. "Oh, hell, maybe I did."

Her back stiffened a bit. "You wouldn't have forced me to do anything I wasn't ready for."

He glanced at her, his eyes dark and unreadable. "You don't know me, Carlie."

"I know you well enough."

"Damn it all anyway!" He rolled over, grabbed the bag he'd let drop to the meadow floor and took her hand again. "We'd better get back. It's getting dark and I don't trust myself alone with you."

"I thought that's what you wanted."

"Don't you get it? I don't know what I want and I was about to do something that might take away all of our options! Hell, what a mess!"

Cheeks inflamed, she adjusted her clothing and walked away from him to the cliff. Staring over the tops of trees, she saw the glimmer of water.

She heard him approaching and tensed when he wrapped his arms around her waist to link his hands beneath her breasts. "Hey, look, I'm sorry. Things were just moving too fast for me."

"I wasn't the one—"

"Shh. I know. Believe me, I take all the blame."

With a sigh, she leaned back against him and wrapped her arms over his. "No blame," she said. "It just happened."

"And it will keep happening unless we use our heads." For a second he was silent and she felt his breath ruffle the hair at her crown.

"You see the lake?" he said, as if trying to change the subject.

"Mmm."

"Now look to the south. Over here." He moved, rotating her body. "The town."

The first lights were beginning to twinkle from the valley, shimmering up against the darkening sky.

"If you look hard enough, or with binoculars, you can see the railroad trestle bridge, city hall and the sawmill."

She followed his gaze and noticed the railroad tracks cutting through the valley. The trestle bridge spanned Gold Creek just on the outskirts of town.

"I didn't think you'd been up here before," she said, once her heart had stopped drumming and she could trust her voice again.

"I'm just telling you what I heard from some of the guys who come into the store. Come on. We'd better get back." He rummaged in his backpack, drew out a flashlight and started leading her down the trail.

Night settled over the forest and by the time they returned to Ben's truck, they were following the steady beam of his flashlight. Carlie heard bats stir in the trees, felt the breeze as they flew low, but she wasn't afraid. Probably because she was with Ben.

Silly, she told herself, but she trusted Ben. It came as a shock to realize that if she didn't stop her runaway emotions, she might just end up falling in love with him.

Chapter Three

"Come on. It's not every day I get the afternoon off!" Carlie said, insisting that Rachelle drop the magazine she was reading as she sat on an old patio chair on the back porch of her mother's house. "I'll buy you French fries and a Coke."

"What if I want lemonade?"

"Whatever!" Carlie blew her bangs out of her eyes and waited as Rachelle told her mother what the girls had planned. Rachelle found a way to avoid dragging her little sister, Heather, with them and they drove into town with the windows down. Carlie's T-shirt clung to her back as she parked her car near the Rexall Drug Store.

Kids on skateboards zoomed along the sidewalk, while mothers pushed strollers and adjusted sunbonnets. Heat waved up from the sidewalk and street.

Inside the store, ceiling fans whirred, but did little to lower the temperature. Carlie fanned herself with her hand as they looked into a glass case filled with costume jewelry.

"You're seeing *Ben* Powell?" Rachelle repeated, lifting her eyebrows as if she hadn't heard her friend correctly. "But I thought—"

"I know. You thought I was dating Kevin. I did for a few weeks. We went out a couple of times and it didn't work out. I thought I told you."

"You didn't say anything about Ben."

"I didn't know Ben." Carlie paused at a rack of sunglasses and tried on a pair with yellow lenses.

"Not you," Rachelle advised.

"I know." She replaced the glasses and turned her attention back to the jewelry case. She fingered a set of turquoise-and-silver earrings, held one of the big hoops up to her ear and frowned at her reflection. "I just met him the other night, at a party. Then . . . well, we took a drive into the mountains."

"Are you going out with him?"

In the mirror, Carlie saw her own eyes cloud. "He hasn't called. It's been nearly a week."

Rachelle tossed a shank of auburn hair over as she eyed the pieces of bargain jewelry on the sale rack. "So you haven't actually dated him."

"Not really," Carlie said. Her time with Ben in the mountains hadn't been much of a date, and yet she'd remembered each second so vividly that even now she tingled a little. She was determined to see Ben again. She'd always been a little boy crazy, or so her mother had claimed, but she'd never been quite so bold. Usually boys had sought her out, as in the case of Ben's older brother, but this time, it looked as if she would have to take the bull by the horns and do a little pursuing. The thought settled like lead in her stomach and she wasn't particularly comfortable with the role. But it was long past the days when girls sat by the phone praying it would ring. Women's lib wasn't a new concept. So it was time to push aside the traditional roles and go for it. Right?

They walked through a section of paperback books and magazines and ended up sitting on the stools at the back counter. The menu was a big marquee positioned over the soda machines with interchangeable letters and numbers that were backlit by flickering fluorescent bulbs.

Carlie waved to her mom, glanced at the menu, but ordered her usual, a chocolate Coke and large order of fries.

"I'll have the same," Rachelle said, "except I'd like a cherry Coke."

"You're making a mistake," Carlie teased and she noticed Rachelle shudder as if the thought of mixing chocolate and cola in a drink concoction was disgusting.

"I thought you had to work today," Thelma said to her daughter as she scribbled their orders onto a pad, ripped off the page and clipped it to a spinning wheel for the fry cook.

"There wasn't much happening at the studio, so Rory gave me a few hours off."

"Are you going home? You could start dinner...."

"I, uh, already have plans. I'm meeting some kids at the lake." She noticed the lines of strain around her mother's eyes and lifted a shoulder. "But I could swing by the house first."

"Would you?"

"Sure."

Thelma busied herself making milk shakes for a crowd of preteen boys. The shake machine whined loudly.

"What's so special about Ben?" Rachelle asked.

"Everything."

"Come on. You can be more specific."

"I wish." Carlie couldn't even explain her fascination with him to herself. "I just saw him a couple of weeks ago and really noticed him. I'd seen him before, of course, but never really paid much attention." She blushed a little. "You know I've never been shy—"

"Amen."

"So... I came up with a way to meet him." She gave a quick version of crashing the party by the lake and Rachelle's good mood seemed to fade, as if she were reliving the night of the Fitzpatrick party.

"I thought you'd learned your lesson."

Carlie grinned. "I guess not."

"So your interest in Ben has nothing to do with the fact that he and Kevin are brothers?"

"Believe me, I wish they weren't."

Thelma placed dewy glasses of soda in front of them. "Fries will be up in a sec," she said with a wink. Carlie fingered her straw until her mother was out of earshot again. "I know that being interested in Ben is...well, kind of strange."

"*Crazy* is the word I'd choose."

"But I can't stop thinking about him."

"You?" Rachelle smiled and Carlie knew what she was thinking.

While Rachelle had barely gone out, and had spent most of her time with her nose in a book, Carlie had dated most of the guys on the basketball and swim teams. Not seriously, of course. She'd never "gone" with any boy for over two months. That had been the problem with Kevin. He'd started talking about the future, their future, here in Gold Creek. When she'd mentioned her dreams of seeing some of the world, he'd pouted, told her that she was setting herself up for a fall, that she should get real and realize that the best she could expect was a small house in Gold Creek, a good husband who worked in the mill and a couple of kids.

No, thank you. She wasn't ready to settle down yet. There were places to see, people to meet and then, someday, maybe, she'd come back. She had the rest of her life to get married and raise a family....

Carlie swirled her straw in her drink. Thelma dropped two plastic baskets of French fries onto the counter. "I'm not supposed to say this around here," she said, "but these are a nutritional disaster."

Grinning, Carlie plucked a hot fry from the basket and dipped it in a tiny cup of catsup. "That's why they're so delicious."

Her mother winked at her. "Don't forget dinner."

"I won't."

She chatted with Rachelle and Carlie until the next wave of patrons came in. "Uh-oh, looks like duty calls." With a friendly smile, she whipped out her order pad and offered coffee to a couple of men who looked as if they'd just got off the early shift at the mill.

Carlie knew why her dreams of leaving Gold Creek were so important to her. Her mother had told Carlie time and time again not to make the same mistakes that she had. "Not that I regret anything, mind you," she'd told her daughter one night as she rubbed a crick from her lower back and reached in the medicine cabinet for the Ben-Gay. Thelma Perkins had once had dreams of being a dancer, but she'd fallen in love with and married Weldon Surrett. She'd gotten pregnant with Carlie and put away her ballet shoes forever.

Rachelle munched on a fry. "Don't you think it's a big mistake getting involved with brothers?"

"First of all, I wasn't 'involved' with Kevin and secondly..." Carlie plucked the cherry out of her drink and dropped it into her friend's glass. "Well, it shouldn't matter."

"It matters when you go out with a guy's best friend. It has to be worse if they're related."

"So now you're the authority."

Rachelle smiled sadly. "I just know that I wouldn't want to share anyone I cared about with Heather."

"Heather's not the type to share."

"Neither am I," Rachelle said and Carlie wondered if Rachelle was thinking of Jackson Moore, the only boy she'd ever cared for. "The way I see it, if they've both dated you, it's got to cause some kind of friction between the two brothers."

She did have a point, Carlie silently conceded, and truth to tell, she'd been concerned about the same thing, but she didn't want to think about it. "I told Kevin it was over weeks ago."

"Did he believe you?"

"Well, it took him a while, but, yeah, he got the message. He's dating someone else now. Some girl from Coleville."

"Ben tell you that?" Rachelle wiped her fingers on a paper napkin.

"No, I heard it from Brenda."

"Ahh, the source of all truth," Rachelle teased.

"Of all gossip," Carlie corrected as they finished their drinks and French fries.

How she felt for Ben didn't have anything to do with his brother, she told herself later as she gathered her hair into a ponytail and made a face at her reflection. After washing her hands, she started on dinner as she'd promised her mother, but she had trouble concentrating.

Ever since being with Ben in the mountains, she'd thought of little else. She had never let another boy touch her—not that way—and she remembered each graze of his finger against her skin, his breath in her hair, the way he cradled her breasts.... "Oh, stop it!" she snapped, causing Shadow to look up from her nap on one of the kitchen chairs.

Carlie threw herself into the task at hand. The chicken was cooked and she was supposed to piece together a potato salad. Not too difficult.

She sliced the already-boiled eggs and added them to the bowl of chopped onions and diced potatoes before starting on the dressing.

Maybe she should just forget about Ben. After all, he hadn't called. He probably wasn't interested in a girl he considered his brother's castoff. Besides, she really didn't have time to get involved with a boy from Gold Creek.... *But who was she kidding?* She was already involved. Up to her eyeballs!

Muttering to herself, she added salt, pepper and paprika to her concoction of mayonnaise and cream. She tasted the dressing and wrinkled her nose. Not quite like Mom's, but it would have to do. Snapping off plastic wrap, she covered the salad and shoved her efforts into the refrigerator before racing upstairs to change.

For Ben.

Not that he even wanted to see her.

However, Carlie was impulsive and she believed in going after something she wanted. Right now, be it right or wrong, she wanted Ben Powell. Despite everyone's advice to the contrary, she knew she'd do whatever she could to make Ben notice her.

Knowing she was asking for trouble, she drove to the Bait and Fish, a small general store perched on the south side of the lake. Built in the 1920s, the store was flanked by a wooden porch and a covered extension that housed two old-fashioned gas pumps. Faded metal signs for Nehi soda and Camel cigarettes were tacked onto the exterior as was an outdoor thermometer.

So this was it. Do or die, she thought when she recognized Ben's pickup parked in the gravel lot. Her fingers were suddenly sweaty on the steering wheel. She parked her car, wiped her hands on her shorts and reminded herself that there wasn't a law against buying soda. She hadn't been in the Bait and Fish for half a year. Pocketing the keys to the car, she walked up the front steps and shoved open the screen door.

A bell tinkled as she stepped inside. Three large rooms connected by archways wandered away from the central area near the cash register where Tina Sedgewick, a spry woman nearing sixty, was working.

Carlie saw Ben from the corner of her eyes. Balanced atop a ladder, he was fiddling with wires to an old paddle fan. He glanced her direction as the door opened and a half smile curved his lips. *As if he'd been expecting her!* She felt suddenly foolish, but there was no turning back.

"Well, hi, stranger," Tina said, catching sight of Carlie. She'd been seated on a stool behind the register and working on a piece of needlepoint. With blue-tinged hair and a weathered complexion, Tina had worked at the Bait and Fish longer than she'd been married to the owner, Eli Sedgewick, which, according to Carlie's mother, was close to forty years.

"How're you, Mrs. Sedgewick?"

"Can't complain, though, Lord knows, I'd like to." She set her needlepoint aside and prattled on, asking about

Carlie's folks, her job in Coleville and her plans after the summer was over. Carlie tried to keep her concentration on the conversation but she could feel Ben's gaze hot against the back of her neck.

"Don't suppose your ma is with you." Tina glanced out the window to check the parking lot, as if she expected Thelma to appear.

"She's at work."

With a sigh, Tina clucked her tongue. "Work, work, work, that's all everybody does anymore. You tell her to come up and visit us once in a while. Eli—hey, look who's come visitin'."

Eli Sedgewick was leaning over a glass display case of fishing equipment, loudly discussing the merits of gray hackles, some kind of fishing fly, with an older man Carlie didn't recognize.

Two other men sat around a potbellied stove in the corner, swapping fishing tales.

Eli, fishing hat studded with different flies, straightened, squinted through thick glasses and smiled as he recognized her. "Well, Carlie girl, about time you showed your face around here," he said. "Your pa retired yet?"

"Not quite."

The customer asked Eli a question and he turned back to his serious discussion.

Carlie walked to the coolers at the rear of the store, eyed the variety of sodas and settled on ginger ale. As she walked back toward the cash register, she stopped at Ben's ladder. "So now you're an electrician?" Carlie asked, her stomach filled with a nest of suddenly very active butterflies.

"Jack-of-all-trades, that's me."

"Or a soldier of fortune?"

He hopped lithely to the ground and dusted off his hands. "Absolutely." Offering her a smile that caused her heart to turn over, he snapped the ladder shut and yelled toward the fishing lure section, "You can try it now, Mr. Sedgewick."

"What? Oh, well, yes..." Sedgewick disappeared behind an open door and flipped on the appropriate switch. The paddle fan started moving slowly.

"What'd I tell ya?" Ben asked, obviously pleased with himself.

"I'll never doubt you again."

His grin widened. "I'll remember that." He turned his intense hazel eyes in her direction. "You come here lookin' for me?"

"No, I...just stopped in for a soda." To prove her point, she flipped open her can of pop.

"Come on, Carlie. You haven't been in the store in months," he said and she couldn't argue, not after he'd obviously overheard her conversation with the Sedgewicks.

"Don't flatter yourself," she said, tossing her hair off her shoulder defensively.

"I'm just telling you what it looks like to me." He carried the ladder back to a storage closet and tucked it inside. Carlie, embarrassed, wondered if the conversation was over and if her relationship, what little there had been of it, with Ben was over, as well.

She paid for her soda and walked outside. She'd been a fool to come by here. She'd known it and yet still she'd come, irresistibly drawn, as if a powerful magnet had forced her to wheel into the Bait and Fish.

"Idiot," she muttered as she climbed into the hot interior of her car. She jammed the keys into the ignition and the motor turned over.

"Hey, wait!" Ben strode out of the store, the screen door slamming behind him.

"For what?" She eyed him through her open window and wondered why she didn't ram the little car into gear and roar out of the lot in a cloud of dust and righteous indignation.

"I didn't mean to embarrass you."

"Well, you did." She just wanted to get away from him. Enough was enough. She couldn't chase him forever and let herself look like an idiot.

"I'm sorry." He stopped by her car and leaned down so that he could stare into her eyes. "I'm glad you came by."

"I'm not."

"Carlie," he said and his voice was like a caress on the soft-blowing breeze. "Look, can we start over?"

She swallowed hard. She didn't want to see the kind side to him, not when she'd made a fool of herself. "Maybe we should just finish. It would be easier."

"But not as much fun," he said and the streaks of silver in his eyes seemed more defined. "I've been meaning to call you—"

"But," she prompted, ready for a string of excuses.

"But I'm working two jobs and well . . . I didn't know if it was such a good idea." He didn't have to mention the passion that had flared between them whenever they were alone, but there it was, still thick in the air, hovering between them. He leaned both arms on the edge of the window and kicked out a hip so that he could stare at her. His fingers grazed her arm and her pulse jumped in anticipation. "I really am glad you stopped by."

She didn't want to hear any platitudes. Not now. "I'm on my way to the lake. I should really go."

Frowning, he checked his watch. "I don't get off until seven. How long are you staying at the lake?"

"Until six-forty-five."

He cocked an interested dark eyebrow. "Not another fifteen minutes?"

"I don't think it's such a good idea," she said, repeating his words and mocking him. With a sigh and a lift of her shoulders, she threw her little car into gear. "I've got to be home for dinner."

"Is that right?" He didn't believe her. The cocksure grin told her he knew she was lying, but he didn't call her on it. At least not yet. Straightening, he slapped the open window with his bare palm. "Well, I guess I'll have to catch you another time." With that he turned on his heel and dashed up the two steps to the porch, leaving Carlie to seethe in her car and wonder why she couldn't just forget him. He was trouble. No two ways about it. She should listen to Rachelle's advice and forget him.

She ripped out of the parking lot in a spray of gravel and imagined Ben laughing at her. So what was she doing chasing after him like a lovesick puppy? He was just playing with her and she certainly didn't need the aggravation. So he'd kissed her. Big deal. Lots of boys had kissed her and she hadn't fantasized about it, made it seem as if the sun and the moon and stars were involved in a simple touching of lips. But she hadn't been willing to let any of the other boys strip her of her blouse or loosen the straps of her swimsuit. No one else had put his lips to her breasts and— "Forget it!" she told herself as she stepped on the gas and pushed the speed limit of the winding road around the lake. At the public boat landing and park, she nosed her compact car into a sliver of a parking space. "Forget him."

She grabbed her towel and beach bag, locked the car and started down the trail through the trees to the swimming hole. She'd cool off, talk with some friends for a while, swim, then go home *before* seven o'clock! She had to forget him. Anything else was just begging for emotional suicide.

"She's a pretty thing, ain't she?" Mrs. Sedgewick said to the world in general as Ben strode back into the store. He didn't comment but saw the old lady swallow a smile at his reaction. Why was everything so complicated when it came to dealing with Carlie? Yes, she was a pretty girl. Yes, he was interested in her. Yes, he'd like to date her. And yes, he couldn't pry her from his mind, try as he might. But all his instincts told him to turn the other way and run anytime he came in contact with her.

Kevin had warned him about her and yet, try as he would, Ben couldn't seem to get the girl out of his blood. Kissing her had been a mistake, a kick-you-in-the-gut kind of mistake that messed with his mind.

He had enough trouble without Carlie. His father had never been the same since his divorce, and his sister, Nadine, seemed about ready to bolt to the altar with Sam

Warne, her boyfriend of the past few years. Kevin, well, he was already screwed up. Ever since he'd lost his basketball scholarship, he hadn't been the same.

Ben needed to keep his wits about him. He was the only Powell left with a lick of sense.

"Why don't you take the rest of the day off?" Tina suggested. "Not much business this afternoon."

"You sure?" Ben was surprised.

"Hell, yes!" Eli said as he straightened a few ten-pound sacks of dog food. "It's slow today."

Ben didn't need any more encouragement. Between his hours working in the woods during the week and his weekend job at the Bait and Fish, he didn't have much time for himself. Not to mention the matter of Carlie Surrett. He should avoid her like the plague, but as he waved to Tina, walked outside and noticed the sun lingering over the horizon, he knew he'd follow Carlie to the lake. "Just like the stupid lemmings," he thought as he ground the gears of his old truck and headed to the public easement where most of the kids hung out.

He saw her car in the parking lot and smiled inwardly. Pocketing his keys, he almost whistled. He had the rest of the day off and didn't have to be back at the tackle shop until noon tomorrow. He considered the ragged pair of cutoffs he kept in a bag on the floor of the cab and decided they'd have to suffice for a swimming suit. *Well, Miss Surrett*, he thought as he climbed out of the hot interior of his old truck, *you're in for one helluva surprise*.

Like a mirror, the lake reflected the forest and surrounding mountains. Speedboats pulling water-skiers, dinghies drifting with fishermen and motorboats trolling through the smooth waters caused the only ripples to appear on the lake's glassy surface.

Carlie ignored a group of kids huddled around a cooler and a radio and walked to the end of the dock. She kicked off her sandals, sat on the edge and dragged one toe through the cold water. What was she doing getting herself tied in emotional knots over Ben Powell? As soon as she had enough money saved, she was leaving Gold Creek and she didn't need any complications—romantic or otherwise—holding her down. Closing her eyes, she pressed her palms to the sun-baked boards of the pier and lolled her head back.

Tranquillity had just settled over her when she felt footsteps reverberating on the tired boards of the dock. She was about to turn around when a pair of hands clamped possessively over her shoulders, thumbs to her back, fingertips resting on the slope of her breasts.

"I didn't think you'd come this early," she said, and a deep-throated chuckle was her response. Blinking open her eyes, she stared upward, where the sun silhouetted the handsome face of a man...but not Ben's. The smell of cigarette smoke and stale beer floated on the breeze. She froze as she recognized Kevin.

"Expecting someone?" he asked with a grin.

She scooted away from him. "What're you doing here?"

"I was with some friends, saw you and thought I'd say hello." He rubbed his chin. "We need to talk."

She tried not to be wary. He was, after all, Ben's brother, as well as a man she'd recently dated. She should give him the benefit of the doubt. Squinting up at him, she said, "What do you want to talk about?"

"Us."

Her throat closed. "There's nothing more to discuss."

"I miss you, Carlie," he said, his expression lifeless.

"I thought you were dating someone else."

"It didn't work out." He shoved a hand through his brown hair and scowled down at the water.

This was getting complicated and she felt a little guilty. "Look, Kevin, I'm seeing someone—"

"Ben. I know." His expression hardened and the look in his eyes was as cold as the depths of the lake. "Hell, don't I know?"

"I don't understand what you want from me, Kevin," she said, wrapping her towel around her shoulders as she stood and faced him. He was tall and intimidating, but he didn't scare her. Kevin wasn't a bad person, just confused.

"I don't know, either. I know it didn't work for us and I suppose I'm as much to blame as anyone, but I'm not sure I can deal with you being Ben's girl. I loved you, Carlie. More than anyone else ever could."

Her heart twisted a little. "You don't, Kevin, and I'm . . . I'm not anyone's girl."

He reached for her, but she stepped away. "Please, don't—"

His lips flattened suddenly. "No one's girl, eh? Oh, right. You're your own woman, going places, off to see the world." When she didn't answer, he cast her a disdainful look filled with pain and anger. "Who're you kidding, Carlie? You don't have any more chance of getting out of this hellhole of a town than the rest of us. You're trapped, baby, just like everyone else."

Trembling a little at the fierceness in his tone, she stepped backward and nearly fell off the dock. She had to scramble to maintain her balance.

"Kevin!" Ben's voice thundered from the parking lot and Carlie wanted to die.

Kevin's expression turned ugly as he watched his younger brother run to the dock. "Big mistake, Carlie," he said, turning back to her and stripping the towel from her fingers. His gaze raked down her body. "If you really want to get out, you'd better not tie yourself down. Especially not to Ben. He'll break your damned heart." With that piece of advice he dropped the towel and strode down the planks of the dock and met his brother who was running toward the pier.

"She's all yours," Kevin said with a dismissive motion of his head.

"I'm not anyone's!" she insisted again, though her face burned with shame.

"Carlie—"

Ben's voice followed her as she turned and dived into the clear, cold water of the lake. Damn the Powell boys. Both of them. Who did they think they were, snarling over her like two tigers coveting a prized piece of meat? Why couldn't she just forget them both? Kevin was bad news and everyone told her that getting involved with Ben would be courting disaster. The writing was already on the wall.

The water caressed her skin and she swam under the surface, determined to put as much distance between herself and anyone named Powell. Who needed them, she thought, and her heart tugged a little as her lungs began to burn. She kicked upward, through the cool depths and, as her head broke the surface, gasped for air. Treading water she looked back at the dock and saw Ben kicking off his shoes.

She felt a little shiver of anticipation as he looked her way and stripped off his shirt. Her throat tightened as he dived neatly into the water and started swimming her way. She had two choices: swim toward him or toward the opposite shore. Gauging the distance, and the rate he was plowing through the water, she knew she didn't have a prayer of reaching the distant bank. Still, she could give him a good run for his money.

Again she dived under the surface and swam toward the middle of the lake, but at an angle, toward the Fitzpatrick place. Within a minute her lungs began to ache, but she kept going and only surfaced when she was starved for air and her lungs were on fire.

Her head emerged and she saw him, still coming, swimming unerringly in her direction. With a kick, she surged away from him, but within a matter of minutes, he was next to her, his hands sliding against her wet skin, his fingers surrounding her arms.

"Wh-what are you doing?" she asked between gasps.

"This." His lips found hers and he tasted of salt and clear water. She had to tread water to stay afloat.

Kicking away from him, she said, "I don't appreciate your getting your big brother's approval to—"

He pulled her roughly against him. "Kevin has nothing to do with us." He kissed her again, and wound his arms around her torso. His body was hot and wet against hers and her heart beat anxiously to a new and wild drum.

"We'll drown out here."

He lifted his head and smiled, a flash of white so devilish that her heart turned over. "I'll keep you safe, Carlie," he vowed. "Come on." He pulled gently on her hand before letting go and swimming back to the dock. With only a second's hesitation, she followed him, swimming in his wake, feeling the ripples splash her face and knowing that she was beginning to fall in love with him.

Not now! her mind screamed. She had plans for her life and those plans didn't include being tied to a hometown boy. But he was different and changed her way of thinking. He wanted to see the world—he'd said as much. Maybe they could see it together.

By the time she reached the dock she was exhausted. He helped her onto the weathered planks and they sat together, side by side, not touching, breathing hard and listening to the sound of crickets and frogs over the constant lapping of the lake.

"Listen, Ben," she said, when she could finally speak again, "I don't like you talking about me to anyone. Especially Kevin."

"I didn't."

"He seems to think we were going together or something." She didn't add that he said he had loved her.

"Are we?"

The question hung between them, unanswered and she dragged her toes through the water. "You tell me," she finally said.

He smiled then and chased away all the doubts in her heart as he kissed her. But he never answered her question.

"Those Powell boys are trouble," Weldon Surrett said as he cleaned his hunting rifle and offered his daughter some unrequested advice. They were seated on the back deck, he drinking a beer, she sipping a tart lemonade. The sun had set, a few stars winked in the sky and the lights of Gold Creek cast a glow into the bank of heavy clouds that were rolling in from the west. "I think you'd best avoid both the boys."

"Who says they're trouble?"

"Ever'body. Now, the old man, George, he's okay. Worked every day of his life for the sawmill, but Kevin's always complaining and showing up late for work. Got the reputation of a troublemaker. I'll just bet his brother's the same." He paused to light a cigarette and let it dangle from his lips.

"You don't work at the mill and besides, just because two people are related doesn't meant they think the same. Look at you and Uncle Sid," she said, feeling a need to defend Ben. They'd started dating just this past week and tonight was the third night they were scheduled to go out to a new action movie at the twin cinemas in Coleville. Obviously her father thought she and Ben were becoming too close.

"But half the people in this town get their paychecks from Monroe Sawmill and our trucks take logs over to the mill all day long. The drivers see and hear things and word filters back. Kevin's a pain in the backside. Always has been. Got himself an attitude that nearly cost him his job a couple of times. The only reason he's still there is Monroe seems to like George. I was worried when you first dated him and I was relieved that it ended so quickly."

"There was nothing there, Dad. We only went out a couple of times."

He drew hard on his cigarette and let smoke drift from his nose. "But now you're with the other kid. Six of one, half a dozen of the other, if you ask me." He took a long swallow from his glass and called over his shoulder. "Thelma, how about another beer?"

"How about you gettin' it yourself and helping with these dishes?"

"I'll get it." Carlie was glad for an excuse to avoid another lecture. She walked through the sliding door into the kitchen and opened the refrigerator. "Leave the dishes, Mom. I'll do 'em."

Her mother smiled. "You vacuum tomorrow. I'll take care of the dishes."

"It's a deal." Carlie popped the cap of a can of beer and walked back outside.

"Thanks," her father said as he stubbed out his cigarette. He poured the brew into his glass, took a sip and set his drink on the table. "Now, about the Powell boy—"

"Dad, please."

"It's not a good idea to date brothers—" He picked up his rifle again and ran his fingers along the barrel.

"I already told you, Ben and Kevin are different."

Her father opened the Remington, snapped it shut and hoisted it to his shoulder, where he squinted through the sight. With a satisfied grunt, he set the rifle on the small table. "Just be careful, honey. Boys are territorial and dating two brothers is—"

"Asking for trouble, I know. Believe me, I've heard the lecture. About a million times," Carlie said as thunderclouds rumbled in the distance.

"Good. Then maybe you learned something. Looks like it might rain." He rubbed the back of his neck. "You know, I saw Thomas Fitzpatrick today and he asked about you."

Carlie squirmed a little. "He's still mad 'cause I stood up for Rachelle and Jackson."

"He didn't seem angry," Weldon said thoughtfully as he gazed over the railing. "He just asked what you planned to do after the summer's over."

She tried to ignore the little chill that scurried down her spine. "I think he might offer you a job," Weldon said hopefully. "You could work for him and go to the community college. Give up all those crazy notions of yours about New York City."

"He wouldn't give me a job."

"Oh, I think he might," Weldon argued. Then as if an unpleasant thought had come to mind, he frowned and snagged his beer. "Sometimes he takes a special interest in a kid from town, helps him out with jobs and loans for college. That sort of thing."

"Helps *him* out?"

"Or her," Weldon said.

"Has he ever helped out a girl before?" she asked, suddenly uneasy. She'd felt the weight of Mr. Fitzpatrick's

stare at company picnics or in church and it made her feel
uncomfortable.

"I don't know." He reached for his pack of cigarettes,
found it empty and crumpled the cellophane wrapper in his
big hand. He settled on his chewing tobacco instead and
twisted open the can. "Come to think of it, I can't say I
ever heard of him working with a girl."

"So why would he want to help me?"

"Maybe 'cause you're my daughter." Her father con-
templated his tin of tobacco. "Who knows? I'm just sayin'
we can't afford to look a gift horse in the mouth." Placing
the tobacco next to his gum, he rubbed his lip pensively.
"You didn't win yourself any points by sidin' with Jackson Moore, but then, Thomas has probably figured it's
time to let bygones be bygones."

Carlie wasn't convinced. Thomas Fitzpatrick's memory
was long and hard. Few people ever crossed him and
though she respected him as her father's employer, there
was something about Fitzpatrick that bothered her. She
hadn't admitted as much to Ben, of course, when the subject had come up because Fitzpatrick had been good to her
family. However, the truth was that she still felt uncomfortable around him. He looked at her a few seconds too
long when he didn't think she noticed and his gaze had
drifted from her face to her chest and lower more than
once.

"Well, I think I'll check on the news," her father said,
grabbing his rifle and walking inside, but Carlie watched as
the night turned black and she shivered despite the day's
heat that lingered.

Chapter Four

"*You're doing what?*" Ben couldn't believe his ears.

"I'm gonna marry Sam," Nadine replied, lifting her chin a notch, daring him to argue with her before she turned her attention back to the dishes in the sink.

"Why?"

She didn't answer, just kept wiping the plates and stacking them in the drainer. She and Ben still lived in the little house by the river with their dad. Kevin had a place of his own, and their mother... Ben didn't want to think of Donna Powell, how she'd left her family all because of Hayden Garreth Monroe III and his scheme to fleece the Powell family out of all their life savings.

Hate burned through his veins and he stared past her through the screen door. Outside, Bonanza, his father's yellow lab, lay in the shade of a maple tree and a bottle-brush bloomed along the porch. The garden, once a source of his mother's pride, was overgrown and dry. Clouds filled the sky and the air filtering through the patched screen door was sultry and hot.

The Powells had once been a happy family. Ben remembered his mother playing the piano and singing as she worked in the house they had in town. She spent her afternoons in the library, earning a little extra income, but her hours had increased when George had sold their house and moved out here, by the river, to this sorry two-storied home that they rented.

The money from their home in town, the savings earmarked for retirement and children's educations, had been invested with the almighty himself: Hayden Garreth Monroe III. Even Monroe's rich brother-in-law, Thomas Fitzpatrick, was part of the scheme to invest in oil wells that turned out to spit only worthless sand. Everything the family had ever saved had been lost, Kevin's dreams had died an agonizing death and he'd lost his scholarship.

Kevin had felt he had no choice but to drop out of college and follow in his father's weary footsteps by working for Garreth Monroe. Everything that had ever gone wrong with the Powell family could be laid at the feet of the Monroes and yet Nadine had seen fit to fall in love with the heir to the Monroe wealth—Hayden Garreth Monroe IV. It hadn't worked out, of course, and Ben was glad, though it would have been sweet irony to see Nadine marry the guy and get a little of their money back.

But Garreth had been engaged to a woman of his social standing. Ben had hoped Nadine had gotten over the jerk, but to marry Sam Warne, a boy she didn't love? That wasn't an answer, it was desperation. "I don't get it," he told her as she wiped her hands on the dish towel.

"Nothing to get." She snapped the wet towel and folded it over the handle of the oven door.

"You set a date?"

"Not yet."

"Good!" Ben kicked out a chair and sat down, glaring at her stiff spine. "You can't marry the guy just because Monroe's not interested."

Her lips compressed and when she looked at him her green eyes sparked with self-righteous fury. "We all have our ways of getting out, don't we, Ben?"

He didn't answer.

"Didn't you go visit the army recruiter today?"

"How'd you know?" All of a sudden, he was on the defensive. That was the trouble with arguing with Nadine; she had an uncanny way of turning the tables on you.

"You don't have to be Sherlock Holmes to figure it out. The recruiter called today, confirming an appointment on…" She ran her finger along the calendar stuck onto the wall next to the kitchen phone. "Let's see … Friday at—"

"I know when."

"Good. Now, do you know when to stick your nose back into your own business? You can sit there and be my judge and jury all day long, but at least I'm not running away to the army and messing around with a woman my older brother's in love with."

Ben's head jerked up. "Kevin's not interested in Carlie."

Nadine let out a snort of disbelief.

"He's been seeing some girl in Coleville—"

"Tracy Niday. Yeah, I know." She slid into the chair next to Ben and arranged the salt and pepper shakers around the napkin holder. "But they broke up and if you ask me, he fell pretty hard for Carlie. The way I see it, his interest in Tracy was all a rebound thing, because Carlie hurt him."

"That's not what he told me," Ben said stubbornly. He didn't want to believe that Kevin was emotionally entangled with Carlie. Not now. Now when he, himself, was becoming involved with her.

Nadine looked him straight in the eye and smiled sadly, as if she thought he were the most stupid beast to ever walk the earth. "You have to read between the lines, Ben. It's hard for you, I know. You like things in black and white, no gray areas. Cut-and-dried. But that's not how the world works."

"And that's why you're gonna marry Sam, because of some gray area?"

She flushed and stared at her hands. "It just seems like the thing to do."

"Isn't it a 'rebound thing' because of Hayden Monroe?"

"It's over between Hayden and me."

Ben clamped his hands under his arms and leaned back in his chair. "Tell me you love Sam."

She opened her mouth, closed it and sighed. "I'm not sure I believe in love anymore."

"Liar. You're still in love with that jerk Monroe, aren't you?"

"He's out of my life," she said, her voice a little husky.

"So Sam's second best."

"Sam has always cared about me," she said simply, lacing her fingers together and biting her lower lip.

"You're settling, Nadine."

Her restless green eyes lifted to meet his. "It's my choice, isn't it, Ben? Don't worry about me, I've learned from my mistakes. Besides, I think you've got your own battles to fight."

The park was nearly empty because of the threat of a thunderstorm. Picnic tables were vacated, the barbecue pits cold, the playground equipment without children.

In a private copse of fir trees, Carlie lay on a blanket with Ben, nibbling at her sandwich of French bread, cream cheese, turkey and sprouts. They'd decided upon a picnic and a few little thunderclouds hadn't changed their plans.

Ben had seemed quiet all afternoon. He smiled rarely, and his eyes were troubled and dark.

"Something's bothering you," she said, tossing pieces of bread to the ducks that were hovering near the edge of the water. With loud squawks and fluttering of wings, two vied for the delicacy.

"I'm fine."

"What you are is a terrible liar." Throwing the final scrap of bread to a brown mallard who had waddled close to the blanket, she glanced up at Ben. His mouth was firm and set, his jaw tight, the skin over his cheekbones stretched thin. Lying across the blanket, leaning on one elbow, he'd brooded for nearly an hour. "What gives?"

"I'm thinking of joining up."

She didn't think she'd heard him right. "You're what?"

"I talked to an army recruiter today."

The bottom dropped out of her world. "But why?"

Avoiding her eyes, he reached into a small cooler and pulled out a Coke. "Things are happening."

"What things?"

"Nadine's going to marry Sam Warne."

"So?"

"So it's a big mistake."

"But really none of your business."

"She said the same thing," he admitted. He twisted off the bottle cap. "But I can't just ignore it. The fact is, he's ruining her life."

"You don't know that."

"She doesn't love him," he said flatly, then nearly drained the bottle.

Carlie shook her hair loose from its braid and considered Ben. So he did believe in love after all, but he didn't want to think that people got married for a lot of different reasons: family pressure, sexual fulfillment, pregnancy. It wasn't a law that two people had to be in love before they signed a certificate of marriage and, from the marriages Carlie had seen, she was certain more often than not, love wasn't a major factor in the decision.

Nadine, the little that Carlie knew of her, was a practical person who knew her own mind. If she wanted to marry Sam Warne, Carlie guessed, Nadine had her reasons. Nonetheless, she wanted to understand the source of Ben's concern, so she played devil's advocate. "Why do you think she's going to marry Sam?"

"Because she can't have the jerk she really loves." He rolled the empty bottle in his hands and stared across the water. A heron skimmed the surface only to fly gracefully away as thunder rumbled over the hills.

"The man she loves?"

"Don't you remember? I thought everyone in town knew the old scandal. Nadine and Hayden Monroe, the younger, were an item not too long ago. He got bored with his so-

cialite girlfriend, Wynona Galveston, messed around with
Nadine and then, when push came to shove, returned to
Wynona's waiting arms and promptly took her on a boat
ride that nearly killed her. Yep, that Hayden Monroe, what
a prince of a guy he is.'' Ben's words were bitter as his eyes
narrowed on the distant shore. ''Good riddance.''

''So what've you got against Sam?''

Ben snorted. ''He's okay, just a little too... normal for
Nadine. And, you've got to admit, Hayden Monroe with
his speedboat and big bucks is a tough act to follow.''

''Maybe it'll work out.'' She pushed herself upright and
scooted close enough so that her shoulder touched his.
Tucking her knees to her chest, she rested her chin on her
arms. ''You can't solve all the world's problems, you
know.''

He glanced at her and offered a self-deprecating grin. ''I
can try.''

''Is that why you think you have to join the army?'' she
asked, trying to ignore the tiny hole in her heart that ripped
a little more each time she thought of Ben tromping
through some humid foreign jungle, or marching across
acres of hot enemy sand, or rappelling down a sheer cliff to
drop into hostile terrain. Her stomach squeezed painfully
and she reminded herself that it was peace time. If Ben
joined the army now, chances were he'd be stationed state-
side or maybe at a base in Europe.

''I'm joining because I can't stay here. Nothing ever
happens in Gold Creek. There's just a lot of broken dreams
and borrowed promises.'' The wind off the lake kicked up,
ruffling his hair, smelling of water. ''I don't think I can sit
around and watch another generation of Fitzpatricks and
Monroes rape the land and make a fortune off the sweat of
other men's backs.'' He cocked his head to look at her.
''Besides, who're you to talk? You don't plan to stick
around.''

She couldn't argue with that, and yet, because of Ben and
the last few weeks she'd shared with him, she'd been second-guessing herself, telling herself that a small town in
California wasn't such a bad place to live. She'd fanta-

sized about staying here and marrying Ben. Would it be so bad? Who needed adventure? Who cared about faraway places—the bustle of Manhattan, the romance of Paris, the exotic allure of the Caribbean? What did the world have to offer that she couldn't find in Gold Creek?

Her train of thought was on a fast track and gathering steam when she put on the brakes. She was ready to change her life and her dreams. All because of Ben. Her throat felt suddenly thick and as she gazed into the hazel depths of his eyes she knew that she would willingly, even gladly, push aside all her dreams of the future just to walk down the aisle with him and become his bride.

As if he could read her thoughts, he brought his face closer to hers and his breath fanned her face. "You're the only doubt I have," he admitted, his voice deep and rough. "If I hadn't met you, I wouldn't think twice about signing on the dotted line and shipping out."

Her heart turned over as the first drops of rain began to fall. "You don't have to say—"

"Shh." He placed a finger against her lips. "I know I don't have to say or do anything. I'm just telling you how I feel, Carlie."

Her throat was suddenly dry as a summer wind.

"And I've never cared for anyone the way I care for you. When I'm with you, I don't want to ever leave and when I'm away from you, I can't stop thinking about you." His gaze searched the contours of her face and his fingers found hers. "I don't understand this and God knows I didn't want it to happen, but I think I'm falling for you, Carlie Surrett, and if there was anything I could do to prevent it, I would."

"Ben—"

The finger pressed harder against her mouth and she kissed the soft pad. Rain drizzled from a darkening sky as he outlined her lips, then pushed against her teeth until her mouth opened. Still staring into her eyes, he explored the recess of her mouth, touching the back of her teeth and lightly rubbing the tip of her tongue.

Carlie moaned softly, opening her mouth as his finger withdrew. He gathered her into his arms and his lips melded over hers with a possession that drew the breath from her lungs. Thoughts swam in her head, but all her doubts were chased away and she was only concerned with the here and now, with this lonely park by the lake and Ben...wonderful Ben. His hands were magic as they slid beneath the hem of her T-shirt and massaged the muscles of her back.

Fires ignited deep in her most secret self, a warmth invaded her blood and a deep, dusky need controlled her.

He kissed her eyes, her lips, her neck, and when he came to the circle of bones at her throat, he pressed his tongue against her skin. A tremor swept through her and she felt heat rise in her blood.

His fingers scaled her ribs to feel the weight of her breast and she arched against him, filling his palm, wanting more. He yanked the T-shirt over her head, then, lying on his back, he drew her down to him, so that she was lying atop him as he took her into his mouth. Through the lace of her bra, he suckled, drawing on her nipple, pressing against the muscles of her back so that he could take more of her into his mouth.

Arching her neck, wanting to fill him with the love that was burning in her soul, she clung to his shoulders. She felt him pause to remove the scrap of cloth that restrained him and then his tongue and teeth and lips were kissing her, on her shoulders, between her breasts, on the flat wall of her abdomen and lower. He drew off her shorts, rimming her navel with his tongue as the fine mist of rain collected on her back.

"Love me, Carlie," he whispered gruffly against her bare stomach and she writhed her answer against him.

She didn't consider the consequences of the step they were about to take, didn't think about how easily she would give him her virginity, nor did she doubt that the union of their bodies was anything but destiny.

Kissing him and feeling the wonder of his sinewy muscles, she stripped him of his shirt and soon they were naked in the darkness, protected by the trees, silently touching and kissing. Feverish, she pressed her tongue into his mouth, felt him stiffen as her hands played with his flat nipples.

There was no turning back. As thunder cracked and lightning sizzled in jagged streaks across the sky, Ben rolled her onto her back, gazed into her eyes and with the determination of a man whose sole purpose is to claim one very special woman, he entered her.

She let out a silent scream at the pain, but soon he was rocking over her, giving of himself only to take away, moving as surely as the sea flows to the sand and then retreats. The pain disappeared and her body swayed in a perfect rhythm with his and the blood in her veins ran hot. With a moan she dug her fingers into his shoulders and danced with him. Ribbons of light fluttered behind her eyes and as lightning streaked the sky she bucked upward, her body convulsing as the ribbons shredded with an explosive wave of heat that flashed behind her eyes and sent her soul soaring to the heavens. Ben fell against her, his body slick with rain and sweat. "Carlie...beautiful, loving Carlie," he cried, expelling ragged breaths against her neck.

Slowly she floated back to earth, still clinging to him as the wind and rain tore at their bodies. When he lifted his head, he smiled down at her and chuckled. Shoving an unruly lock of wet black hair from her cheek, he sighed loudly and shook his head. "You usually have all the answers. Now what're we going to do?"

She giggled and wiped a drip of rain from the tip of his nose. With a gruff voice that she didn't recognize as her own, she whispered, "Hey, soldier, what about an encore?"

They ran to the pickup. Their clothes were streaked with mud, their hair sopping wet, their spirits laughing upward to the dark clouds that had the nerve to block the moon.

Carlie cuddled close to Ben as he flipped on the radio and pulled out of the empty lot. Stephen Stills was singing "Love the One You're With" as the windshield wipers slapped raindrops from the glass. Ben's truck splashed through puddles on the road back to town and the sky was inky black. Only the occasional oncoming headlight flashed over the interior of the cab, giving Carlie a chance to stare at Ben's handsome features. Would he really sign his life away and join the army, leaving Gold Creek forever? Her heart squeezed though she knew she was being foolish; she, too, was planning to shake the dust of this small town from her heels.

But now, after making love, after realizing what it was to give yourself to one person, she wondered if she would have the guts to leave. What if Ben didn't go? What if he stayed here and worked for Thomas Fitzpatrick or Hayden Monroe, putting in hour after hour, shift after shift, day after day and year after tedious year?

Her throat tightened. She could never ask him to give up his dreams, to stay here forever.

So what if you get pregnant? her wayward mind nagged. She hadn't planned on making love with him, nor had either of them taken precautions. Though she knew the chances of it happening were slim, there were people who conceived children the first time they made love.

Made love.

She bit her lip and wondered about a baby possibly growing inside her: Ben's child. Oh, Lord. She was torn between being in awe of the miracle of life and knowing that neither she nor Ben were emotionally equipped to raise a child.

The truck sped along the road, toward the glow of lights that shimmered up against the heavy clouds, the town of Gold Creek. Hadn't she sworn that she'd never live her life here, that she'd see the world before she settled down to raise a family, that she wouldn't make the same mistakes her parents had? And yet, a part of her would give up all her glamorous plans for a future of adventure and fantasy if she could know that Ben Powell would love her forever.

They drove down Main Street and stopped at a red light. He glanced in her direction and must've read the confusion in her eyes. "Regrets?" he asked, touching her hand.

"None," she assured him. "You?"

He laughed and kissed her cheek. "What do you think?"

The light changed and Ben crossed traffic just as the sound of sirens split the night.

Two police cars, lights flashing, sirens screaming gained on the old pickup.

"Great," Ben said, pulling over, but the cruisers sped past, sirens wailing shrilly. "Accident," Ben said and Carlie felt a cold drip of fear slide down her spine. She watched as the police cars rounded the corner of Main Street and Spruce. Ben stepped on the throttle. "That's Kevin's street," he said with a shrug though his brows drew into a worried line.

Of course nothing was wrong with Kevin. Just because he lived on Spruce Street was no reason to believe the police were after him.

But Ben didn't turn onto the side street leading to the Lakeview Apartments complex. Instead, as if drawn by some kind of morbid magnet, he turned onto Spruce and a ball of ice tightened in Carlie's stomach. "What're you— Oh, God!"

The cruisers were parked cockeyed in front of the house Kevin shared with a roommate. Colored lights strobed the sky. A fire truck and rescue van were already pulled into the driveway. Several firemen and police officers were scattered around the yard. Some talked into walkie-talkies, some huddled together, others were in the garage huddled around Kevin's shiny Corvette.

Neighbors filtered out of their houses and the whole scene played out in slow motion.

Ben yanked out the keys and jumped out of the pickup before the truck had come to a complete stop. Carlie scrambled out behind him. "What's going on here?" Ben demanded of the first policeman.

"Get back, boy!"

Ben ignored him. "My brother lives here!" he said when the officer tried to restrain him.

"Who's your brother?"

"Kevin Powell. He—" His voice broke when he stared into the officer's grim face and Carlie's lungs seemed to give out. She couldn't breathe. Her blood pounded in her ears.

"Your brother's dead, son," the officer said, sadness etched on his features. "Your sister found him. They took him over to County General, but it was too late."

"Oh, God," Carlie whispered, her knees threatening to buckle. This was all a horrid dream. That was it... a dream. She watched as if from a distance.

"No, you're wrong!" Ben threw off the policeman's arm. "Kevin—he's here. He lives here!"

"Son, I'm telling you—"

"You're a liar!" Ben screamed.

Carlie thought she might be sick. She tried to reach for Ben, but he twisted away from her.

"Kevin's okay, Carlie! He's okay!" Ben yelled. "He's okay!"

"I'm sorry, kid. Maybe I should get you a ride—"

"Like hell. Kevin's okay! He's okay!" Ben repeated. His features were etched in fury and disbelief, his body tense and spoiling for a fight as rain sheeted from the sky. "I don't know why you're lying to me!"

"Look, son, if you don't believe me—"

"What's going on here?" a senior officer intervened and Carlie, willing her knees not to give out, stood next to Ben.

"There's been some kind of mistake," she said, her voice nearly failing her. Kevin couldn't be dead. He just couldn't. "This is Ben Powell, Kevin's brother, and—"

"Then you've got your work cut out for you," the officer cut in, staring at Ben. "Your sister's not dealing with this very well and your father has been taken to the hospital with chest pains. I know this is difficult, but you've got to face it."

Carlie's legs turned to water. Deputy Zalinski caught her before she slid onto the muddy ground.

"You're wrong!" Ben said, backing away from the policemen. Rain flattened his hair and ran from the tip of his nose and his chin. "You're wrong! Kevin's okay! He has to be!"

"Get a grip, Powell," the officer said evenly. "We can take you to the hospital—"

"No way!"

"Ben," Carlie said, walking up to him and touching his arm. Her lips were trembling and tears filled her eyes. "Come on—"

"Let go of me," he snarled, yanking his arm away, his eyes filled with dark, unspoken accusations. Carlie's heart turned to stone when she saw the sudden hatred in the angry line of his mouth.

"We're investigating this as a possible suicide," the officer said. "But we're not certain of anything. Not yet. It looks like alcohol could've been involved and—"

"No! Man, this is crazy—" Ben cried, but the anger left his features, replaced by cold, certain fear. "No!" he screamed, his fists clenched as he turned his head to the sky. "No! No! No!"

Tears washed down Carlie's cheeks. She reached for Ben again, but he backed away, nearly stumbling on the curb before he turned around and ran through the night, abandoning her and racing under the street lamps, faster and faster through the rain. She took a step forward to chase him, but Zalinski restrained her.

"Give him time to deal with this."

"But I—"

"He needs some space. He's had a helluva shock."

But I love him, she cried mutely, feeling the officer's strong hands restraining her as Ben disappeared around a corner.

"He'll be okay," the officer assured her. "It'll just take a little time. He needs to be alone for a few minutes, but don't worry about him, I'll send a squad car after him."

Carlie, numb, couldn't say a word.

The officer motioned for one of the paramedics. "Hey, Joe, you got a blanket and a cup of coffee?"

"Comin' right up."

Carlie barely heard the exchange. She was still staring down Spruce Street where neighbors had clustered and stood whispering and shaking their heads, but her eyes were still searching for Ben.

A blanket was tossed over her shoulders and a disposable cup of warm coffee placed between her fingers, but she didn't move. She wanted to run after Ben, to hold him, to kiss him, to make love to him again and tell him everything would be all right. But he didn't want to hear her lies, nor did he want her comforting touch.

Shivering, Carlie began to sob. Deep, racking, pain-filled sobs. For Kevin. For the Powell family. But mostly for Ben.

BOOK TWO

Gold Creek, California

The Present

Chapter Five

Carlie slid her Jeep between two cars and told herself she just had to get through the ceremony, then she could leave. Watch Nadine Powell Warne become Mrs. Hayden Monroe, say congratulations and be off.

Except that she'd have to see Ben again! Ben the Impossible. Ben the Cruel. Ben the Terrible. She could give him a thousand names but it wouldn't change the fact that she'd have to pretend that he meant nothing to her, that the past was dead and buried and that she was content to live her life without him. Which, of course, she reminded herself, she was.

How ironic that they were both back in Gold Creek after years away. She hoped that he was just passing through, staying only long enough to watch the wedding ceremony, then climbing back into his beat-up pickup and taking off for parts unknown.

She'd leave, too, if she could, but her father's health wasn't what it once was. The doctors thought he'd had a series of tiny strokes, and he'd been forced to stop working for a while, maybe forever. Carlie's mother was sick with worry. Carlie, as the only child, had offered to stick around until things were settled.

And she'd found a job. Not just a job. A "career opportunity" Rory Jaeger, her old boss, had told her when she'd approached him about working part-time. He'd scoffed at her proposal. Hadn't she been a New York model? Hadn't she seen Paris? What could she possibly want with his little business? She'd explained that though she didn't need work, not desperately, quite yet, she needed a studio to develop her pictures. *As well as a place to put down a few roots—shallow ones perhaps, but roots nonetheless.*

Rory had become more interested and they'd struck a deal. For a small investment, she could own half the shop. He was close to retiring anyway and they'd shook hands on their agreement, sealing her fate to stay in Gold Creek for at least a year, probably longer, at which time she could sell her interest back to Rory or to someone else, upon Rory's approval.

The documents were being drawn up by the lawyers and within the week she would become part owner of the shop. If she needed extra income, she could drive to San Francisco and talk to a modelling agency there and she'd called her old agency in New York, giving the owner, Constance, her telephone number and address. The modeling was a long shot; she hadn't been in front of a camera in years and she didn't have much interest in trying to revive a career that had barely gotten off the ground. Still, she couldn't afford not to keep all her options open.

So she was stuck in Gold Creek for a while and she'd just have to be able to face Ben if she ran into him again, which, in a town this size, was a foregone conclusion.

She locked her Jeep and started walking to one of the largest houses built upon the shores of Whitefire Lake. The house was cozy, despite its size. Now, in the coming twilight, Monroe Manor looked like something out of an old-fashioned Christmas card. Snow was piled on the third-floor dormers, golden light glowed warmly through frosted windows and smoke drifted lazily from a chimney. Icicles hung like crystal teardrops from the gutters that separated the house from the garage. Two dogs, one black-and-white, the other a yellow lab, wandered through the tree-covered acres.

It's now or never, she thought, wondering what she would say to George Powell. Before she could second-guess herself, she rang the doorbell and prayed that she would be inside before Ben arrived.

She heard the rumble of a truck's engine as the door opened and a boy of about seven or eight, with red-blond hair, freckles and mischievous hazel eyes stood before her. Dressed in a black suit and white shirt, he shoved out his hand in a gesture that looked as if it had been practiced a hundred times over. "Hi, I'm Bobby."

Ah. Nadine's younger son. "Pleased to meet you. I'm Carlie." She shook his hand firmly.

His nose wrinkled thoughtfully. "You're the model, aren't you?"

Laughing a little, she said, "I was, but that was quite a while ago."

"Wow! Wait until I tell Katie Osgood. She said you wouldn't show up and that—"

"Robert!" A short, blond woman whom Carlie recognized as Ben and Nadine's aunt Velma, came to the rescue. "We're glad you could come," she said with a smile, then shooting a warning look to Bobby.

"Thanks."

Bobby, suddenly remembering his manners said, "Oh...um, can I take your coat?"

"Sure." Carlie peeled out of the coat and watched as the boy tried diligently not to let the hem drag as he carried it upstairs. He looked over his shoulder at the landing. "You're s'posed to sign the book!"

"The guest register," Velma clarified, "when you have a minute. Now, come on in." She touched Carlie on the arm. "The ceremony's going to start in about ten minutes, so you might want to grab a seat pretty quick."

The doorbell chimed and Carlie's stomach tightened, thinking that the next guest might be Ben. Rather than wait for round two of their argument, she walked through the foyer to the living room where folding chairs had been set up to face the fireplace. Soft music drifted through hidden speakers to vie with the sounds of laughter and conversation flowing through the spacious rooms. Flowers and ribbons decorated the walls and stair railing and the scents of carnations, roses and lilacs mingled with an underlying smell of burning wood.

She recognized more than a few people. The Fitzpatricks, though separated, were together. Despite rumors of impending divorce, Thomas sat by his wife, June, and their daughter, Toni. As Carlie walked in, Thomas glanced in her direction. Beneath his mustache, his lips curved into a quick smile of recognition, but quickly faded and Carlie was reminded of all the times she'd met him as a girl—and how uncomfortable he'd made her feel.

Along with the Fitzpatricks, the Reverend Osgood and his family, as well as the Nelsons, Pattons, McDonalds and Sedgewicks, were already taking seats.

"About time," a voice called from the stairs. Carlie's best friend, Rachelle, was hurrying down the steps. Her mahogany-colored hair was curled and fell to the middle of her back. "I was afraid you were going to chicken out," Rachelle teased. "Looks like I lost that bet."

"You *bet* on whether I'd come or not?"

Rachelle winked. "Couldn't help myself. There was this pool, you see. Heather, Turner, Jackson and I—"

"I don't want to hear it!" Carlie said, though she relaxed a little at her friend's gentle teasing. "And I hope you lost big-time—thousands of dollars. You deserve it. Besides, I wouldn't have missed this for the world."

"Oh, sure. Remember, Carlie, I know you. I can just imagine how desperately you wanted to be here." Grinning, Rachelle grabbed Carlie's hand, "Jeez, you're freezing!"

"I stopped for a walk around the lake."

Rachelle's eyes narrowed a fraction, but the smile didn't leave her lips. "Getting your nerve together?"

"Something like that."

"Think you can handle seeing Ben again?"

Carlie lifted a shoulder in nonchalance. "Now that I'm here, I guess I don't have much choice, do I?"

"It won't kill you," Rachelle predicted with a knowing smile. "In fact, it could be fun."

"Fun? Yeah, about as fun as having all my teeth extracted."

"You might be surprised."

"Don't count on it." But Carlie felt more relaxed than she had since she'd decided to attend the wedding. She'd been friends with Rachelle for as long as she could remember. "Friends for life," they'd once pledged and so far, despite the miles and years that had separated them, they were still as close as sisters.

"Come on," Rachelle urged, "Heather and Turner have saved us seats up near the front."

Rachelle pulled on her hand and soon Carlie was standing in front of a folding chair facing the fireplace. She didn't see Ben come in, but she knew the moment he entered, sensed his presence, as surely as if she'd watched him stride across the threshold. The air against the back of her neck felt suddenly chilled, but her shoulders burned where his gaze bored into her. Cold and hot—like dry ice. Ignoring the temptation to glance over her shoulder, she sat in her chair and watched the ceremony unfold.

Reverend Osgood stood before the fire as Nadine's older son, John, gave the bride away. Then, while Carlie's throat grew tight, Nadine Powell Warne and Hayden Monroe IV stared into each other's eyes and pledged their lives and their love for all time.

To have and hold... from this day forward. Bits and pieces of the traditional words filtered through her mind, and she thought back to her own wedding day, so distant now. She and Paul had stood before a judge and the entire ceremony had lasted less than ten minutes. Cold, stark, without feeling.

Just like her short-lived marriage.

Blinking rapidly, she turned her attention back to the preacher. "You may kiss the bride."

Reverend Osgood didn't have to repeat himself. With a rakish grin, Hayden took Nadine into his arms and kissed her with a passion and love that nearly melted Carlie's bones.

Only one man had kissed her with the same blinding passion that Hayden so obviously felt for his wife, and that man was standing somewhere near the back of the room, regarding the ritual with jaded eyes.

Holding his bride at arm's length, Hayden winked at her, then, as the piano player began playing, they walked between the beribboned chairs and mingled with their guests.

"Don't you just love a wedding?" Heather said on a sigh. Her blond hair was curled away from her face and she wore a shimmery pale blue dress that didn't hide the fact that she was pregnant again. Dabbing at her eyes with a handkerchief, she sighed. "It's so romantic."

Her husband, Turner, looked at his wife and clucked his tongue. "Women. Emotional." He grinned irreverently and Heather rolled her eyes.

"Men. Stoic."

"That's me," Turner replied, but he linked her hand with his as their son, Adam, ran toward the tiered cake and punch bowl to take stock of the refreshments.

Jackson laughed as they walked past the den. "Bring back memories?" he whispered to his wife, though Carlie overheard and understood that he was talking about this very room where Jackson and Rachelle had taken refuge, where they'd first spent the night together, where Jackson had been hiding when he'd been hauled into the sheriff's office for questioning the next morning.

"Great memories," Rachelle said, blushing slightly. Her hazel eyes twinkled wickedly. "I just wonder why Deputy Zalinski wasn't invited."

"You're trouble, Mrs. Moore," Jackson said as he guided her away from the crowd.

"Absolutely," she replied while Carlie, wanting some time alone, wandered toward the stairs where Nadine and Hayden were posing for "spontaneous" snapshots. Velma clicked off a picture as Nadine's boys, John and Bobby, rushed into the foyer.

Bobby tugged on his mother's skirt. "Katie Osgood's trying to sneak some of the champagne," he said, his eyes wide.

"Is she?" Hayden said. "Well, we'll just have to see about that."

"That girl's a wagonload of trouble," Velma said, rewinding her film.

John yanked at his bow tie. "Troublemaker," he snarled at his younger brother.

"It's true!"

"Yeah, and it's true that you're a dweeb!"

"Later, boys," Nadine said, but Hayden glanced pointedly toward the fountain and a girl of about nine or ten dashed quickly out of the room.

The older boy, John, saw Carlie for the first time. "You're—"

"John, this is Carlie Surrett," Nadine said. "We're really glad you could come."

"Thank you," Carlie replied, then shook John's hand. "Nice to meet you."

"She's a model," Bobby supplied.

John's face wrinkled and he glanced up at his mom. "Is she the one who posed for the swimsuit issue of *Sports Illustrated?*"

"Don't I wish," Carlie said, and John grinned.

"Forgive them," Nadine said as her sons caught up with a group of other children about their age.

"Nothing to forgive."

"They're pretty impressed with your life."

"If they only knew," Carlie replied, thinking of the loneliness she'd felt in New York. "Believe me, it's not as glamorous as it seems."

Nadine and Hayden were called away and Carlie found herself alone. She wondered where Ben was, decided it didn't matter and wandered over to the fountain for a glass of champagne. *Just a little while longer,* she told herself as she sipped from a fluted glass and took a seat on a window ledge near the stairs. Then the ordeal would be over.

Ben tried to keep his eyes off Carlie. After all, there was no reason to torture himself. If she felt she had to make a statement and show up, who gave a rip?

His father, for one. George had declined giving his daughter away, proclaiming that one time was enough. He'd blamed every member of the Monroe family for stripping him of his life savings. Though Hayden Garreth Monroe III and Thomas Fitzpatrick were solely responsible for the scheme, George still blamed everyone associated with the rich men. Including Nadine's new husband whom he considered "a spoiled playboy with too much money and too little sense."

George had watched the ceremony without any trace of emotion. His lips had tightened when he'd noticed Carlie, but he'd held his tongue and only stayed long enough to shake Hayden's hand and hug his daughter, then had asked his new friend, Ellen Tremont Little, the woman who had sat with him and been the only person to coax a smile from his lips, to take him back to town.

Nadine, for her part, had braved her father's disapproval and had refused to let anyone spoil her day. She'd gone upstairs for a moment, returned to the landing and, to the surprise of everyone, thrown her bridal bouquet into the group of guests milling around the base of the stairs.

Girls squealed, hands raised, fingers extended, but the airborne nosegay had landed squarely in Carlie's lap. She'd been sitting on the window seat, staring out the window when the bouquet had soared over the anxious fingers to rest against the blue of her dress. So startled she nearly dropped the flowers, she'd blushed a dozen shades of red.

Fitting, Ben thought, his jaw tightening a little. Hadn't Carlie always been the center of attention? Even now, at Nadine's wedding, she'd somehow managed to steal the show. Hell, what a mess. He would have walked up to Carlie and made a comment, but he didn't want to ruin Nadine's happiness by causing a scene. So he held his tongue and glowered at the woman who had been on the edge of his thoughts for too many years.

Leaning a shoulder against the archway separating the living room from the foyer, he kept his distance—from Carlie and the dangerous emotions that always surfaced when he thought of her. He snatched a glass of champagne off a silver tray carried by a waiter, then drained the drink in one swallow. Restless, he had to keep moving. He walked into the living room and noticed that the folding chairs had been stacked, the carpet rolled back, and Hayden and Nadine were dancing together for the first time as man and wife. He couldn't stand it. He needed some air. Turning his back on the bride and groom, he shoved open the front door and strode outside.

Carlie watched him leave and let out her breath. Maybe now she could relax a little. She forced her fingers, wrapped tightly around the stem of the bridal bouquet, to loosen.

From a baby grand piano tucked in a corner of the living room, strains of the "Anniversary Waltz" drifted through the hallways. Nadine and Hayden glided across the soft patina of the old oak floors. The guests, citizens of Gold Creek, dressed in suits or tuxedos and dresses of vibrant silk or simple cotton, talked among themselves, watching the newlyweds, laughing and sipping champagne that flowed endlessly from the fountain.

Hayden and Nadine danced as one. He whispered something in his bride's ear and Nadine tossed her head and smiled up at him, her green eyes flashing impishly, her red hair reflecting the soft illumination of the tiny lights.

Carlie saw the exchange, noticed Hayden brush Nadine's forehead with his lips as he guided her around the floor. Other couples joined the newlyweds.

Heather and Turner swept by. They looked like a cowboy and a lady, he in a black Western-cut suit and polished boots, she in quivering pale silk. They swayed around plants decorated with a thousand tiny lights and behind them, even though it was long past the season, the Christmas tree loomed twelve feet to the ceiling.

As the dance floor became more crowded, Hayden and Nadine disappeared through the French doors. No one but Carlie seemed to notice.

At last she could go home. She'd done her duty. She found her coat in the closet of an upstairs bedroom and, after saying hasty goodbyes to Rachelle and Heather, she started for the door.

"Carlie?" Thomas Fitzpatrick was wending his way through a crowd of guests and making his way toward her. Her muscles tightened, though he posed no threat. A distinguished-looking man with patrician features, silver hair and a clipped mustache, he smiled evenly as he approached her and she told herself that she'd imagined his leers all those years ago.

Still, she didn't completely trust him. She'd seen what his hatred could do—even to his own kin. Hadn't he tried to blame Jackson Moore, his illegitimate son, for the death of Roy, his favorite child? He'd pitted one of his sons against the other, never recognizing Jackson, then allowing him to take the blame for a murder he didn't commit. No, Thomas Fitzpatrick was no saint, but only a few people had ever had the nerve to stand up to him and Carlie had been one of those very few.

"Can I have a few minutes of your time?" he asked, touching her arm with the familiarity of a favorite uncle.

"I was just leaving."

"Please...it will only take a few minutes. It's about your father."

Her heart nearly stopped. What was wrong with Dad? Surely Thomas wouldn't lay him off now, not while he was still recuperating. Dread inching its way into her heart, she followed the richest man in Gold Creek into the kitchen, where there were only a few caterers filling trays.

"I know things are difficult right now for Thelma and Weldon," Thomas said, his forehead furrowing in worry.

Carlie braced herself against the counter. "It's hard. Dad doesn't like being cooped up."

"Understandable." Thomas smiled, that cold snakelike smile that chilled Carlie to her bones. "He's been a valued employee at the company for years."

Here it comes! Carlie's fingers curled over the smooth marble edge of the counter.

"This is difficult for me, you understand, and I'm willing to do anything I can to help out, but I can't leave his job open indefinitely."

Oh, God.

"I don't think Weldon would expect that and the man who's taken over his position temporarily is willing to stay on indefinitely. In fact, he's insisting that he needs more job security and that's not an unreasonable request as he has a family to support."

"Don't you think you should be discussing this with my father?" she said, unable to hide her irritation. Her parents weren't rich; they, too, needed the job security Fitzpatrick Logging had always provided. There was no way her mother's small salary and tips from working at the soda counter at the drugstore would begin to pay their bills.

"I'll speak to Weldon tomorrow," Fitzpatrick agreed. He stroked the corner of his mustache with a long finger. "And you have to understand that it's hard for me to make a decision like this. Your father could retire, of course—"

"But not at full benefits."

Thomas sighed. He seemed genuinely unhappy. "Unfortunately, no."

"What's he supposed to do?" she asked, anger beginning to burn through her blood.

"As soon as he's well enough, I'll find him a job—a decent job, mind you—with the company. However, he won't have the same responsibilities as he did while he was foreman."

"Or the same salary."

Thomas lifted the shoulder of his expensive wool suit. "I do have a way to help out."

She didn't believe him and she didn't bother hiding it. "My folks aren't interested in your charity, Mr. Fitzpatrick."

"Of course not." He offered her a tentative smile. "The reason I'm bringing this all up to you is that the company annual report is due in a couple of months. We always had the photographs taken by Rory Jaeger."

Was it her imagination or was Thomas smirking behind his cool blue eyes? She nearly shivered, for she was certain that he already knew every intimate detail of her life.

"I worked for him a long time ago."

"And, as I understand it, you'll be working with him again."

So he did know! Carlie wondered if there was any word of gossip in Gold Creek that Thomas Fitzpatrick didn't hear. "It looks that way. If things work out."

"Good. Then I was hoping I could ask you to do the pictures for this year's report. We'd need shots of the logging camps, the trees that are growing through reforestation, and photographs of the other phases of our business—oil wells and the like."

"Have you talked to Rory about this?"

"He insisted on throwing the business your way and, in light of your father's situation, I thought it was a good idea."

As if he ever did anything noble. She itched to tell him to take his business and shove it, but she was more practical than that. She was in no position to turn away a job. Any job.

"What do you say?"

She hesitated, then looked him squarely in the eye. "I'll call you once I set up shop."

"Looking forward to it," Thomas said amiably as he handed her his business card. His gaze lingered on hers a second longer than was normal and Carlie swallowed hard. Was it her imagination? He placed his hand on her shoulder, as if feeling the texture of her dress. The touch was intimate and Carlie took a step away. "Give my best to your dad."

He walked back to the living room to join his wife and daughter. June stiffened at his touch on her elbow and Toni didn't even look his way.

Wealth didn't guarantee happiness, Carlie thought, tapping the narrow edge of his card against the counter, grateful her interview with him was over. Thomas Fitzpatrick might be one of the richest men in Gold Creek, but he'd already buried one son, and his second was in the legal battle of his life and his third—his bastard—Jackson Moore, refused to even speak with him. That left Antoinette "Toni" Fitzpatrick, pretty and petite, with dark blond hair and blue eyes and an attitude that wouldn't quit.

It was rumored that Toni was more trouble than his other children combined.

Yes, Thomas was an unhappy man. Carlie stuffed his card into her purse and walked through the back door.

Outside, the night was still and snow continued to fall. Thousands of tiny lights illuminated the gazebo and boathouse, to reflect in the dark, shimmering waters of the lake. Somewhere overhead an owl hooted softly.

It was peaceful here. Serene. If she let herself she could forget all her problems with her family. With the Powells. With Thomas Fitzpatrick. With Ben. She frowned at the thought of him—handsome and rigid in his military best. A man who saw the world in terms of black and white, wrong or right, good or bad. No in-between for Ben Powell.

She turned, intending to slip through the breezeway when she saw him, standing near the far side of the gazebo, snow collecting on his shoulders and in his hair.

"Just can't tear yourself away, can you?" he said without bothering to hide his animosity.

"I was about to leave."

"*After* your little chat with Fitzpatrick."

She glanced to the house and the kitchen window where the lights cast squares of light onto the snow. Inside, the caterers were busy refilling trays. Carlie could watch their movements as clearly as if she were in the room. Obviously Ben had seen all of her exchange with Fitzpatrick. "We had business to discuss."

His lips tightened at the corners. "He's trouble, Carlie."

"So you've finished insulting me and now you're giving me warnings?"

He lifted his shoulder, as if he really didn't give a care, but the rigid set of his jaw said otherwise.

"You know, the same could be said about you," she pointed out.

He leaned one hand against a leafless oak sapling, then dusted off the snow that clung tenaciously to the bark. "I just thought you should know."

"'Forewarned is forearmed'—isn't that an old army saying?"

"Take it any way you like," he said hotly. He moved dangerously close to her. "Besides, what do you care, from the looks of it, you've got Thomas Fitzpatrick wrapped around your little finger."

"I don't even know him."

"It won't be long, Carlie," Ben predicted harshly. "I saw him with you. He's on the scent and a man like that usually gets what he wants."

"You're crazy." Thomas Fitzpatrick? Interested in her? The idea was outlandish. Or was it? Her skin crawled.

"Just watch out."

"You're serious."

"Absolutely, and you'd better open your eyes or quit playing that you don't know what's going on."

"He's a married man and old—"

"—enough to be your father. I know. Big deal. He wants you, Ms. Surrett. So the question is whether you're going to go for the bait. Fancy house, all those businesses, more money than you can count. What about it, Carlie?"

"You're unbelievable."

"Tell me that in a couple of weeks. The way I figure it, Fitzpatrick will make another move by then."

She lifted her hand as if to slap him, but he caught her wrist and his eyes flashed fire. "Don't even think about it!"

"You bastard."

His mouth twitched into a sarcastic grin. "Now we're getting somewhere." He let go of her hand.

Shaken, Carlie decided to have it out with him. Obviously they couldn't both live in this tiny little town, trying to avoid each other, hoping to steer clear of the other person's path. Tilting her chin, she eyed him speculatively. "You know, you don't have to hate me, Ben." Her words seemed to echo across the lake. "It's not part of the rules."

Ben winced and looked at her sharply, his eyes narrowing on her face. "I don't—" He moved back, snapped his mouth closed and glowered angrily, as if he were suddenly mad at the world.

"You don't what? Hate me?" She almost laughed. But her heart soared at the thought that there was a chance they could, at the very least, be civil to each other. "You have a funny way of showing it." Shoving her hands in her pockets, she walked through the tiny drifts of snow to get closer to him. "It would be a lot easier if we could get along."

"I don't think so."

"You'd rather despise me."

He raked fingers through his hair and squared his cap on his head. "It just makes things easier."

"You don't believe that," she said, feeling suddenly bold. There was anger in his dark gaze but something else, as well. Doubts? Passion? Memories of the love they'd shared? She wondered what he'd think if he knew the truth—all of the painful truth.

"I don't think it matters."

"How long are you staying in Gold Creek?"

He wanted to lie, to tell her that he'd be on the next bus out of town, but the deceit would catch up with him. "I don't know."

"A few days?" She stepped closer. Too close. The scent of her perfume wafted through the cold air. "A week?" Her face turned up to his, defying him, challenging him to lie to her. "A month?" She was so near that he saw the reflection of the Christmas lights in her eyes.

"Why does it matter?"

"I just wonder how often I'll run into you and how I'm supposed to act? Like a complete stranger? Or maybe just an acquaintance, someone you've heard of but don't really know? Or maybe a friend? No—that wouldn't be right, now would it? We'd be bending the rules.'' Her nostrils flared just a fraction. ''I know,'' she said, tossing from her face the few strands of hair that had fallen out of her braid. ''I'll act like a jilted ex-lover. You know, a girl who had all her hopes and dreams pinned on the boy she loved only to find out that he didn't care about her at all. Yeah, that's it. Like someone who was unjustly accused of something and who didn't even get the chance to defend herself.'' There was more she wanted to say, but thoughts along those particular lines were dangerous, made her vulnerable, which, right now, she could ill afford.

His back teeth ground together, and as she stared up at him with those damned blue eyes it was all he could do not to touch her, not to grab her by the arms and shake some sense into her, not to drag her body close to his and shut her up by kissing her so long and hard, she could barely breathe. Instead he just stared down at her, like a statue, the trained soldier he was, his face a mask of disinterest. ''Act any way you like, Carlie,'' he said harshly and winced a little inside when he saw the color drain from her face. ''You can do whatever you want, 'cause I really don't give a damn.''

Chapter Six

Thomas Fitzpatrick swirled a drink in his hand and stood near the window of his office. He tossed back a large swallow of Scotch, felt the alcohol hit the back of his throat and burn all the way down to his stomach. It was still morning. Ten-fifteen. Too early for a drink except on special occasions: birthdays, anniversaries, the signing of a particularly good deal. Or the day a man's served with divorce papers. From the corner of his eye he glimpsed the neatly typed documents from some high-powered lawyer in San Francisco. James T. Bennington. A tiger. The best. June was going for blood.

He swallowed the rest of his drink and poured another. Two would be his limit. Sitting at the desk, he stared down at the divorce papers. Signed, sealed and delivered. His wife had actually filed. She had more guts—and pride—than he'd ever given her credit for.

Being served had been humiliating, but not surprising. His reconciliation efforts with June had been feeble. They'd just gone through the motions of seeing a marriage counselor, engaging in a few "dates," trying to figure out what to do with the rest of their lives. All that time and money had been wasted. June wanted out. She was tired of Thomas's deals and his women. When Jackson Moore had come back to town and discovered that Thomas was really his father, all hell had broken loose. June had known the truth, of course, but it had been a well-kept secret. The boy had even been kept in the dark and Thomas had continued his on-again, off-again affair with Sandra Moore, Jackson's sexy, loose-moraled mother. He smiled as he thought of her. Sandra, of all his mistresses, had most touched his heart.

June had found the strength to move out and take their daughter, Toni, with her. Though Toni was old enough to be on her own, she'd still been living at home, here in Gold Creek. Thomas's baby. His little girl. His princess.

He sighed. He didn't really blame his wife. The love they'd once shared had died a long time ago. Sandra Moore wasn't his first mistress, nor had she been his last.

There had been lots of other women. Bosomy, beautiful females he'd met when he'd been out of town. Young women who had pretended an interest in him but were really impressed with his wealth.

He sipped this drink slowly and set the glass on the table as he settled deeper in his chair. The old leather creaked.

He thought of Carlie Surrett. Lord, she'd turned into a beauty. His fingers moved slowly up and down his sweaty glass. Years ago she'd caught his eye, but he'd drawn the line at girls still in their teens. If he remembered correctly, she'd left town because of that scandal with the older Powell boy, Ken or Conrad...no, Kevin. That was it. He'd committed suicide, or so everyone thought, because he'd loved Carlie and she'd broken up with him and became involved with his younger brother—that arrogant kid who ended up joining the army. There had even been some scandal about pregnancy, but no one knew for sure if that was true. Carlie certainly hadn't come back to town with a kid tagging behind her.

Pulling on his mustache, he thought long and hard, as he always did when he considered something he wanted. Without realizing what he was doing, he shoved back his chair, walked to the bar and plopped a couple of ice cubes into his glass. He caught his reflection in the mirror and scowled. Age was creeping up on him. Age and disappointment. He hadn't wanted to lose Roy years ago, and he didn't want to suffer the pain and financial strain of a divorce now. He'd hoped Jackson would forgive him and that somehow he'd end up with Turner Brooks's ranch. He'd even tried to wrangle the sawmills from his nephew, Hayden. Nothing had worked. He seemed to have lost the Midas touch he'd once possessed.

So now he wanted Carlie. She was old enough, and he was soon to be single. Nothing was standing in his way. Unless she was involved with someone; he'd have to check. It wouldn't be hard to find out all about her.

Carlie's father, Weldon, worked for him as a foreman at the logging company. Good man. Steady worker. Company man. Carlie was Weldon's only daughter and he'd disapproved when she'd taken off for the city. Weldon had grumbled about her getting too big for her britches though Thomas suspected that Weldon was covering up because he was hurt that his only daughter had run off to the city.

Rumor had it that she'd been married, briefly, but that wasn't confirmed. Thomas didn't really know much about her except that she and Rachelle Tremont had backed up Jackson Moore to prove that he hadn't killed Thomas's eldest son, Roy. Grief stole into his heart as it always did when he thought of Roy. God, he'd loved that boy. So had June. He'd been so bright, so athletic, and Thomas was sure there wasn't anything Roy couldn't do if he set his mind on it.

While Roy was alive, June had been a different person. Afterward, she was a shell of the woman she had been—a bitter shell. She had no longer turned a blind eye to Thomas's affairs.

The whole family had started to unravel when Roy was killed. Brian... Hell, Brian was never half the boy Roy had been and then he'd married that tramp, Laura Chandler, who'd trapped him into marriage and who, it turned out years later, had actually killed Roy.

So Carlie Surrett had been right, and grudgingly Thomas admired her principles. Among other things. Her long legs, her blue eyes, her perfect face. No wonder she'd been a model. He felt a restless stirring between his legs, something he hadn't felt in a long, long time and in his mind's eye he saw himself seducing Carlie, lying with her on silk sheets.

It didn't matter that she was less than half his age. She was an adult, a gorgeous adult, and she was single. Rumor had it that she wasn't rich and after all, her father was still working at the mill, struggling to make ends meet.

He folded the neatly typed documents and shoved them into his desk drawer. He decided to find out everything there was to know about Carlie and her family. The strengths and, more importantly, the weaknesses. He pushed the button on his intercom and told Melanie, his secretary, to get Robert Sands, a slick private investigator, on the line. For the right amount of money, Sands would leave no stone unturned and would find out all the dirt there was on the Surretts—finances, illegitimate children, affairs and any other little skeleton they'd like to keep locked in their closets.

For the first time all morning, Thomas Fitzpatrick smiled.

"We'll send a crew over to clean up the debris at the lakeside site." Ralph Katcher, Ben's foreman, reached into the back pocket of his jeans for his tin of chewing tobacco and propped one leg on the small step stool in the trailer Ben used as the official offices of his new company. It had been nearly two weeks since Nadine's wedding—two weeks since he'd seen Carlie—and Ben had spent that time buried in his work, trying to start his own construction business. "The Hardesty brothers are looking for work and they'll be able to salvage whatever's left," Ralph added.

"It's not much." Ben stood and stretched. He'd been sitting behind his beat-up desk for hours and his neck ached. He reached for the coffeepot still warming on a hot plate. "Nothin' much but the chimney. I was over there the other day."

"Leave it to Lyle and Lee. Believe me, they can find something out of nothing. 'Sides, the Hardestys work cheap. Best scrappers in the county."

"Good enough. Coffee?"

Ralph shook his head, and chuckled. "I'll pass. I'm about to head out for a beer. Besides, that sludge looks deadly."

"It is," Ben agreed, pouring the coffee into a chipped cup and taking a sip. Scowling at the bitter taste, he set his cup on the clutter of paperwork strewn over his desk and picked up his pencil again. The best decision Ben had made since he'd returned to Gold Creek was to hire Ralph. A hard worker who was supporting an ex-wife and a son, Ralph was glad for the work and had pointed Ben in the direction of several potential jobs.

Ralph pinched out some tobacco and laid it against his gum.

Ben pointed to the tin with his pencil. "*That's* the stuff that'll kill you."

"Yeah, but if it's not this, somethin' else will," Ralph replied with a grin that showed off flecks of brown against incredibly white teeth.

"I guess you're right."

"What about the house on Bitner? Mrs. Hunter's place?"

"It's a go. I'll start looking things over today and let you know what needs to be done. She seems to know what she wants."

"That's Dora for ya."

Ben rotated his neck and heard some disquieting pops. "I'll talk to Fitzpatrick tomorrow. There's got to be some repair work at the camp." Ben hated to ask for work from old Thomas. Ever since seeing him with Carlie at Nadine's wedding... The pencil he'd been holding snapped between his fingers.

"It would be nice to get a little money out of that old skinflint." Ralph had been out of work for nearly a year since a back injury had sidelined him from his last job with a major construction company, which was owned in part by Thomas Fitzpatrick. Since the accident, the company had laid off more people than it hired and Ralph hadn't been offered his old job because it had no longer existed: the company had gone out of business. Since then, Ralph had worked doing odd jobs—carpentry, chopping wood, even general yard work before he'd been introduced to Ben over a beer at the Silver Horseshoe. They'd struck a deal and he'd been working for Ben ever since. Ralph was grateful for the job and Ben was sure that he'd found the best foreman in the county. A burly man with muttonchop sideburns and slight paunch that hid his belt buckle, Ralph worked hard and was honest. Ben couldn't ask for more.

Ralph grabbed a dusty Mets cap off the rack near the door, then slung his denim jacket over his shoulder. "Well, it looks like we're gonna be busy."

"That's the plan."

"You won't hear me complainin'." Ralph stepped out of the old trailer and jogged to his pickup.

Ben took another swallow of bitter coffee, before dumping the rest of the foul stuff down the toilet. He'd start a fresh pot in the morning.

Stretching so that his back creaked, he thought about leaving, then sat down again in the worn swivel chair behind his metal desk. He shuffled a few papers, and wondered when he'd feel confident enough to hire a secretary. Not right away. He picked up a manila folder and let the check fall into the mess that was his desk. Fifty-thousand big ones. More money than he'd ever seen in his life and he hadn't even had to sign for it. All because he was now related to Hayden Monroe IV. Ben shouldn't take it—just stuff the damned piece of paper into an envelope and send it back, but he was too practical not to realize the value of this—a peace offering—from his sister's new husband.

"I just want to set things straight," Hayden had told him when he and Nadine had returned from their week-long honeymoon in the Bahamas. "For the past."

"That had nothing to do with me," Ben had replied.

Hayden's jaw had clamped tight. "This was my idea, not Nadine's. Hell, she doesn't even know about it."

"Deal with my dad."

Hayden had leveled him a gaze that could cut through solid steel. "I did, Powell. Now this is between us. Just you and me. Think of this money as an advance or a loan or a damned gift, I don't care, but rebuild Nadine's cabin the way she wants it. You can take your profit off the top, then pay me back when you can." Hayden's gaze had brooked no argument and the nostrils of his nose—a nose Ben had nearly broken just a few weeks ago—had flared with indignation.

It was a generous offer, one Ben could hardly refuse, so he'd agreed, but he'd had the proper legal papers drawn so that it was duly recorded that he was borrowing money from Monroe and the debt would be repaid within four years.

Ben had grown up believing that a person earned his way in the world, that he couldn't expect something for nothing, and he wasn't going to accept Hayden Monroe's money just to ease his new brother-in-law's conscience. This was a business matter. And a chance to rebuild his sister's cabin, so family loyalty was involved. However, the sooner he paid back the debt, the better he'd feel.

Satisfied, he filled out the deposit slip for his new business and stuffed the paperwork into his briefcase. His father had called him a fool, referred to Hayden's investment as "blood money." Well, maybe George was right. It didn't matter. For once Ben wasn't going to kick the golden goose out of his path.

He'd been frugal, picking up this old trailer from Fitzpatrick Logging for a song, and putting it on an empty lot on the outskirts of town zoned for commercial use. He'd bought the weed-infested lot from a man who lived in Seattle and who had once planned to retire in the area.

Later, because of the downturn in the California economy, the owner had changed his mind about his retirement plans and gladly sold the piece of ground to Ben. Once the lot was paid off, Ben planned to build himself an office complex, but that dream was a long way off. First he needed to line up more work than just the construction of a lakeside cabin for his sister and the renovation of the old Victorian house on Bitner Street.

Ben's bid for the Bitner job had been lower than any of his competitors' because he was hungrier and he wanted a real job, not a handout from his brother-in-law. Mrs. Hunter, the owner of the building, wanted it to be brought up to date: cleaned, repaired, remodeled, "whatever it takes" to get it ready to sell. She was a sly woman who had a vacancy that she hoped to fill and she'd decided Ben would make a perfect tenant for her downstairs studio. "We could do a trade. You get free rent and I get a little knocked off the bill?" She'd smiled sweetly, bobbing her head of blue-gray curls, but Ben had declined, preferring to keep a little distance between himself and the people who hired him.

However, Dora Hunter wasn't to be outmaneuvered. "You think about it," she'd told him during their last conversation. "It could be mighty convenient and I could come up with a deal you'd be a fool to pass up."

Ben had decided right then and there that there was a shrewd businesswoman with a will of iron lurking behind the grandmotherly persona of apple cheeks and rimless spectacles. At seventy-eight, Mrs. Hunter was tired of the problems associated with owning and managing an apartment building and was ready to retire to Palm Springs to be closer to her daughter and good-for-nothing son-in-law. She'd confided in Ben as she'd signed their contract. "He's a bum, but Sonja loves him, so what does it matter what I think? Besides, there's the grandchildren..." She'd clucked her tongue. "Hard to believe that man could father such adorable boys. Ahh, well..." She'd put down the pen, looked up at Ben with a twinkle in her blue eyes and stuck out her hand. "Looks like we have a bargain, Mr. Powell."

"Ben." Her grip was amazingly strong.

"Only if you call me Dora."

"It's a deal."

So Ben had a contract for his first "real job," and it felt good, damned good, even if he wouldn't make a ton of money. He had a chance to prove himself and, if Mrs. Hunter—Dora—was satisfied with the quality of his work, word would get out. In a town the size of Gold Creek word of mouth was worth more than thousands of dollars of paid advertising in the *Clarion*.

The Hunter apartments and Nadine's cabin were just the beginning of his plan. He figured there were ample opportunities in Gold Creek, Coleville and the neighboring communities. He intended to specialize in remodeling rather than developing new projects. A lot of the buildings in Gold Creek were steeped in history and charm but nearly desolate in the way of modern conveniences. Most of the commercial property in the center of town had been built in the early part of the century and though attractive and quaint, needed new wiring, plumbing, insulation, heating and cooling systems or face-lifts.

Ben was determined to find work, even if he had to swallow his pride and offer his services to Fitzpatrick Logging, though that particular thought stuck in his gut. He locked the single-wide trailer behind him. In the army, he'd learned about construction and had taken enough college courses at different universities and through correspondence to graduate as a building engineer.

Now all he needed was a break or two. Hayden Monroe had given him his first. Dora Hunter had provided the second. It was just a matter of time, then maybe he'd settle down in this town, find himself a wife and ... Thoughts of Carlie crashed through his cozy little dreams and he threw a dark look at the sky. Why couldn't he get her out of his mind? Ever since the day of Nadine's wedding, when he'd first spied her through the binoculars, he hadn't been able to quit thinking about her. She was on his mind morning, noon and night.

And, as before, nights were definitely the worst, he thought, grimacing as he strode across the gravel to his pickup. He'd spent the past week tossing and sweating in his bed or under the spray of an ice-cold shower. Whether he wanted to admit it or not, Carlie Surrett had gotten into his blood again.

But not for long. She definitely wasn't the kind of woman he intended to spend the rest of his life with. A hot-tempered New York model, a sophisticated photographer—an *artiste,* for God's sake. No, the woman he'd finally ask to marry him would be a simple girl, born and raised in this small town with no ambitions other than to have a couple of kids and enjoy life. He knew it was an antiquated picture of the American family, but it was exactly the kind of family he'd wanted ever since he'd left the army.

He had no room for Carlie in his life.

Besides, she was the last woman he should want. He had only to remember back to that horror-riddled night of Kevin's death....

"Don't!" he told himself as he noticed the first fat drops of rain fall from the sky.

Muttering under his breath, he threw his briefcase onto the seat of the old truck and had started the engine when he saw the dog—a dusty black German shepherd—lying near the side of the trailer. He hesitated, knowing he was taking on more than he'd bargained for, then let the truck idle.

Whistling softly, he climbed out of the cab. The shepherd's ears pricked forward for a second and he snarled.

Ben lowered himself to one knee and began talking softly.

The dog growled.

"This is not a way to make friends and influence people," he told the animal.

They didn't move for a while, each staring the other down, before Ben whistled again.

The dog didn't respond.

"Come on, boy." Ben inched closer and watched the shepherd. Balanced on the balls of his feet, Ben was ready to spring backward if the dog decided to lunge. "Okay, now what's going on here?" he asked as the animal issued a low warning. The shepherd tried to get up, stumbled and Ben saw the blood, a sticky purple pool, beneath the animal's belly. With surprising speed, the dog attacked, snapping, and Ben jumped back. Now what? He couldn't leave the animal there to die.

Knowing he was probably making a mistake, he climbed into the truck, found his leather gloves, a shank of rope and a thick rawhide jacket. After spreading a tattered blanket in the bed of the truck, he approached the dog calmly as he worked the rope into a slip knot.

"Okay, boy, let's see what you've got," he said.

The animal lunged again, but Ben was ready for him, avoiding the sharp teeth as he slipped the noose over the dog's head and barked out his own command. "No!"

The animal froze.

"Down!"

Still no movement.

"That's better." Ben fashioned a muzzle with some hemp and braved the snarling jaws to quiet the animal. For his efforts he was nipped on the sleeve. "You are a bastard," Ben ground out, enjoying the fight a little. "I'm gonna win, you know. Whether you like it or not, I'm taking you to the nearest vet and you're going to be stitched up so you can bite the next idiot who tries to take care of you."

Carefully Ben carried the writhing dog to the truck and laid him, snarling and frustrated, on the tattered blanket. "Stay!" Ben commanded, knowing the dog was too weak to stand or leap from the vehicle. He climbed in the front, snapped on the wipers, threw the rig into gear and headed into town, hoping that Doc Vance and the veterinary clinic were still on the west end of town.

What was wrong with him? Ever since he'd landed in Gold Creek, he seemed destined on some sort of collision course with fate. First his battle with Hayden Monroe, then

Carlie—hell, what a mess that was—and now the dog. The damned dog. One more problem that he didn't need.

Carlie rubbed the kinks out of her neck. She'd spent a long day in the dark room and couldn't wait to get home to a hot shower, a glass of wine and a good book.

Just before leaving the studio, she'd called Thomas Fitzpatrick, agreed to take the photographs for the logging company's annual report, and wondered why she felt as if she'd sold her soul to the devil. The man was just offering her work, after all; it wasn't as if he'd committed a major sin. He'd visited her father, as promised, and broken the news to Weldon that his job couldn't be held. Her father, always a prideful man, hadn't fallen apart. In fact he'd been grateful that Fitzpatrick had promised to find another position for him as soon as Weldon was fit enough to spend four or five hours at the logging company. "You can work as many hours as you want, kind of ease into the job again," Thomas had told Weldon as he'd clapped him on the back. "The logging company's just not the same without you."

Her father had eaten it up, but Carlie had been unsettled by Fitzpatrick's practiced smile and easy charm. She remembered that he'd once planned a career in politics and she didn't trust him any more than she would a king cobra. He was too smooth to be real. And then there was all that trouble and scandal concerning Jackson.

So why are you planning to do business with him? her tired mind demanded. *For the money.* Pure and simple. Just in case the bastard had lied to her father.

As for Ben's insinuations about the man, they were just plain false. She'd spoken to Fitzpatrick several times, her senses on guard, and each time he'd been a gentleman. Ben, damn him, had been wrong.

But he'd been wrong about a lot of things, she thought darkly, wondering if he had an inkling of the fact that he'd nearly been a father.... The pain in her heart ached and she shoved those agonizing thoughts far away, where no one could ever find them.

She drove to her parents' apartment and managed a smile as she opened the door. "Hi! Thought I'd stop by—" She stopped in midsentence as she felt in the air that something was wrong—dreadfully wrong.

"Carlie?" Her mother's voice shook a little and her footsteps were quick as they carried her down the stairs. White lines of strain bracketed her mouth and she looked as if she'd been crying.

"What's wrong?" Carlie asked, her heart knocking.

"Thank God you're here." Thelma's voice cracked and she had to blink against an onslaught of tears. "It's your father. He's... he's in the hospital."

"The hospital?" Carlie whispered, her heart pounding with dread.

"He...he got that numb feeling again—you know, I told you it happened a couple of times before—and he couldn't move very well and I called the emergency number and an ambulance took him to County General.... Oh, Lord, it was awful, Carlie. I stayed with him for a couple of hours, just to make sure he was resting, but then the doctor convinced me I should go home, that there wasn't anything more I could do. I didn't want to leave him—" Her voice cracked and Carlie hugged her mother tightly.

"Shh. He'll be fine," Carlie said, hoping for the best and knowing that her words held a hollow ring.

"They're sayin' it might be a stroke—a bigger one. Oh, Lord, I can't imagine your father all crippled up. It'll kill him, sure as I'm standin' here."

"Oh, come on, Mom, don't think that way," Carlie said, though she was smiling through her tears. *A stroke?*

Thelma sniffed, attempted a smile and failed miserably. "I tried to call you, but by that time, you were already gone."

"So what did the doctor say? What exactly?"

"A lot of things I didn't understand," she admitted and wiped her eyes with the back of her hand. "The gist of it is that your father's out of immediate danger, whatever that means."

"Well, it sounds encouraging."

"I'm not so sure." Thelma wrung her hands and walked into the kitchen with Carlie, fearing the worst, following behind. "They've taken more tests and well, they practically wore poor Weldon out with all their poking and prodding...." Her voice faded and she stared out the window to the rainy winter night. "All we can do is pray."

Carlie's heart seemed to drop to her knees. Her father couldn't be seriously ill, could he? He'd always been so big and strapping—a man's man. Now he was frail?

"Come on, Mom," she heard herself saying as she walked on wooden legs. "Let's go see how he is and I'll talk to the doctors. Then, if we think we can leave him, I'll buy you dinner."

"You don't have to—"

"Don't be silly, Mom. I *want* to. Now get your coat."

Thelma didn't argue and Carlie ushered her out to the Jeep. The ride to the hospital took less than thirty minutes and Carlie spent the entire time willing her father to live, to be as strong as he once was.

She'd always depended upon her father. Whenever she had been in trouble, she'd turned to him, listening to his advice. He was kind and strong, not well educated, but wise to the world and she'd adored him. Even when they'd argued, which had happened more frequently in her teenaged years, they had never lost respect for each other because of the special bond they shared.

It had been he, not her mother, who had been hurt when Carlie had turned her back on Gold Creek. He, who had in those first few months when she'd been starving in Manhattan, sent her checks, "a little something extra to help out," though she knew he'd grumbled loudly and often about her decision to move to New York. He'd never liked the idea of her modeling, wearing scanty clothing and being photographed; he'd felt personally violated somehow. However, Weldon Surrett had offered a hefty shoulder when she'd needed to cry on one and then been baffled when she no longer reached for him.

He hadn't approved of her love for Ben. Years ago he'd warned her about both Powell boys. She'd ignored him and when, in the end, he'd been right, he'd never mentioned the fact. Of course, he hadn't known that she'd been pregnant when she'd left Gold Creek. That little secret was hers and hers alone.

Her father had been hurt badly enough when she'd gotten married on the spur of the moment but had tried his best to like his new son-in-law, though they'd met only once and Paul had been disagreeable. But Weldon hadn't so much as said "I told you so" when the marriage had failed.

Oh, Dad, don't die, she thought desperately. She wasn't done needing a father. For the past few months she'd convinced herself that she'd returned to Gold Creek to help him, when, she decided as she squinted through the drizzle on the windshield, it had been she who had needed help to figure out what to do with the rest of her life.

One thing was certain. It was time she stopped running. Time to face her past. Time to mend fences. Time to start a new life. Time to tell her father she loved him and time to deal with the one loose end in her life, the one dangling thread that still had the ability to coil around and squeeze her heart: her feelings for Ben.

But she couldn't think of Ben now, not when her father was battling for his life. She drove the Cherokee into a spot near the emergency entrance, slid out of the Jeep and hunched her shoulders against the rain as she and her mother dashed across the puddles forming on the asphalt of the parking lot.

On the third floor of the hospital, in a semiprivate room, Weldon Surrett lay in the bed, his face slightly ashen, the left side slack. He was sleeping and his breathing was labored.

"Dad?" Carlie whispered, and he blinked his eyes open. It took him a second to focus before he smiled a little. "How are you?"

"Still kickin'," he replied though he coughed a little and his tongue seemed thick.

"You gave us both a scare."

He chuckled and coughed again. "Keeps you on your toes."

"Sure does." She grabbed his hand and held it tightly between her own. His grip was weak, but he was still the man who, singing in a deep baritone as he arrived home from work each evening, would scoop her up in his arms and swing her in the air. He'd smell of smoke and the outdoors and he would force her to sing along with him while her mother clucked her tongue and told them they were both mindless.

"Don't suppose you brought me a beer?"

"Not this time."

"Smokes?" he asked hopefully.

"The doctor would kill me, and I thought you gave those up years ago."

"Smokeless ain't the same," he said. "But I'll take chew if ya got it."

"Like I always carry around a can of tobacco," she said with a smile.

"You should've today," he managed to get out.

"Don't talk," she said, still holding his hand. "You go back to sleep and we'll stay with you awhile."

"Sorry I'm such lousy company."

Her throat clogged. "You're good company, Dad. You always have been."

He squeezed her fingers before closing his eyes again and Carlie fought the hot sting of tears. "I love you, Daddy," she whispered and though he didn't open his eyes again, she felt him try to squeeze her hand a second time.

They waited until he'd drifted off, then Carlie decided it was time she spoke to the doctor. Her parents had led her to believe that her father had suffered a "mild stroke," which was stronger than the smaller ones he'd experienced. The doctors hoped that after a little recovery, some intensive physical therapy, new medication and a change in diet, he'd be able to resume most of his usual activities. But seeing her father looking so weak, as if he'd just walked a thousand miles, she knew better. And it scared the living daylights out of her.

* * *

Ben sat at the computer, the one luxury he'd afforded himself, and worked with the rough drawings Nadine had given him. At first she'd wanted to rebuild the cabin as it was, but Hayden and Ben, agreeing for the first time in years, had suggested that she'd need something a little more modern, with two bathrooms instead of one and a couple of bedrooms rather than a single. She could still keep the loft, but she'd have an expanded kitchen and a fireplace that served as a room divider so that it could be seen from both the kitchen/nook area as well as the living room.

"Looks like I'm outnumbered," she'd responded, with a slight trace of irritation in her voice.

"It's just more practical," Ben had explained.

"But I liked it the way it was."

"So did I." Hayden had wrapped his arms around his wife's waist and kissed her on the neck. "This will be essentially the same floor plan, but a little more modern."

"You can even have a laundry room," Ben had quipped.

"And a sewing room with enough space for your machine, a desk and—"

"Okay, okay, already! I'm convinced," she'd said with a smile. "Just as long as I get to design the room layout."

So here he was, struggling with her rough sketch, adjusting the size of rooms and placement of walls for duct work, support beams, plumbing, electrical wiring and taking into consideration the slope of the land, watershed and a million other things that would be required before the county would approve her plans.

By noon he was stiff from sitting, so he drove into town to the Buckeye Restaurant and Lounge. The establishment hadn't changed much in the years that he'd been away. The booths were still covered in a time-smoothed Naugahyde.

"Ben Powell!" Tracy Niday, dressed in a gingham dress and brown apron, slid a plastic menu onto the table in front of him. "I heard you were back in town."

"You heard right."

"Just passing through?" she asked.

"I think I'll be sticking around for a while."

"Coffee?"

"Please. Black."

He opened the menu as she hurried back to the kitchen. He'd known that Tracy was in town, of course; Nadine and his father had written him while he was in the service. She'd been nearly destroyed after Kevin had died. Three weeks later she'd dropped the bomb with a mind-numbing announcement that she was pregnant with Kevin's baby. Ben had already left Gold Creek when Tracy had told his father the news.

She'd given birth to a healthy baby boy eight months after Kevin had been buried. George had helped her out a little as her own family had nearly disowned her. Things were better now, or so Nadine had told him. Tracy worked at the bank during the week and put in a shift or two at the Buckeye on the weekends.

She returned, flipped over his coffee cup and poured the coffee from a fat glass pot. "You know," she said as she set the pot on the table and grabbed her pad, "Randy would love to meet you."

Randy was her son. His nephew. He felt a jab of guilt. "Sure. Anytime."

"You mean it?"

"Give me a call." He reached into his wallet and drew out a business card. "I'd like to see Kevin's boy."

For a second he thought she might cry. Her brown eyes glistened and she cleared her throat before taking his order and moving on to wait on the next booth.

Tracy had never married, though, according to Nadine she'd dated several men seriously. She'd spent the past ten years taking care of her boy and trying to better herself. She was pretty, one of those kind of women who seemed to get more good-looking as the years passed.

She returned to Ben's table, talked with him, laughing and joking, smiling a little more than she did with the other patrons as she served him a ham sandwich, potato salad and a crisp dill pickle.

"Don't make yourself scarce," she said when he'd taken the final swallow from a coffee cup she seemed determined to keep filled.

"I won't." He left her a decent tip and waved as he walked out the door. A weak winter sun was trying to break through the clouds and the puddles of water, left over from the rain, shimmered in the pale light. He climbed into his pickup and drove to the veterinary clinic where he was told that the shepherd, though dehydrated and suffering from malnutrition, was on the mend. The hole in his belly was probably compliments of a fight with another dog or a wild animal and though the beast had lost a lot of blood, he would survive.

"I've called around," Doc Vance said as he rubbed the lenses of his glasses with the tail of his lab coat. "None of the shelters or other vets have any anxious owners looking for their pets. I even checked with the police department. He's got a collar, but no license, so there's no way of knowin' where he comes from." He patted the groggy animal on the head. "But my guess is that the dog is a pure-bred and someone's taken care of him. He's been neutered and had his teeth cleaned within the last year, and look at this—" he showed him the dog's feet "—his toenails have been clipped, fairly recently, so I don't think there's a worry of rabies, though I'd inoculate him."

"If I decide to keep him."

The round vet smiled, showing off a gold tooth that winked in the fluorescent lights dangling from the ceiling. "You've got yourself a hefty bill here for a dog you're gonna turn loose on the streets." Again he patted the shepherd and the dog yawned. "Besides, every bachelor needs a dog. Someone to come home and talk to. Believe me, a dog's better than a wife. This here shepherd won't talk back."

"I heard that," Lorna, the doctor's wife and assistant, called from the back room.

"Listenin' in again?" he yelled back at her.

"Hard not to overhear you griping."

Doc Vance rolled his eyes and mouthed, "Women!" as if that said it all.

Ben agreed to have the dog vaccinated, then paid his bill. It took most of his patience not to be offended when the shepherd growled at him. "Okay, Attila," he said, leading the animal outside and to his truck, "if you so much as snarl at me while I'm driving, I'm letting you off right then and there. You're history." The dog snorted as Ben helped him onto the sagging bench seat, but he didn't bare his teeth, nor did he try to bite which, Ben decided, was an improvement over the day Ben had first found him.

"Just for the record," he said, as if the beast could understand him, "I don't want a dog."

Settling behind the steering wheel, Ben thought of Doc Vance's words of wisdom about marriage. Vance was probably kidding; he'd been married forever.

Ben had already decided he needed a wife—but not Carlie Surrett. Yet, just at the thought of her clear blue eyes, lustrous black hair and intelligent smile, his gut tightened.

He wanted her. It was that simple. And though he could deny it to himself a thousand times, he had to admit the truth. "Damn it all," he muttered, slapping on the radio. The dog let out a low growl of disapproval which Ben ignored.

His house, a rental, was located on the outskirts of town. Once inside, he offered the dog food and water, then left him on a blanket in the laundry room. He had to meet some of the men who were going to clean the debris from Nadine's lot, then he had to do a little work over at the Hunter Victorian. He'd figure out what to do about the dog a little later.

As for Carlie—God only knew what he'd do about her.

Carlie was bone weary. The past couple of nights she'd spent hours at the hospital with her father or talking with the doctors who attended him. Though Weldon Surrett had suffered a mild stroke, he would recover. His speech had already improved and he had partial use of his left hand and arm. He was frustrated and cranky, but if he changed his life-style, gave up high-cholesterol food, avoided cigarettes and kept active, the prognosis was encouraging.

However, he was stuck with months of physical therapy. He would eventually be released from the hospital, but he wouldn't be able to work at any kind of strenuous labor for a long, long while.

He was too old to retrain for a desk job, and even if he were a younger man, he would never be happy cooped up inside, shuffling papers, filing and working with figures.

It looked as if he would have to retire early, as Thomas Fitzpatrick had suggested, and hope that whatever savings he and his wife had accumulated over the years would be enough to get them through. Thelma would still work of course, and Carlie intended to help out, though her father had been adamantly against the suggestion. Eventually, he'd collect Social Security, but those checks were still a few years away.

"We'll manage," he'd said from his hospital bed.

"But I can help—"

"This is my problem, Carlie, and I'll handle it. Now don't you say a word to your mother or go getting her upset. We've made it through rough times before, we can do it again."

Reluctantly Carlie had dropped the argument when she'd seen the determined set of his jaw. Any further discussion would only have made him angrier and more upset and might have brought on another attack.

Now her stomach grumbled at her as she walked through the foyer to her apartment and noticed that the baseboards had been stripped from the walls. Mrs. Hunter, Carlie's landlady, had told her that she was going to renovate the old place in hopes of selling out. She'd even approached Carlie about buying the old Victorian house on the hill.

At the time, Carlie hadn't been sure she wanted to stay in Gold Creek; now, with her father ill, she'd decided to stay, at least for a while. She'd seen a lot of the world and was surprised at the feeling of coming home she'd experienced upon returning to this cozy little town, a town she'd once left without a backward glance.

"Well, hello there!" Mrs. Hunter opened the door to her apartment to walk into the vestibule. She was dressed in a raincoat and carried a floral umbrella of purple and pink. "I thought you were my ride down to the center," she said, peering out one of the tall leaded-glass windows that flanked the front door. "Smorgasbord tonight, you know."

"You'll have a good time."

"I hope so. Last time the food was overcooked, you know, tasted like shoe leather, but the company's usually good. Let's just hope Leo Phelps doesn't drag out his harmonica. Why they let him play after dinner, when everyone else wants to get on with cards or bingo, I'll never know." She pulled a plastic bonnet from her behemoth of a bag and spread it over her newly permed gray curls. "Oh, here they are now. By the way, the workmen are still here, probably just finishing up, so if you run across a handsome man in your room..." She let the sentence trail off and laughed.

"I'll know what to do," Carlie teased as Mrs. Hunter walked onto the porch and closed the door behind her.

Still smiling to herself, Carlie gathered her mail and started up the stairs. She lived on the third floor, the "crow's nest" Mrs. Hunter called it, and Carlie had come to love her apartment. The turret, where she kept her desk, had nearly a three-hundred-and-sixty-degree view, and the old wooden floors, and hand-carved window frames held a charm that she'd found lacking in more modern apartments. Running her fingers along the time-worn rail, she hiked her way up the steep stairs and told herself that the climb would keep her in shape. There were drawbacks to living here—the heating and cooling systems were ancient, the windows rattled and she'd seen more than one mouse sharing her living quarters, but she still loved her tiny rooms tucked high in the eaves of the old house.

On the landing, she stepped over an electrical cord strung across the hall before it snaked through her front door.

"Hello?" she called, not wanting to scare the workman as she entered.

Ben stood near one of the windows, his hip thrown out, his arms crossed over his chest.

Her heart missed a beat and she stopped dead in her tracks.

A tool belt was slung low over his hips and the sleeves of his work shirt were rolled over his forearms displaying tanned skin dusted with dark hair.

"Well, Carlie," he said with a brazen smile that touched a dark corner of her heart. "I wondered when you'd show up."

Chapter Seven

Carlie couldn't believe her eyes. Ben? Ben was the contractor—the workman who was going to be walking in and out of the house, with his own set of keys, his own set of rules and his own damned swagger? She felt suddenly violated and insecure. The fact that he was in her apartment, her private sanctuary, made her blood boil. After the way he'd treated her, he was the last person she wanted prowling about her home. Let the windows rattle. Let the faucet drip. Let the damned roof leak, but for God's sake, never let Ben Powell in here. "What're you doing here?" she demanded as he placed a screwdriver to her window frame and played with the pulleys in the old casing.

"What does it look like?"

She ground her teeth in frustration. "I *know* about the work that has to be done, I just don't understand why *you* had to do it!"

"I got the job." He grimaced a little as the rope slid between his fingers and the window dropped suddenly. With a grunt, he shoved the old pane up again and tightened the screw.

"But you're not living here, are you?" she asked, her world suddenly tilting as she remembered the empty studio apartment on the first floor that Mrs. Hunter had wanted to rent. Mrs. Hunter had mentioned that she might trade the rent for work around the house.... Oh, no! He couldn't live here—no way, no how! This small set of rooms was her private place, her shelter! She wasn't going to share it with the one man who had the ability to wound her.

"I'd be moving in tomorrow if your landlady had her way." He shoved his screwdriver back into his tool belt and his eyes glinted a bit. "However, so far I've resisted."

"She can be pretty persuasive." Carlie tossed her purse on the couch.

"Can she?" he asked, one corner of his mouth lifting skeptically.

"Very."

"I guess I'd better avoid her."

"Like you do with all women," she challenged, and his head jerked up, his smile fading quickly away.

"Only the ones that I think will be trouble." He reached into his open toolbox, withdrew a plane and turned back to the sill, as if he planned to fix the damned window this very night.

"And that doesn't take in the entire female population?" Carlie was spoiling for a fight and she couldn't control her tongue. It had been a long week, worrying about her parents, thinking about Ben, wishing she could just start over.

"Not quite." He glared pointedly at her and she blushed. He seemed so much more real today. The last time she'd seen him at Nadine's wedding, he'd worn his military uniform and he'd seemed untouchable and remote. Distant. A soldier on a three-day pass. But today, dressed in faded jeans with worn knees and thin fabric over his buttocks, a tool belt and work shirt with the sleeves rolled over his forearms, he was decidedly more human and, therefore, more dangerous.

"You obviously don't want me here," he said as he shaved off some of the casing. Sawdust and wood curls fell to the floor.

"You got that right."

"Look, it's just a job, okay?" He scowled, as if he felt uncomfortable.

"A job in my house."

"Live with it, lady." He uncinched his belt and it fell to the floor with a thud that echoed in her heart. She averted her eyes for a second; she couldn't even stand to watch him remove one article of clothing without thinking back to a time when she would have liked nothing more than to lie naked with him in a field of summer wildflowers.

But she couldn't afford to feel this way; the strain on her already stretched emotions would be too much. She couldn't be around him until they'd dealt with the past, cleared the air and started fresh. She wasn't in the mood to pick up the old pieces of her life and start fitting them together, but she didn't have much of a choice. Not if she was being forced to see Ben on a daily basis.

"This job going to take long?"

"Are you asking if I'm gonna be underfoot for the next couple of weeks?" He frowned, then ran his fingers over the newly smoothed wood. "That's a distinct possibility."

"I'm not crazy about the idea."

"Neither am I." He glanced up at her, and when their gazes touched, the breath seemed knocked from her throat. Damn the man, he had no right to look so sexy. "Couldn't one of your men—"

"So far I *am* my men." He set the plane back in the toolbox. "Does it bother you so much—that I'm here in your apartment?"

"It makes me uncomfortable."

"Why?"

"Why?" She rested one hip against the back of the couch. "I guess there're about a million reasons," she admitted.

"Name one."

"You're an arrogant bastard."

He grinned. "Name two."

"You've tried your best to do nothing but insult me from the minute you stepped into town." Crossing her arms over her chest, she added, "I can read all sorts of accusations in your eyes, Ben, but I don't understand them."

"I'm not accusing you of anything."

"Like hell! Every time we're together you insinuate that I'm some kind of... of criminal or something—that I did something terrible and wrong and God only knows what else." She took in a long breath and asked the question that had haunted her for so many years. "Just what was it I did to hurt you so badly?"

"You didn't hurt me."

"I damned well did something. You took off out of town like a dog with his tail tucked between his legs."

"My brother was dead, damn it!" He kicked the tool belt across the floor, sending it crashing into an ottoman. "Dead! And you... you..."

"I what?" she demanded, her lungs constricting, old memories burning through her mind.

"You didn't care."

"Oh, Ben—"

He held up a hand, to cut off further conversation. "Forget it, Carlie. Let's just start back at square one. You didn't do anything. Okay? Not a damned thing!" But a tic jumped near his left eye and the muscles in the back of his neck grew rigid.

"Wrong." She shook her head and thought hard, rolling back the years, allowing the blinding pain of the past to surface. For over a decade she'd kept it bottled up, tucked away in a dark corner of her mind, collecting cobwebs, but now she let all of her suspicions surface. "It was because of Kevin," she said quietly, finally saying the words that she'd denied so long. "Somehow you blame me for what happened to him."

Ben didn't say a word, just stared at her as if she were Eve in the Garden of Eden, offering him forbidden fruit, trying to open his eyes to things better left unseen, forcing him to face the truth.

Shoving away from the couch, she picked up his heavy belt and walked the short distance that separated them, her footsteps muffled on the worn Oriental carpet. He never stopped staring at her and she only quit moving when the toe of her shoe nudged the tip of his worn sneakers. She dropped the belt at his feet. "You've blamed me, though I don't know why. There was nothing I could do. Nothing either of us could do. We couldn't have stopped Kevin from driving into that garage and letting the engine run."

The air grew thick with cold. Rain pelted the windows and dripped down the sill into the house. Ben's eyes narrowed a fraction and a deep anguish shadowed his eyes.

"Whether it was an accident or suicide, we weren't to blame," she said wishing she could touch him and erase the pain that still lingered in his gaze.

"You don't know that."

Her heart ached for all the years they'd let the past keep them apart, for all the misunderstandings, the hatred and mistrust. "What could either of us have done?"

"I could have been there for him. I knew he was having problems," Ben said gruffly. His throat worked and he stared at her with a venom so intense, she shuddered.

"Did you think he'd take his life?"

"No."

"Neither did I."

Ben snorted. "But I suspected he was in love with you and I didn't care. Nadine even warned me, but I still took you out, bragged about it, even told him I thought I might marry you," Ben said. His face was filled with self-loathing.

"Marry me?" she whispered, her heart aching.

"I'd thought about it. He'd tried to talk me out of it, claimed that you weren't the marrying type—too interested in seeing the world." He slammed the window shut and the room seemed suddenly still.

"Ben, I didn't know—"

"You knew a lot, Carlie," he said, his lips curling into a sneer of disgust, his gaze suddenly dark and menacing. He grabbed her by the shoulders, his eyes fierce, his expression haunted. "He loved you, Carlie. We both should have known it, but we didn't want to. We were too wrapped up in each other to care about someone else. I rationalized everything—he was dating Tracy so it was okay for me to start seeing the girl that he couldn't forget."

"You've got it all turned around," she said, but she remembered the day on the dock when Kevin had surprised her and professed his love. She'd conveniently forgotten how wounded he'd been.

"Do I?" Ben snarled, his face flushed in anger, his hands clenching and stretching in frustration. "Why didn't you tell me about the letters, Carlie?"

"The letters?" she repeated. "What letters?"

He offered her a smile that chilled her to the bones. "You know the letters. The ones that Kevin wrote to you."

"I didn't get any—"

"Liar!" His fingers dug into the soft flesh of her upper arms. "We found some of the letters he hadn't gotten around to sending to you and they were pretty explicit about your relationship."

"There was no relationship!" she said. "I'd broken up with him, if you can even call it that. There wasn't even a reason to break up. We only had a few dates and I just told him I couldn't go out with him anymore."

"But those dates . . . they were powerful, weren't they?" he said, his hold punishing.

"I don't know what you're getting at, Ben."

"I know about the baby."

Her heart stopped suddenly and she hardly dared breathe. "*What* baby?"

"The baby you wouldn't have. Kevin's baby."

"Kevin's baby? What are you talking about? I never had a baby. . . ." Her voice failed her as her heart tightened in painful knots.

"Because you wouldn't," he snarled in disgust. The look he sent her was pure hatred.

"Oh, Ben, if you only knew."

"I do know. You were too selfish—"

"Hey wait a minute!" She shoved hard on his chest. "You don't know me, Ben Powell! Not at all. You didn't stick around long enough to find out, did you?"

"I know you wanted to get rid of the baby."

"I didn't want to get rid of any baby," she said, her throat closing as she shook her head in misery. Anger rushed through her veins. "You've got everything all twisted around. You think I was pregnant with Kevin's child and...and that I had an abortion?"

Horrified at his accusations, she watched the play of emotions contort his face. He was serious! He really believed this insane bunch of lies. He didn't say a word, but condemnation sizzled in his gaze and she died a little inside. If only she could reach out, touch his hand, explain...but the censure on his face was devastating.

Her knees nearly gave way when she thought of all the wasted years. All the lies. All the pain. Leaning against the wall for support, she shook her head. "I didn't...I never...Kevin and I...we didn't ever get that far."

"Don't lie to me, Carlie. It's too late."

"You should know better, Ben," she said, fury taking hold of her tongue again. Eyes shimmering with unshed tears, she inched her chin up a notch and pinned him with her furious gaze. "You are the one man who should know the truth!" Her heart shredded a little. It wasn't Kevin's baby she'd wanted all those years ago, it was Ben's. She'd hoped for a miracle, that though they'd made love only one night, that she would become pregnant. At the time, she'd wanted desperately to bear his child, and she'd been ecstatic when she'd skipped her period. But her euphoria had been short-lived. Though she'd taken an in-home pregnancy test that had showed positive, within weeks, she'd miscarried. Alone. The doctor had kept her secret and she'd never felt more miserable in her life.

A tear drizzled down her cheek, but she sniffed hard before any other traces of her regret tracked from her eyes. "Don't you remember?" she demanded, pride stiffening her spine. "I couldn't have been pregnant, Ben, because when I was seeing Kevin, I was still a virgin."

He had been reaching for his toolbox, but he froze.

"That night on the lake. In the rain? That's the night I lost my virginity, Ben!" she said, wounded and furious all in one instant. "And I didn't give it to Kevin. I gave it to his brother." *And I got pregnant. With your baby. Our baby!*

He stared at her in disbelief and she shook her head. "I don't know why you want to believe this ridiculous story—"

His face drained of color. "You were a—"

"Too bad you weren't paying attention," she said bitterly. "You could have saved yourself a whole lot of time and trouble hating me for something that was so obviously a lie!"

"I don't believe—"

"I don't care what you believe," she said in righteous fury. "You can think what you want! But the truth of the matter is that I gave my virginity to you, Ben, and if I'd been lucky enough to get pregnant it would have been with your child!" *It had been with your child!*

"But—"

"Kevin never touched me!"

His jaw clamped tightly together.

"I can't believe that you let some lie and your own guilt twist things around so that you hated me for all these years. Why didn't you come to me, Ben? Why didn't you let me explain rather than set yourself up as judge and jury?" Trembling inside, she motioned to the door. "You've always been wrong about me. You were wrong then and you're wrong now. I think you'd better go," she said firmly. "This is my place—my private place—and I don't want you here."

"I don't believe you."

She smiled bitterly. "Then you're a fool."

His lips curled and she thought he might grab her and shake her, but he muttered something under his breath, snapped his jaw shut, grabbed his toolbox and strode past. The door slammed behind him with a bang that rattled the old timbers of the house and caused the suspended light fixture to swing from the ceiling.

Carlie collapsed on the couch. *Ben had thought she'd been pregnant with Kevin's child and then had aborted the baby?* She let her head fall into her hands and the tears she'd held at bay ran from her eyes. How could he have believed that she could have been that heartless? Shuddering, she drew an old afghan to her neck. God, what a mess! She wished she could stop the cold that settled deep in her soul. She'd loved Ben, believed he'd loved her and yet he could be swayed by such vicious lies. And he didn't even know the truth. She supposed that he never would.

So why would he believe such horrid lies?

Because his brother died and he felt guilty. But he didn't have the right to believe the distortions of Kevin's letters. The least he could have done was face her.

Closing her eyes, she remembered all the guilt, all the pain that had seared through her soul. She'd felt somehow responsible for Kevin's death because she hadn't loved him, because she'd never felt for him what he'd sworn he felt for her, because she'd fallen in love with his younger brother.

Though Kevin had left no suicide note, the general consensus in town was that Kevin had killed himself. He'd been unhappy and troubled for years. Some final straw had caused him to drive into the dilapidated garage of his tiny house, close the door and leave the Corvette running.

Carlie had gone to the funeral hoping to speak with Ben, but the Powells had kept their distance from the rest of the mourners and the icy glares she received from Ben's parents kept her from approaching the grieving family. Donna had returned from the Midwest to bury her son, and George, looking pale and wan, had made his wishes clear: no one was to bother the family. Especially not Carlie Surrett.

Carlie hadn't wanted to intrude; she'd just wanted to talk to Ben. She'd seen him in the funeral parlor and again at the grave site but he'd never so much as glanced her way. Standing still and straight, like the soldier he would soon become, he'd stared at a point far in the distant hills while Reverend Osgood had given a final blessing over the coffin.

The entire town had been stunned by Kevin's unfortunate death. Gold Creek was a small community and the loss of one of its young citizens was a shock. Friends, family and acquaintances had come out in droves, paying their respects and grieving. For weeks after Kevin was buried people had spoken of the Powells' "tragic loss" while shaking their heads.

Carlie had tried to see Ben, before and after the funeral, but he'd refused her calls, and sent back her letters, unopened. Desperate, she'd even plotted to go to the Powells' home on the outskirts of town where Ben was rumored to be staying with his father and demand that he see her.

Rachelle had tried to talk her out of it. Brenda had advised her to let time go by. Her parents had told her that the Powells deserved their privacy in their time of loss.

So Carlie had waited, working up her nerve, planning what she would say to Ben. By the time she'd found her courage and was ready to tell him that they were going to be parents, Ben had already taken off. She heard through the grapevine that he'd left town for the army. "That's what Patty Osgood says," her friend, Brenda, had told her three weeks after the funeral. They'd been seated at the counter in the drugstore and sipping lemonade. Brenda had swirled her ice cubes with her straw. "I usually take what Patty says as gospel, if you know what I mean. She hears all the gossip in town in church, y'know. If I were you, I'd forget him."

But he's the father of my child, Carlie had wanted to scream and had held a protective hand over her abdomen.

The rumor that Ben had joined up had proved true and Carlie had been left trying to mend her broken heart, hoping that Ben would call or write.

She'd started cramping the day after she found out that he was gone. The bleeding, just a few drops at first, followed. She'd lost the baby that one night and her romantic dreams of Ben had turned out to be the foolish wishes of a girl caught in a one-sided love affair: she'd never heard from him again.

"Oh, Lord," she whispered, refusing to shed any more tears for a past that could never be changed. "Stop it, Carlie! Get a grip, would you?" Angry with her runaway emotions, she shoved herself upright and walked to the kitchen where she found a bottle of wine and poured herself a glass of Chablis.

"Not a good sign," she told herself as she took an experimental sip and felt the cool wine slide down her throat. "Not a good sign at all. Drinking alone." But she didn't care, not tonight, and she wasn't going to sit here in the dark crying over Ben Powell or his ridiculous accusations. Let him think what he wanted. It didn't matter.

So why couldn't she convince herself?

Her stomach rumbled though it was barely five o'clock and she remembered that she missed lunch. The photography shop had been busy and during the noon hour, she'd driven to the hospital and visited her father. Later, there hadn't been any time to grab anything to eat.

Still, food wasn't appealing. Without a lot of enthusiasm she fixed herself a small dinner of crackers, cheese and apple slices. Sipping her wine, she ate the less-than-exciting meal and didn't taste anything, not realizing how the time was passing as she wasted the evening thinking about Ben, the man who had sworn he'd never wanted her. Not then. Not now. Not ever.

Wrong? He'd been wrong about Carlie? For long over a decade? Ben drove through the rain-washed streets and swore under his breath. He couldn't trust her, of course. She was probably lying again, but the anguish in her clear blue eyes had nearly convinced him. She might be lying but she believed her lies!

"Damn," he muttered, his eyes narrowing against the rain drizzling down his windshield. Could he have been so stupid not to realize that Carlie had given him her virginity that night so long ago? Had he been deluding himself, wasting time hating her for a decade? Not that he'd had all that much experience himself and he'd been so caught up in his own passion that he hadn't been thinking clearly. She hadn't said anything and he hadn't asked.

Later, upon finding the letters in Kevin's house and reading between the lines, thus learning of Carlie's pregnancy, Ben had felt as if a hot knife of betrayal had been twisted in his heart. The thought that she'd made love to Kevin had burned like acid in his gut and he'd thrown up. What had been so special between them suddenly seemed dirty and incestuous and ugly. His blossoming love for her had withered quickly into hatred, a hatred his family had helped nurture.

So why was he half believing her and second-guessing himself? Because he wanted her. Even though he professed to hate her, he couldn't help remembering the feel of her body against his, the way her lips rounded when she moaned, the curve of her neck when he held her close. His fingers clenched hard over the steering wheel and he nearly missed stopping for a red light. At the last minute he slammed on his brakes. A furious horn blasted from behind him.

"Damn," he said under his breath.

Another impatient honk warned him that the light had changed yet again, and he tromped on the accelerator, the back wheels spinning on the wet pavement. At the next corner, he wheeled into the parking lot of a gas station and cut the engine.

He climbed out of the cab and waved to the attendant, Joe Knapp, a man who'd gone to school with him years before. Joe had been captain of the football team way back when and after school, when he'd had his leg crushed while working in the woods for Fitzpatrick Logging, Joe's dreams of a career in football had been destroyed, as well. Kind of like Kevin. Only Joe had survived, married a hometown girl, Mary Beth Carter, and seemed happy enough with his wife and kids.

Scowling to himself, Ben shoved the nozzle of the pump into the gas tank and listened as the liquid poured into his truck.

He couldn't trust Carlie. *Couldn't!* Oh, but a part of him would love to. That same rebellious part that still wanted to kiss her senseless and make love to her forever.

That thought caused him to start and he nearly let the gas overflow.

"You're losing it, Powell," he growled to himself as he turned off the pump. With thoughts of Carlie trailing after him like a shadow, he walked inside the small Texaco station that had been on the corner of Hearst and Pine for as long as he could remember. The building had changed hands, but it still smelled of grease and stale cigarette smoke and oil.

"Good to see you around here again," Joe said as he took Ben's credit card in his grimy fingers. "I thought you'd said *adios* to Gold Creek forever."

"So did I."

Joe flashed him a toothy smile as he ran Ben's card through the verification machine. "So you feel like the prodigal son?"

"Nope. Just the black sheep."

Joe laughed and Ben signed the receipt. The conversation turned to football. The usual stuff. If the 49ers were going to the Super Bowl the following season, or if L.A. had a better chance. As if it mattered.

Later, as Ben drove away from the station and through the heart of town, he couldn't remember any of the conversation. Retail buildings gave way to houses that bordered the eastern hills, but he didn't notice any of the landmarks that had been a part of his hometown.

Because of Carlie. Damn that woman! Why couldn't he get her out of his head?

Ben liked things cut-and-dried, clear and to the point and structured. That's why he'd felt comfortable in the army, working his way up through the rank and file, and that's why he'd planned to come back to Gold Creek, start his own business, settle down with a *sensible* small-town girl and raise his family. His future had seemed so clear.

Until he'd seen Carlie again.

And until he'd listened to her side of the story. Her lies. Or her truth?

"Hell," he growled as he turned into the drive of his little house that wasn't far from the city limits of Gold Creek. Ben had rented the place from an elderly woman, Mrs. Trover, who lived at Rosewood Terrace in an apartment just down the hall from his father. Ben promised to keep the house up, including minor and major repairs, which he could deduct from the monthly rent. It wasn't much, two bedrooms, living room, single bath, kitchen, laundry room and a basement that leaked in the winter, but it had become home and he was certain, when the time was right, he could probably buy the house, outbuildings and half acre of land from Mrs. Trover on a contract.

He turned off the ignition and sat in the pickup for a second. The cottage needed more than a little repair— "TLC" he'd heard it called, but Ben knew it was just plain hard work. Even when it was brought up to code, the house wouldn't be ritzy and Ben couldn't picture Carlie living here with a tiny bathroom and a kitchen so small, only one person could work in it. Rubbing his jaw, he wondered why he kept trying to picture her in his future. She was all wrong for him. Kevin had told him as much long ago.

He should have listened. Maybe then Kevin would still be alive and Ben wouldn't walk around with a load of guilt on his shoulders for falling for his older brother's girl.

Trying to shove Carlie and all the emotional baggage she brought with her from his mind, he grabbed the sack of dog food he'd purchased earlier in the day and hauled the bag to the back door. "Honey, I'm home," he said as he unlocked the door.

Attila growled from the darkened interior.

"Well, at least you still have your sweet disposition."

A deep-throated bark.

"Come on, get out of here and do your business," Ben said leaving the outside door open as he walked into the kitchen and found a mixing bowl. The dog padded after him, hackles raised, but not emitting a sound. "Go on. You don't have to follow me around." He sliced open the sack, poured the dry dog food into the bowl and set it on the kitchen floor.

Attila just looked at him.

"Go on. Dig in." Ben waited and the dog slowly, as if he expected to be kicked or poisoned, cautiously approached the food. "Be paranoid if you want," Ben said.

The shepherd cocked his head, then hurried outside. Within seconds he was back, his nose deep in dog food.

"That's better." Ben grabbed a beer from the refrigerator and walked into the living room. Flicking on the remote control to the television, he dropped into a chair near an old rolltop desk he'd shoved into the corner. The message light on his telephone was blinking. "Hopefully, this is about a dozen clients begging me to come work for them," he said with a glance to the dog.

Attila didn't respond.

He pressed the button, the tape rewound and a series of clicks were followed by the first message.

"This is Bill with General Drywall. We can be at the house on Bitner next week on Tuesday. I'll send a crew unless I hear from you."

The phone clicked again.

"Ben?" a female voice asked. "This is Tracy. I saw you today at the restaurant and I . . . we, Randy and I . . . were wondering if you'd like to stop by for dinner tonight. Nothing special—but we'd love to have you." She paused for a second, then said, "How about seven? And if I don't hear from you by six, I'll just figure you had other plans. It was great seeing you today. Hope you can make it."

He glanced at his watch. Five-forty-five. Why not have dinner with Tracy? A small-town girl. A woman who was content to live here with her son. Kevin's son.

Carlie's face flashed before his eyes and he felt like a Judas. But that was crazy. Even if she were telling the truth about her relationship with Kevin, she'd thrown him out of her house. Gritting his teeth, he reached for the receiver.

He owed Carlie Surrett nothing!

* * *

"This is your uncle Ben," Tracy said to a young red-headed freckle-faced boy. His hair was straight and fell over his forehead in a way that reminded Ben of Kevin a long, long time ago.

Randy wrinkled his nose. "Uncle Ben? You mean like the guy on the rice box?"

Ben laughed and stretched out his hand. "Not exactly," he replied, shaking Randy's hand.

"Don't give Ben a hard time," Tracy gently chastised her son. They lived in a nice apartment in Coleville, as modern as Carlie's was rustic. White rug, white walls, white appliances and white furniture with a few throw pillows of mauve and blue.

"He's not giving me a bad time," Ben said. "What grade are you in?"

"Fourth."

"Same as Nadine's oldest boy," Tracy said, turning back to the sink. "But they don't see each other much since we don't live in Gold Creek."

"Are you talking about John Warne?" Randy asked.

"You know we are."

"He's a creep."

Tracy visibly stiffened. "That's not very nice—"

"Hey, it's the truth," Randy said. "And I don't care if he is my cousin because he's a jerk."

"You don't really know him."

"Well, I know Katie Osgood. I see her in Sunday school and she tells me all about John—like how he's the biggest dweeb in the whole school. He's always in the principal's office."

"That's enough, Randy," Tracy said, managing a forced smile. "Why don't you show Ben your baseball-card collection?"

"He won't want to see—"

"Sure, I will," Ben said, anxious to diffuse the tension between mother and son.

Hanging his head, Randy led Ben down a short hallway to a small room covered with posters of baseball players. Within minutes, he'd opened several albums and was tell-

ing Ben about all the players. He was particularly proud of
a few old cards of Mickey Mantle and Whitey Ford, "you
know, those old famous guys," he said to Ben, his face
lighting up. "My dad had these cards when he was a kid.
Grandpa kept them for me."

Ben's heart twisted. This boy was Kevin's bastard, a kid
George Powell had accepted. He spent half an hour with
Randy and the cards before Tracy called from the kitchen,
"How about something to drink?"

"I'll have a Coke!" Randy yelled back.

"I was talking to Ben," she replied, wiping her hands as
she appeared in the doorway. "But I'll get you something,
too. By the way, it's seven." She glanced at Ben as Randy
turned on a small black-and-white television. "There's
some sports show he always watches about this time. Come
on into the kitchen."

While Randy settled back on his bed, his cards spread
around him, his eyes glued to the little black-and-white
screen, Ben followed Tracy back to the kitchen. She was a
pretty woman, but as he watched her hips sway beneath her
black skirt, he felt nothing.

"Okay, the selection isn't all that great but I've got beer
and wine and . . . a bottle of Irish whiskey, I think."

"A beer'll do," he said, feeling suddenly awkward. The
apartment was clean and neat, not a magazine out of place,
and on a table near the couch was a gold-framed picture of
Kevin, a picture Ben recognized as having been taken only
a few weeks before his brother's death. Ben stared at the
photograph and felt that same mixture of pain and anger
build in him as it always did when he was reminded of his
older brother.

"Belly up to the bar," Tracy invited as she placed a bottle and empty glass on the counter that separated the
kitchen from the eating area. She held up a frosty mug of
dark soda. "I'll run this down to His Highness and be back
in a flash."

He drank his beer and watched her work in the kitchen.
She was efficient and smiled and laughed a lot, but there

were emotions that ran deep in her brown eyes, something false, as if the layer of lightheartedness she displayed covered up other, darker feelings. Her smile seemed a little forced and there was a hardness to her that bothered him.

They ate at a little table by the sliding door and the food was delicious: steak, baked potatoes and steamed broccoli smothered in a packaged cheese sauce. She poured them each a glass of wine and made sure that Randy's manners were impeccable. Ben had the feeling that the kid had been coached for hours. "No elbows," she said when Randy set his arm on the table. "What did I say about your hat?" she asked, noticing the fact that Randy's Giants' cap was resting on his head. "Oh, Randy, you know better! Please . . . use the butter knife. That's what it's there for."

When Randy finally asked to be excused, Ben let out a silent sigh of relief. "He really is a good boy," she said as Randy ambled down the hall.

"Of course he is."

"Straight A's and pitcher for his Little League team. They won the pennant last year." She smiled, all filled with pride and Ben got an uneasy feeling that she was trying to sell the kid to him. "He's in the school choir, too. Last year he had the lead in their little play. It wasn't much, you understand, only third graders, but he was the one they chose. Probably because of his voice and the fact that he's smart as a whip. I've been into that school five times this year already, asking them to move him up a grade or two in math. He's bored with what they're teaching."

Ben shoved his chair from the table. "Ever thought of private school?"

She sighed. "All the time. But that takes money and, well, being a single mother, we don't have a lot of extra cash." She picked up her plate and when Ben tried to carry his to the sink, she waved him back in his chair. "Sit, sit. I can handle this."

"So can I."

"But you've been working all day."

"Haven't you?"

She smiled and seemed flustered. "Just let me do it, all right? It's been a long time since I've had a man to pamper."

Warning bells went off in his head, but he ignored them. She was just trying to be nice. Nothing to worry about. She stacked the dishes in the sink and cut him a thick slab of chocolate cake.

"Won't Randy want some of this?" he asked, when she sliced a sliver for herself and sat back down at the table.

"He's in training. No sweets."

"But—"

She shook her head and took a bite. "Baseball starts in a few weeks and tryouts are just around the corner. He's got to be in shape. He's lucky I let him have a soft drink tonight."

"He's barely ten."

"Doesn't matter," she said, that underlying hardness surfacing in her eyes. "You, of all people, should understand. It's kind of like being in the military. Randy wants to be the ace pitcher again this year and I told him that I'll support him in that goal, but only if he works hard for it. No junk food. Lots of rest. Exercise. And he's got to keep his grades up."

"And sing in the choir and do higher-level math," Ben added, unable to hide the sarcasm in his voice.

"Why not? He can do it all."

"When does he have a chance to be a little kid?"

She sat on the couch and frowned when he slid into a white chair in the corner of the living room. "He *is* a little kid. A disciplined little kid."

"But when does he build forts and play in the woods and ride his bike and swim and—"

"When he trains, he swims on the weekends in the Coleville pool and there are no woods right around here. Riding his bike is dangerous—too much traffic. Besides we have a stationary bike in my room. If he wants to work out—"

"I'm not talking about working out. I'm talking about just hanging around," Ben said, his insides clenching when he considered how much pressure the kid had to live up to.

She was about to argue, thought better of it and kicked off her high heels. Tucking her feet beneath her on the couch, she sipped her wine slowly. "I suppose it does look like Randy's on a pretty tough regimen, doesn't it?" Sighing, she ran the fingers of one hand through her hair. "And part of the reason is that it's easier for me to have him on a schedule. I work two jobs and don't have a lot of free time so I have to depend on other people to give him rides. I don't want him to spend too much time alone—that's not good—so I encourage him to participate and be with kids his own age."

"And win."

She smiled. "Because he can, Ben. He's got so much potential." Her eyes glazed for a second, she licked her lips, and she whispered, "Just like Kevin."

Ben's stomach turned to stone. He suddenly realized why Tracy had never married; no one could compare to his brother. She didn't give another man a chance. And over the years she'd created a myth about Kevin, the myth being that he was perfect.

"Kevin was an average student, Tracy."

"He had a basketball scholarship."

"That was taken away when he couldn't keep up his grades."

"He just had some bad breaks," she said quickly. "How about a cup of coffee?"

"I can't." He stood, glad for an excuse to leave. "I've got a million calls to make before it gets too late. But thanks."

"Anytime," she said as if she meant it. She walked to him and touched his arm with feather-light fingers. "The door's always open for you, Ben. It does Randy a world of good. He...he needs a...man. Just wait a minute and I'll get him. He'll want to say good-night."

She hurried down the hall and a few minutes later, she practically pushed Randy forward to shake Ben's hand.

The boy licked his lips nervously. "Glad to meet you—" he shifted his eyes to his mother, struggled for the words and added "—Uncle Ben."

"You, too, Randy. Maybe I'll see you at the ball field." Ben clasped the kid's hand.

His sullen face broke into a smile. "Would you?"

"You bet. Can I bring my dog?"

"You've got a dog?" Randy's eyes widened and all evidence of his pained expression disappeared. "What kind?"

"A mean one."

"Really."

"I call him Attila."

Tracy's lips tightened.

"He just showed up at the office with his belly sliced open."

Randy's eyes were wide. "Wow!"

"He's a German shepherd—a black long-haired one."

"Cool!" Randy said, grinning ear to ear.

"You're allergic to dogs, Randy," his mother reminded him gently as she nudged him back down the hallway. "And so am I—at least I'm allergic to big dogs that shed." She walked with Ben to the front porch and Ben felt as if she expected something from him, something he couldn't give her.

"Thanks for dinner. It was great."

"We could do it again," she suggested, her lips curved into a satisfied smile.

"I'll let you know." He felt a jab of guilt when he recognized the hope in her eyes.

"Good night, Ben," she said as he started across the parking lot. "Call me."

He didn't bother to turn around and lie to her. He wasn't about to start a romance with Tracy and he felt that whether she realized it or not, Tracy hoped to use Ben as a replacement for his dead brother.

"What a mess," he growled as he climbed into his truck and let out the clutch. He thought of Carlie again. Beautiful Carlie. Seductive Carlie. Lying Carlie.

The old Dodge leapt forward and he flicked on the windshield wipers. *Women,* he thought unkindly. *Why were they so much damned trouble?*

Chapter Eight

"When you left town, you thought Carlie was pregnant—with Kevin's baby?" Nadine was clearly astonished. Hauling a huge suitcase out of her new Mercedes, a wedding gift from her husband, she shook her head, then slammed the door shut with her hip.

"That's what the letters said."

"No way." Shaking her head in disgust, she unlocked the front door. "Sometimes, Ben, I don't understand you. Come in. I think we need to talk. But first things first. Bring in those other bags, will ya?" She tossed him her keys and he found two suitcases in the back seat. "Hayden will park it in the garage later—there's some stuff he's got to move around in there—things left over from the wedding."

Ben grabbed the other two bags, locked the sleek car and walked back into the house. The Christmas tree was still standing in the corner but some of the lights had been stripped from the stairs and all the flowers had begun to wilt.

Nadine sighed loudly as she walked to the den, dropped her large case and kicked off her shoes. "Oooh, that's better. I've been dragging my latest inventory all over the place. Heather Brooks hooked me up with some art dealers who are expanding into jewelry and jackets, you know...'wearable art.' Now I'm afraid I'm going to end up with more orders than I can fill." She led him into the kitchen where she opened the refrigerator door and peered at the contents. "How about some sparkling apple juice?"

"I don't think so," he said with more than a trace of sarcasm.

"Might brighten your mood."

"I doubt it."

"A cola?" She didn't bother waiting for an answer, just grabbed two cans and handed him one. As she sat in one of the kitchen chairs and popped the lid, she rested her heel on one of the empty chairs and said, "Now let's start over. You thought *Carlie* was pregnant—by Kevin, right?"

Was she deaf? "We already discussed this."

"But *why,* Ben?"

"Because of the letters."

"The letters?" she repeated, then caught on. "Oh, we're talking about the letters you found in Kevin's bedroom, right?"

"Yep." He didn't like talking about the subject, but knew there was no other way to get to the truth. Ben had been seated in his pickup, waiting for Nadine, brooding about Carlie for over an hour, wondering what was truth and what was fiction.

"Are you serious?" She actually had the gall to laugh.

"This isn't a joke."

"Yes, it is!" Rolling her eyes, she took a long swallow of her drink. "You really thought—"

"Yes, I did. Now what's so damned funny?"

"It's pathetic really." Her green eyes turned sober. "I think you read too much between the lines."

"What do you mean?" he asked, surprised at the hope leaping in his heart.

She massaged her foot as she shook her head. "I read those letters and yes, Kevin was in love with Carlie—that much was obvious. He was really hurt that she was seeing you and he felt betrayed by both of you."

The old pain knotted Ben's stomach, but he'd expected as much. Nadine never pulled any punches. You asked her a question, she gave you a straight answer.

She was still talking. " . . . but the pregnancy he wrote about had to have been Tracy's." Nadine reached across the table and touched the back of Ben's hand. "Don't you remember? *Tracy* was pregnant. Not Carlie. And the abortion you read about was just hopeful thinking on Kevin's part," she said with a twist of the lips. "He didn't want the baby. We're talking about Randy, you know. It took a lot of guts for Tracy to have that baby and raise him on her own. Kevin was dead and the tongues in this town were wagging like crazy. But she did and Randy's a super kid. In fact," she said wryly, "with his grades and all, he certainly shows mine up, not that I'd change anything about John and Bobby. My boys are just more . . . trouble."

"Like their mother," Ben said, though he didn't feel much like joking. Had he been so blind? For all these years. "Those letters were addressed to Carlie."

"But never mailed. They were just a way for Kevin to let off steam, or maybe someday he would have had the nerve to send them to her, I don't know, but you turned everything around in your head." She took a long swallow of her soda and settled back in her chair.

Was that possible? Had he been so much a fool? So quick to judge? Blaming Carlie for something that wasn't her fault? He lapsed into dark silence and his thoughts were like demons in his head, poking and prodding with painful memories.

"Look, it was a rough time for all of us," she said, "but if you've been hating Carlie because of those letters, you'd better let it go. It's just not fair."

"That's what she said," he admitted, remembering her fury.

"Oh." Nadine's breath whistled through her teeth. "You didn't go charging over there half-cocked and accuse her of all sorts of vile deeds, did you?" When he didn't answer she rolled her eyes again. "Oh, Ben, why? I wanted to blame her, too. She was an easy target, but the fact of the matter is, Kevin took his own life. It's a damned shame. God, I still miss him. But that's what happened."

At that moment Hayden and the boys arrived home. The back door banged open and two dogs, muddy feet and all, bounded into the kitchen in a swirl of rain-dampened air.

"Hershel—Leo—out!" Nadine commanded, but the animals paid no heed. They raced through the kitchen and down the hallway leading to the foyer. "That's what I like about this place, the way I have absolute control," she muttered under her breath.

John and Bobby barreled in through the back door. They were hurling insults at each other at the top of their lungs.

"Nerd!"

"Baby!"

"At least I didn't kiss Katie Osgood!" Bobby said, tossing Nadine a superior glance.

"You kissed—"

"Aw, Mom, she kissed me!" John said, his face mottling red.

"So much for peace and quiet," Nadine said, reaching for Bobby as he tried to race out of the room. She captured him and planted a kiss on his cheek. He giggled loudly. "That's what you get, mister, for not even saying 'hi' to your mom."

He smiled and nuzzled her cheek. "Hi."

"And you—" She turned to John but he was backpedaling out of the room.

"I'm too old for that sissy stuff," he said, disappearing into the hall.

"Yeah, that's because you got enough kissing for the day," Bobby crowed.

"Not me. I haven't had nearly enough sissy stuff!" Hayden leaned over and kissed his wife's crown. "The older I get the more of the 'sissy stuff' I want."

"You're incorrigible."

"And you're irresistible." He kissed her again, then glanced up at Ben. "Hi—I suppose you came with the blueprints," he said, obviously hopeful to see how the plans for Nadine's cabin were progressing.

"Nope, he just brought the blues," Nadine quipped. "But I think I can twist his arm and convince him to stay for dinner."

"With your wild bunch? No way."

"Come on—"

"Not tonight," Ben said, draining his can and shoving his chair away from the table.

"Got a lot to think about?" she asked, shooting him a knowing look.

"Too much," he admitted as he walked out the back door and cut through the breezeway to his pickup. He climbed in and fired up the old truck.

Somehow he had to figure out the truth. Had he been so naive, so insensitive that he hadn't realized that he was making love to a virgin? Had he just assumed that she'd been experienced and then ignored the signs of her own naiveté?

He felt like a fool. He remembered their night of lovemaking in the rain. He still felt a wonder at the thrill of it.

Never had he felt so alive and never, with the women he'd been with since that fateful night, had he ever felt so completely undone. The joining of his body and Carlie's had been unique and earth-shattering and passionate. Even Kevin's death hadn't turned that spectacular memory bitter.

He'd blamed Kevin's death for his inability to feel the same exhilaration with a woman, but now he knew differently. The reason sex had never been the same was that he'd never again allowed himself to become so emotionally attached to his partner.

Fool! he told himself as he drove home through the misting rain.

He hadn't even realized that she'd been a virgin. He'd been so caught up in his own pleasure that he hadn't noticed any sign of her discomfort, or any breakage of tissue or any pain.

"Damn it all." He felt like a complete idiot. An idiot who had falsely blamed a woman for too many years. "Hell, Powell, who did you think you were?"

Never had he considered Carlie's feelings. After Kevin's death, he'd turned her phone calls and letters callously away, never once explaining, refusing to listen to her side of the story. He'd just blamed her for Kevin's death and condemned her to his family and friends. And when he'd joined the army, he'd run as fast and as far away from her as possible.

The truck bounced along the rutted drive to his little rental house, a house he'd hoped to share with a woman someday.

He wondered if Carlie would ever be that woman and snorted at the thought. She'd be out of her mind to trust him again.

Thomas Fitzpatrick's office was quietly understated. Located on the third floor of one of the oldest buildings in town, the original Gold Creek Hotel, the offices of Fitzpatrick, Incorporated were plush without being ostentatious.

Carlie was seated in a chair near the window and Thomas was speaking, his even voice well modulated from years of public oration.

"...So I don't want any studio shots or pictures that are obviously posed. I want to show the men at work, doing their jobs, the American worker at his best." Thomas Fitzpatrick leaned back in his leather chair, seemingly pleased with his eloquence. His hands were tented under his chin and, from the far side of his desk, he watched Carlie over his fingertips. His gaze was speculative and thoughtful and it bothered Carlie more than it should.

She didn't know why she felt like a bird with a broken wing under the fixed stare of the neighborhood tomcat. She shook off the feeling. He was a man, a wealthy man, but he had no power over her.

Carlie hoped her smile didn't look as brittle as it felt. "No mugging for the camera?"

"Absolutely," Thomas said, a smile curving beneath his clipped mustache. "Now, mind you, I don't want anything that looks the least bit...dangerous...or uncomfortable for the men. I want to show the logging company as an exciting but safe workplace, where we, at Fitzpatrick, Incorporated are concerned with the environment and working conditions as well as the bottom line." He raised his eyebrows as if expecting her to comment.

"Is that possible?"

His lips twitched. "I think you can make it possible, Miss Surrett."

She wanted to tell him that she was a photographer, not a magician, but she decided discretion was the better part of valor in this case. "I'll give it a shot," she agreed, feeling like a traitor.

"Good. Now tell me, how is your father?" He had the decency to look genuinely concerned.

"Better. He should be going home in a couple of days."

Thomas sighed heavily. "When he's up to it, have him call me. I've already talked to the corporate attorneys and accountants about the possibility of his early retirement, but I wanted to speak to Weldon again first."

"That's a good idea," she said stiffly.

"Look, he knows that there are desk jobs available, but—"

"He doesn't want your charity, Mr. Fitzpatrick. Nor your pity." Deciding she shouldn't discuss her father's health with the man who was stripping away all of Weldon's dreams, she slung the strap of her purse over her shoulder and stood. "I can start working at the logging company offices at the beginning of next week."

"Perfect. Just check in with Marge, the secretary over there, and she'll let Brian know what's going on."

She started to turn to leave, but his voice stopped her. "There are a couple of other things."

She tensed, but willed her body to relax as she turned to face him again.

"My daughter, Toni—you know her, I believe."

"We've met."

Thomas's face clouded over. "She may be getting married soon—within the next couple of months—and we might need a photographer for the wedding. I wondered if you'd be interested."

She wanted to tell him no, that she was already regretting working for him, that she didn't want anything more to do with the Fitzpatricks and their money, but she couldn't. She was too practical and until her father was home, the hospital and doctor bills paid, and his future a little more certain, Carlie couldn't afford to turn down any offers. "I'd be very interested," she said. "Have Toni give me a call."

"I will. Now the other." He set his feet on the floor and placed his elbows on the desktop. "It's more personal. I was hoping you could find time in your busy schedule for dinner. With me."

Uncertain she'd heard correctly, she hesitated for just a heartbeat. "I don't think that would be such a good idea."

His grin was self-deprecating. "Don't get the wrong idea, Ms. Surrett. This would be strictly business. I am, after all, still married." A dark shadow passed behind his eyes for just a second, then disappeared.

"As long as we understand each other."

"Absolutely. How about a week from Friday? Seven?"

Carlie felt uncomfortable. She was used to handling passes from men of all ages; she'd had more than her share of offers when she was modeling, but she couldn't afford to offend Fitzpatrick. "Let me check my calendar."

"Fine. I'll give you a call," he said, as she made her way out of his office and into his secretary's, Melanie Patton's, sanctuary. Melanie hardly glanced up as Carlie breezed by and swept through another set of doors to the reception area where a young girl was talking on the phone. The elevator took her down three floors to the foyer of the elegant old hotel.

Thomas Fitzpatrick had done the town one good turn, she decided. Rather than call in the wrecking ball, he'd spent the money necessary to restore one of the oldest buildings in Gold Creek and returned the gold-brick building to its original charm. Thick Oriental carpets covered glossy floors and, three stories over the lobby, a skylight of stained glass allowed sunlight to pool in muted shades upon the walls and floor.

However there wasn't enough charm in the building to alleviate her distaste at dealing with the man. He was too smooth, almost oily, and she had the gut feeling that anything he did was with one sole intention: the promotion and profit of Thomas Fitzpatrick.

She had lunch with her mother at the drugstore, visited her father for the remainder of her lunch hour, then spent the rest of the day at the shop. By the time she was finished with a studio sitting with four-year-old triplets, it was nearly seven and she was exhausted.

The last person she wanted to deal with was Ben Powell, but as she pulled into the parking lot, she recognized his truck parked in between the twin spruce trees. "Great," she muttered, remembering the disaster of the night before. She was tired and cranky and didn't want to face him.

Hopefully, he was working in another apartment.

No such luck.

When she shoved the door to her unit open she found him, sprawled across her old sofa, his shoes kicked off, his head propped against the overstuffed arm. As if he belonged. As if she'd invited him. As if she wanted him.

"I'd about given up on you," he drawled.

"What're you doing here?"

His smile was slow and sexy. "Waiting for you."

"So you could come back and insult me again?" she asked, all the old anger chasing through her blood. "No way. I'm tired and I don't think I should have to make a nightly ritual of throwing you out of my apartment. So why don't you take the hint and I won't have to get rude?"

"We need to talk."

"Talk? I don't think so. We said plenty last night. More than we should have."

"That's where you're wrong." He swung his feet to the floor and stood, studying his fingernails for a second. "We've got a lot more to say to each other."

She waited.

"Okay, I'll go first. I'm sorry, Carlie," he said, though the words seemed to lodge in his throat for a second.

"You're sorry?" She couldn't believe her ears. Ben Powell was apologizing. To her? After all this time? Damn hard to believe.

"For jumping to conclusions." He glanced up at her and his expression was sober. "I made a lot of mistakes and I have no excuses. I could say that I was just a kid, that I was confused, that I was naive enough to believe lies, but the truth of the matter is I guess I wanted to believe the worst about you. You were an easy target. You made it possible for me to shrug off some of the guilt."

She felt hot tears threatening the back of her eyes again. "You believe me?" she whispered.

"I didn't want to. To tell you the truth, I wanted to go on thinking that you were a lying, callous, coldhearted woman."

"Why?"

"Because it was easier," he said. "Less complicated." He walked up to her and touched her shoulder. Quickly she drew away, crossing the room to the window and stared out at the gathering night. "I've spent the last twenty-four hours soul-searching, trying to convince myself that you're trouble, that you're the last woman in the world for me and that I'd be a fool to come back." He hesitated a minute, then let out a long sigh. "But I couldn't. Not until we straightened things out. I think there's a chance I haven't been fair to you."

"A big chance."

His jaw tightened. "As I said, I came here to apologize."

She knew she should point him in the direction of the door and shove him hard, but there was a part of her, a very small and determined part, that wanted to hear him out. For years she'd fantasized about him groveling in front of her, begging her forgiveness, but those were just girlhood dreams of vindication. "I don't want or need your apologies, Ben," she said slowly. "There's been too much time...too many years..." She lifted her hands and dropped them again. "Too much pain. I just want to be left alone."

Shaking his head slowly, never letting his gaze move from the contours of her face, he said, "I don't believe you."

"Then you're a fool."

His smile was irreverently cocky. "Been called worse."

"I'll bet." She swallowed hard and her pulse thundered in her brain as he approached her, his eyes glimmering with a silver fire. The way he was staring at her turned her blood to warm honey and she had to remind herself that he was dangerous, that spending any more time with him would only cause her more heartache than she would ever be able to bear. Until today he'd believed the most hideous lies about her. "You...you have to leave."

"Not yet."

"Please, Ben, do us both a favor."

"In a minute."

"You have to leave—" Throat so dry she could barely speak, she whispered, "Please, Ben, if you really want to make things right, just walk out the door and don't ever come back."

"If only I could," he said as his arms suddenly surrounded her and he lowered his head. For an instant he hesitated, as if he, too, were afraid to take the next step. His lips were poised over hers, bare inches from her mouth.

"Don't do this."

"I have to." Her breath caught and she thought she might die as desire and disgust warred deep within her soul. "I've wanted to do this from the minute I saw you at the lake before the wedding," he said as his lips found hers in a kiss that was hard, and hot and filled with years of repression. She told herself to squirm away, to fight, but the gentle pressure of his mouth, the sweet sensual tickle of his tongue against her teeth and lips, the hard contours of his muscles fitting perfectly against hers, kept her silently pressed against him.

She knew this was wrong, that right now she was vulnerable and that she couldn't let Ben back into her heart or her life. Yet she couldn't pull away, and the harder he kissed her, his tongue and hands becoming more demanding, the more distant the warning bells sounded.

She was wrapped in the warm, seductive haze of yesterday. The winter wind was no longer lashing at the house and rattling the windows; no, a soft summer breeze, scented with lilacs and honeysuckle played upon the air. And she was a girl again, a girl in love. Her arms wound around his neck and she didn't stop him when his hands clamped over the lowest part of her rib cage, holding her close, letting her feel the heat of desire burning through his flesh.

When at last he lifted his head, he let out a long rush of air. "It's always been like this between us," he said, as he dropped his forehead to rest against hers. "I don't understand it."

"Neither do I." Her senses began to clear and she struggled away from him. "But it's got to stop."

"Why?"

"Because it's wrong, Ben. We both know it. You use me when it's convenient and when it's not, you hurl insults at me and accuse me of things I had no part in."

She took a step backward, but his strong arms surrounded her again, more tightly this time. He yanked her back against him. "Carlie, don't—"

"You don't!" she insisted, refusing to be one of those kind of women who went weak around a man regardless of how he treated her. "A few days ago you accused me of... Oh, Lord, this isn't worth thinking about. Just let go of me!"

Ben refused. Determination and grit clamped his jaw shut. "I came here to sort things out."

"They're sorted. We both know we're wrong for each other."

"What we know is that we were young and impetuous and couldn't keep our hands off each other."

"You thought I slept with your brother," she reminded him, trying to keep her voice steady. "You thought I got pregnant by him and got rid of the baby. You thought I used him to get to you and you thought he killed himself over me. Oh, God, Ben," she whispered, blinking against the rush of unwanted tears that filled her eyes. "You blamed me for everything that went wrong in your life." She had the urge to tell him the truth, to let him know that at one time he, not Kevin, could have become a father, but she couldn't trust that very private secret to him. Not yet. Probably not ever. "I wasn't at fault and neither were you. So stop beating yourself up and while you're at it, do the same for me."

He didn't flinch, didn't move a muscle, but she could see by the hardening of his features that she'd finally gotten through to him. He looked as if he were grappling with an inner struggle, and a tiny muscle ticked above his eye. "I know I've made my share of mistakes. Big ones. But I just want a chance to start over with you, Carlie. We can't pretend that the past didn't happen, we'd be foolish to believe that it won't affect the rest of our lives, but I want to try... to find a way that we can become friends."

"Friends?" she repeated, refusing to cry though her heart was twisting painfully. "Oh, Ben, it's gone too far for that. We'll *never* be friends."

"Then lovers."

"Too late," she said, though the pulse at the base of her throat throbbed with ancient memories.

"Don't you know it's never too late, Carlie?" he said, drawing her body even closer and kissing her with lips that were demanding and hard.

She felt something uncoil within her though she fought the feeling. She could never fall for Ben again. Never! When he lifted his head, his eyes were glazed and his breath stirred her hair. "I wish I didn't feel this way," he said roughly.

"So do I."

"You can't deny it, Carlie." He kissed her again.

She wanted to stop him, to protect her heart, but all thoughts of protest fled as his fingers twined in the strands of her hair and his body, long and lean, drew her down to the couch. Her arms wound around his neck and her body molded to his, instinctively fitting intimately against the hard planes and angles. No words of love were spoken, no vows of forever passed his lips, but he kissed her with a passion that was answered only by her own hot desire.

He found the zipper on the back of her dress and it slid downward in a quiet hiss. She felt cold air on her back, but soon his hands were caressing her, bringing back the warmth, molding anxiously against her skin.

Still he kissed her, his tongue thrusting boldly through her parted lips, his mouth supple and strong. Emotions, old and new, brought a soft moan from her throat.

His weight carried them both to the floor and she closed her eyes against the protests forming in her mind as they tumbled onto her old Oriental carpet. *This is wrong,* her brain screamed, *wrong and dangerous. Stop him now, while you still can!*

But she couldn't. Or wouldn't. Instead she silenced those awful doubts and thrilled to the wonder of being with him. His hands, rough and callused, rubbed anxiously across her skin and he lowered the top of her dress slowly to reveal a lacy camisole and filmy bra.

"Oh, Carlie," he murmured as he kissed her cheek and neck, lowering himself leisurely, letting his lips and tongue trail along her collarbones before drifting lower and leaving a dewy path that chilled when the air touched that sensitive film. "You're so incredibly beautiful." His breath whispered across the dusky hollow of her breasts as he tasted of the lace that covered her nipples. "I've missed you."

She arched off the rug and he took more of her into his mouth, licking and sucking, gently teasing.

Liquid heat swirled deep inside her and her fingers delved deep into his hair, holding his head in place, offering more of herself.

Don't do this! Carlie, think! her desperate mind screamed as he lowered the straps of lace that were small protection against his seductive assault.

He doesn't love you. Doesn't even like you. You're setting yourself up for more pain than you can imagine.

Moaning, she felt her bra and camisole slip away, knew she was naked from the waist up and reveled in the feel of his hands and mouth slowly moving over her flesh, stoking the flames of desire already running rampant in her blood. "Ben," she whispered.

He slid one hand inside her dress, pushing it over her hips while he suckled at her breast.

Writhing with desire, she worked on the buttons of his shirt. Her mind was blurry with emotion, her heart pounding, the ache deep within her crying to be filled.

He's using you! He's playing you for a fool! Remember what happened before. Oh, Carlie, think! Before it's too late!

His hand slid lower, beneath the waistband of her panties.

Remember the baby! For God's sake, Carlie, remember the baby! "Ben, no!" she said, alarm bells clanging wildly in her mind.

He froze, every muscle strident and taut.

"We...we can't. *I* can't!" Tears welled from nowhere in her eyes as he gazed down at her. "This is...this is too fast," she said, feeling like a fool as she lay, half-naked beneath him. "Way too fast." His shirt was open and his chest rose and fell with the effort of his breathing. A fine sheen of sweat glistened on his skin.

Slowly he rolled off her. She watched as he drew in long, mind-clearing breaths. "Too fast?" he said, once his voice worked again. "It's been eleven years!" With a sigh, he stared at the ceiling. "What do you want from me, Carlie? Hearts and flowers? Champagne and moonlit walks, diamonds and promises—the whole ball of wax?"

"I—" She struggled back into her clothes. "I don't want to make a mistake."

"I've got news for you, darlin'," he said, rolling onto his side and staring at her. His mouth curved into a self-deprecating smile. "We're way past making our first mistake, or our second or third. The way I figure it, we're in double-digits, maybe triple."

Carlie couldn't argue with his logic, cynical though it may be, but she wasn't a girl any longer. She was a woman determined to control her own destiny. Ben was making it difficult—damned difficult. "Okay, so I don't want to make any more, or at least I don't want to make one that will follow me for the rest of my life."

"Like sleeping with me?"

She swallowed hard against that painful lump. "Yes." Her voice was barely a whisper.

"Seems to me we already crossed that bridge," he pointed out, his hazel eyes sharpening as he stared at her.

"Not in recent history."

He snorted. "Taking it slow with you is like trying to stop a runaway train."

She had the urge to scream. It was all she could do to control her tongue. "Look, I'm not blaming you, okay? I'm here. A responsible adult. I'm supposed to know what I'm doing and so . . . I think we should just be careful."

He stared at her long and hard, his eyes roving over her body. She was stretched out on the thick Oriental carpet, her body only inches from his and she felt a flood of embarrassment wash up her neck. He touched her cheek and brushed her hair out of her eyes. "Okay, Carlie, you win. I didn't come over here to try and seduce you. I just wanted to apologize and get to know you again—not necessarily in the Biblical sense, although—" his eyes sparkled with a seductive gleam "—that would have been nice."

"Forget it, Powell," she said, finally able to laugh as she levered up on one elbow and tossed her hair over her shoulders. "This is probably the same old line you told every girl you met all over the world when you were in the army."

"I didn't have time for girls, or women for that matter, while I served."

She shook her head. "I've heard about soldiers and sailors and marines. You're not going to convince me that you never had a date—"

"Okay, I had a few," he conceded. "Well, more than a few, but nothing that lasted over a couple of weeks." She narrowed her eyes skeptically and he lifted a shoulder. "It's true. I was pretty dedicated and I moved around a lot and whenever a woman got too serious, I stopped seeing her."

"So you broke a million hearts all over the world."

"Not quite a million." He shoved himself upright and pulled her to her feet. "Come on. I'll buy you dinner while I tell you my life story."

"You don't have to—"

"I *want* to." His fingers closed over hers. "What will it hurt?"

She was afraid to answer that one.

He chose a restaurant in Coleville, the Blue Lobster, which specialized in seafood. Rough plank walls adorned with black-and-white photographs of fishing crews and whaling boats were complemented by fishing nets strung over individual booths. Dried starfish and sea horses were cast into the nets and colorful glass floats completed the decor.

A waitress showed them to a private booth near a fireplace. Glassed candles and fresh flowers graced a varnished table constructed from the hatch cover of a small boat.

Ben ordered a plate of seafood appetizers as well as wine for Carlie and a beer for himself.

When the drinks and hors d'oeuvres arrived, he touched the neck of his beer bottle to her glass of Chablis. "To new beginnings," he toasted.

"Here's mud in your eye," she responded, then laughed, remembering so many years ago when she'd laughed with Ben and shared her most intimate secrets with him. She'd told him her dreams, her fears and made love to him without a worry for the future.

"Nice, Carlie," he said, but laughed. The candlelight flickered, casting golden shadows on his face, and she wondered what it would be like to fall in love with him again. Gone was any trace of the boy she'd once cared for. Seated across from her was a man, one with lines around his eyes, a leg that sometimes pained him and years of military service. A man who had seen action in deserts and jungles and cities of the Third World. While she'd been in New York and Paris, he'd been in the Middle East, Africa and Central America.

Worlds apart.

She sipped her wine, studied the menu and ordered baked halibut with rice. He chose steak and prawns.

"You were telling me about your love life," she reminded him as the main course was served and the waitress disappeared.

"There was no 'love' to it," he assured her.

"No special girl?"

His head lifted and he stared at her, his hazel eyes sending her a message that caused goose bumps to rise on her arms. "No special woman," he said.

Carlie's throat nearly closed on a piece of halibut.

"What about you?" He broke off a piece of garlic bread. "You're divorced, right? Who was the lucky guy who walked you down the aisle?"

An old ache settled in her heart and the food suddenly lost its taste. She didn't like discussing her failed marriage and had barely mentioned it to anyone. Her parents knew most of the story, of course, and Rachelle, from various conversations, had pieced together the most telling details, but now, seated across from the only man she'd ever loved, she didn't know if she could face the pain. "I, um, don't talk about it much."

"Why?"

"It's . . . history."

Ben's lips tightened. "Does it hurt too much?"

"I suppose."

His brows lifted slowly. "You still love him."

"Oh, no! I mean…that's the problem." No time like the present to be honest. She'd convinced herself that she would be straight with any man she became involved with, that she would tell him everything that had happened in her life. But she hadn't expected to start a relationship with Ben, the very man who had caused her the greatest heartache of her life. "I didn't love Paul as much as I should have."

"Paul was your husband."

"Yes, Paul Durant. He was a struggling actor and I had just started modeling. Neither one of us had a dime to our names and we started seeing each other. I guess he caught me on the rebound from you," she admitted, and noticed Ben's mouth tighten at the corners. "He wasn't handsome, but very cute. Blond and wiry…" She smiled sadly and pushed around the uneaten portion of her fish into her rice. "Well, before I really had time to think about it, we decided to get married."

"Why?"

It seemed like a sensible question. "You know the old saying, two can live as cheaply as one? Well, we both needed roommates—Manhattan was so expensive. We, um, liked each other a lot. Even convinced each other that we were in love."

"But you weren't?"

She dropped her fork and stared at him. "I'd only been in love once before, Ben, and it hadn't worked out all that well for me." His jaw tightened perceptibly, but she plunged on. After all, he'd asked. "I don't think passion is a driving force for two people planning to spend the rest of their lives together. I just wanted to…not be alone and to spend my time with someone I liked. Someone who cared about me."

"Sounds perfect," he said sarcastically.

"It wasn't." She finished her wine in one gulp. "I started getting more jobs than he did. While he was still waiting tables in an Italian restaurant two blocks from our apartment, I was getting more work than I could handle and making a lot more money. He went to audition after audition and only landed a few parts—nothing to speak of."

"So jealousy and money drove you apart?"

She ran the tip of her finger around the rim of her glass. Somehow it seemed a violation, a betrayal of a trust to tell him any more. "That was most of it."

"And the rest?"

"He fell in love with someone else. My best—and only—friend in New York. You might have heard of her. She's starting to make a name for herself on- and off-Broadway. Angela Rivers." She didn't add that she'd walked in on Paul and Angela, twisted in the bedsheets, making love with such passion that they hadn't heard her come into the room. She'd been horrified and embarrassed and had promptly thrown up.

Paul's biggest fear had been that Carlie might be pregnant and he would be tied to her forever, but fate had saved him that particular embarrassment. He'd told her that the marriage had been a big mistake from the get-go, that he loved Angela and that he wanted a divorce. He filed the next morning and Carlie hadn't fought him. She'd just wanted out.

Licking her wounds, she'd given up her life in Manhattan, started taking photography classes again and spent a lot of time in different cities, finally spending the last few years in Alaska where she'd taken shots of wildlife and quaint villages and natives. Her photographs had been commissioned by the state as well as bought for a book about America's rugged northern wilderness.

She'd cut all ties with Paul and knew nothing of his life. That's the way they'd both wanted it.

"I'm sorry," Ben said, though his gaze belied his words.

"I'm not. It's over. Probably never had a chance to really get started. Besides, it was all for the best."

"How so?"

"I gave up all those silly dreams about the big city," she said.

"You didn't like New York?"

"I *loved* it, but I was younger then, had different ideas about what I wanted out of life."

The waitress came with dessert and coffee and while Carlie picked at a strawberry mousse, Ben devoured a thick wedge of apple pie. He wondered about her marriage to the actor. She'd obviously glossed over her relationship and Ben sensed she wasn't being completely honest with him, but he really didn't care. Everyone was entitled to a few secrets. What bothered him was the sadness in her eyes as she'd talked of the man she'd married, and he couldn't help but feel a spurt of jealousy run hot through his blood.

At one time in his life he'd hoped to marry Carlie, dreamed of sleeping with her every night and waking with her snuggled safely in his arms. After Kevin had died, he'd convinced himself that Carlie was the wrong kind of woman for him, a schemer, a user, a woman who would stop at nothing to get what she wanted. She was too beautiful, too flighty, too interested in the bright lights of a big city.

He paid the bill and ushered her back to his pickup.

On the way home, he flipped on the radio and told himself that Carlie was still a woman to avoid. True, he'd misjudged her in the past, but although she now seemed to know what she wanted out of life, he suspected that she still flew by the seat of her pants, took chances that were unnecessary and didn't know the meaning of the words *discipline* and *structure*. Her apartment, though charming, was an eclectic blend of antiques, period pieces and modern furniture. She wore anything from high-fashion designer labels to jeans or faded "granny dresses" right out of the seventies. She was confident and secure and fascinating, but she wasn't the woman for him.

So why did you try to make love to her? his imperious mind demanded and he scowled to himself. Despite all his rational thoughts, all the reasons he should avoid her like the proverbial plague, he was entranced by her.

Shifting down, he glanced in her direction. She was certainly the most beautiful woman he'd ever met, but her looks were only a part of her allure. Sophisticated and sexy, she still smiled easily and her eyes were warm with humor and intelligence.

Boy, have you got it bad!

Swearing under his breath he wheeled into the drive of Mrs. Hunter's apartment house and let the pickup idle.

"Thanks for dinner," Carlie said, reaching for the handle of the door. She seemed anxious to escape and he had the overpowering urge to drag her into his arms and make love to her forever.

"I enjoyed it," he admitted and she offered him a fleeting smile. A darkness shadowed her eyes and he imagined that he'd hurt her more than he could remember. She was as enigmatic and mysteriously beautiful as ever.

"Next time it's on me," she said as the door opened.

"Carlie?"

"Hmm?"

He couldn't stop himself. His arms surrounded her and he drew her close. His lips found hers and though he told himself to go slow, to kiss her gently, the passion that still burned through his blood exploded and his mouth moved urgently against her lips.

She wound her arms around his neck and kissed him with the fever that seemed to have infected them both. As the windows began to steam, her tongue mated and danced with his and the swelling in his jeans ached so badly, he thought he'd go crazy.

Shifting to get closer to her, he pressed against the small of her back, urgently dragging her atop him.

Carlie lifted her head and breathing raggedly, whispered, "Slow down, soldier."

"You're going to drive me crazy," he said in frustration. With a groan he released her.

"That works two ways."

"Does it?" His hands tangled in her hair and his breath whispered across her face.

"We've got time, Ben. We're not kids anymore." Again the pained shadow appeared in her eyes. She seemed about to tell him something vital, then forced a smile and kissed him quickly and chastely on the cheek.

"How much time do we have?"

"As long as you want." She slid out of the truck and left Ben with an ache in his groin that refused to wither.

Half lying across the seat, he watched as she let herself into the building and closed the door tightly in her wake. Within a few minutes the lights of her apartment were switched on and she appeared in one of the windows of the turret.

She threw the sash open and stuck out her head. Ben rolled down his window and watched in fascination as the wind blew her hair, a black and gleaming banner, away from her face. "Go home, Ben," she said, her laughter light as a summer breeze. She'd tucked her sadness away again.

"What if I refuse?"

"You'll freeze."

It was his turn to laugh. "Not likely, lady. Not if I'm anywhere near you!"

He rolled his window back up and put the old truck into gear. All the way home he reminded himself that she wasn't the kind of woman he wanted, but by the time he opened his back door and his dog, barking and growling, raced out to the yard, he still hadn't convinced himself.

Like it or not, he wanted Carlie Surrett.

Chapter Nine

Tracy stared at her reflection in the mirror over her sink in the bathroom. She frowned at the pinch of little lines near her eyes. Whether she wanted to admit it or not, she wasn't getting any younger.

"Hey, Mom, I'm outta here!" Randy called from his bedroom.

"Got your lunch money?"

"Yeah, and my book report."

"You have a good day," she yelled at him.

"I'm gonna have a *spectacular* day," he teased, using one of the vocabulary words he'd studied the night before.

"Good." She smiled as she thought of Randy—the one joy in her miserable life. She turned that thought away; Tracy didn't like feeling sorry for herself. Both she and Randy were healthy, she made enough money that life wasn't the struggle it once was and now...Ben Powell was back in town. *And still single.*

Randy appeared in the doorway, gave her a quick kiss on the cheek, then took off with his backpack swinging from one arm. Her heart squeezed as she followed him to the front hall and watched as he hurried to the bus stop where twenty kids from the apartment complex had gathered.

Maybe she'd made a mistake in not marrying. Randy had never known his father and the men that Tracy had dated, usually men who had picked her up at the Buckeye Restaurant and Lounge, had never shown the least bit of interest in her boy. Well, there had been a couple of guys who had acted as if Randy were something special, but those men, Red Langford and Terry Knapp, weren't the marrying kind. Red was nearly fifteen years older than she was and worked as a driver for Fitzpatrick Logging. He had a steady job, but also kids from a first marriage who were nearly grown. Terry was closer to her age but spent his Friday and Saturday nights on the third stool of the Buckeye Restaurant and Lounge, sitting, watching the big screen, smoking and closing down the place. He'd been picked up by the police for driving under the influence of alcohol on more than one occasion.

Nope, not marriage material.

But things were looking up. Ever since Ben showed up again in Gold Creek. Tracy smiled to herself and closed the door. She finished with her makeup, adding extra lip gloss and heading downstairs to her job at the bank. She worked weekdays as a teller at the Bank of The Greater Bay in Coleville and a couple of nights a week in the lounge at the Buckeye. Sometimes, on Saturdays, she put in an extra shift for the lunch crowd. During her usual schedule, she was home for Randy in the morning and late afternoon and had a sitter come and watch him on the nights when she worked the late shift at the Buckeye.

She hadn't had much time for men, but she planned on making time for Ben. The only problem was that about the same time he'd landed back in Gold Creek, so had Carlie Surrett. Gossip had been spreading around town—gossip that the old romance between Carlie and Ben was heating up.

Tracy frowned as she tilted her head and slid a teardrop-shaped earring through the tiny hole in her earlobe. She didn't like thinking about Carlie, the woman who had everything that was lacking in Tracy's life. Carlie was drop-dead gorgeous, while Tracy was merely pretty. Carlie had experienced a fleeting brush with fame while Tracy, bearing her illegitimate son in a small town had been infamous for a while—the target of any jerk who had the mistaken impression that she was easy. Also, Carlie had her independence, Tracy thought with a mild twang of envy. Carlie could do what she wanted, go where she wanted and when she wanted without worrying about a child.

Tracy grabbed her purse and jacket and locked the door behind her. Years ago, Carlie had found a way to sink her claws into the Powell boys with a tenacity that was awesome. But Tracy was older and smarter than she had been then. Also, she had an ace up her sleeve: her son. Ben, with all his lofty morals, wouldn't stay clear of his brother's boy. He couldn't. His conscience would kill him if he did.

Also, Tracy had always made time for Ben's father. George adored Randy and often teased Tracy about settling down with the right man. What George didn't know was that Ben just happened to be that very man. With just a little pressure, George would be in her corner. Besides, he'd never liked Carlie and still blamed her for Kevin's death.

There was also the little secret Tracy knew about Carlie, a secret no one else in Gold Creek knew. She smiled to herself as she remembered the day she'd seen Carlie at the Coleville Women's Clinic. She'd been reading a magazine in the waiting room and had been screened from the hall by a potted palm. Carlie had rushed out of the doors leading to the examining rooms and she'd been white as a sheet. Her eyes were red and she looked scared out of her mind. A nurse had run after her. "Miss Surrett, please. The doctor thinks you should make another appointment. Next week—"

Carlie had disappeared and Tracy, acting unconcerned, had been led into an examining room. She had a few minutes before her appointment with Dr. Dodd and so she'd casually walked to the rest room and noticed Carlie's chart obviously left on a desk near the scales when the nurse had taken off after the distressed girl.

Tracy hadn't felt a single moment's guilt as she read the report and figured out that Carlie had been pregnant but lost the baby. So far, she'd kept that information to herself. At the time she'd been worried that Carlie's baby, like her own, had been fathered by Kevin, but she'd quickly changed her mind. According to Carlie's chart, the timing wasn't right. And Kevin was dead.

So the baby had to have been Ben's.

He probably never knew how close he'd come to being a father. Tracy wondered how he would feel if, and when, he ever found out. She smiled a little wickedly and was grateful that Carlie hadn't been able to carry the kid to term.

So, now, Tracy wasn't really too worried about Carlie Surrett. Concerned, but not worried. She climbed into her little Pontiac. Humming to herself, she started the ignition. If Ben didn't call tonight, well, she'd just have to drum up a reason to contact him. It was as simple as that.

Carlie braced herself. Her father had been moved home and, according to her mother, was cranky and irritable, tired of being cooped up. Opening the door, she heard the argument drifting from the dining room.

"I'll talk to him myself!" her father bellowed. "Fitzpatrick can't pull the rug out from under me. Not after all the years I've put in with the company! Damn it all, where are my cigarettes?"

Carlie started through the living room.

"The doctor told you—"

"I know what he told me and I said I'd cut down. But I'm not about to stop cold turkey."

"Weldon, it's been nearly two weeks and you haven't had one. Why start now and—"

"Hi!" Carlie interrupted brightly as she breezed into the room. The dining room table had been shoved against the wall and a hospital bed had been set under the window.

Her father, half reclining, was glowering at his wife.

"You don't really want to smoke, do you?" Carlie's mom asked anxiously.

"Damn straight I want a smoke."

"Dad—"

"Don't you get on me, too. You women!" Muttering under his breath Weldon reached into the drawer of the night table that had been placed near his bed, but came up empty. As he scowled angrily, he slammed the drawer shut and muttered under his breath. "And where the hell's my chew?"

"Weldon—" Thelma said.

"Hell!"

Carlie sat on the foot of the bed. "Hey, Dad, give it a rest, will ya?"

"Take it easy. Give it a rest. A lot you know," he grumbled. His color was back to normal and he was talking much more clearly. His face, too, had improved, though there was a little droop at one corner of his mouth.

"Let me handle Fitzpatrick," Carlie said, smoothing the folds of the old quilt.

"This is my fight, kid."

"I know, but I'm out there anyway, taking pictures."

"You stay out of it." His tone brooked no argument and his eyes, sunken farther into his head than they should have been, sent her a glare that could have cut through steel. "I mean it."

"Don't worry about Thomas Fitzpatrick."

"I'm not concerned about that old buzzard, but I sure as hell want my job back!" He let out an angry puff of indignation. "And now the bastard has the gall to invite us to an engagement party for his daughter!" Weldon glared at his wife. "We're not going. Not unless I get my job back!"

Thelma's lips pursed. "Don't be rash."

"I'll be anything I damned well please, and I sure would like a smoke!" He started coughing then settled back on the pillows. "It's hell to get old, Carlie-girl."

"You're not that old, Dad."

He smiled. "What's that they say—it's not the years, it's the miles? Damn it all anyway."

Carlie sat down and held her father's work-roughened hand. She wanted to set him straight about his job and his health, to beg him to take care of himself, to ease his mind about his finances, but the arguments forming on her tongue went silent when she saw the nearly imperceptible wag of her mother's head, cautioning her that it would be best to let the subject drop.

"What've you been doing?" Thelma asked, turning the conversation in a new direction.

Carlie spent the next hour talking about her job, avoiding mention of the logging company and keeping Ben's name from the discussion. The less her family knew about her tenuous relationship with Ben, the better. She stayed another forty-five minutes with her folks, but felt more than a little depressed when she was leaving. Her father had refused to be jollied into a good humor and her mother was obviously worried about him.

"He'll be better in a few days," Thelma said, hope in her voice as she held open the screen door for her daughter. "The physical therapist says he's improving much faster than they'd expected."

"It's his will of iron," Carlie replied.

"We'll just have to give him time to get used to all this. It's new to him, you know. And he's worried that we might have to move into something a little cheaper, something with only one level." Thelma sighed and leaned on the door. "It's not as bad as he makes out. We've saved all our lives, and we have a little nest egg. Unfortunately, your father thinks it's the size of a hummingbird egg and he thinks we need an ostrich egg." Thelma managed a thin smile. "Things'll get better."

"I'll stop by tomorrow," Carlie promised as she dashed through the rain, sidestepping puddles on the way to her Jeep. She rammed the rig into reverse, turned around and tried not to let her father's depression settle on her shoulders. It was times like these when she wished she had a sister or a brother to share the load. She envied Rachelle and Heather. Even though they'd fought like cats and dogs while growing up, the bond between them was deep and when the family had split up, the two sisters had rallied together.

Carlie stared through the raindrops gathering on the windshield and flipped on the wipers. Even Ben had Nadine, a sister who was as stubborn as he was bullheaded. Though Kevin was dead and their family had been ripped to shreds, brother and sister were still friends, still staunch allies.

Nadine's marriage to Hayden Monroe had been a strain on the relationship, but it seemed as if Ben was now grudgingly accepting his new brother-in-law.

Carlie blew her bangs out of her eyes as she thought of Ben. Despite everything she'd told herself about protecting her heart, about avoiding him because he was trouble with a capital *T,* about staying away from a man who was as dangerous as a loaded gun, she still found excuses to be with him.

He'd called and invited her to a movie. She'd accepted and though the picture had been dull, they'd laughed about it together. They'd met for lunch in Coleville twice in the past week and they'd even bumped into each other at Fitzpatrick Logging where Ben had been contracted to restore some of the company buildings that needed work. Thomas had told her not to take any photographs of the buildings until Ben's crew had given the offices a "face-lift."

They hadn't so much as kissed since the night she'd found him in her apartment, hadn't even touched. Nor had he surprised her again in her own home. She'd met a couple members of his crew, subcontractors hired to update the plumbing and wiring, others who were scheduled to paint and refinish the floors, but Ben himself hadn't been around and she was surprised at the disappointment she'd felt that he hadn't bothered to stop by.

"That's the way you wanted it," she told herself as she got home and unlocked the door of her apartment. Shrugging out of her coat, she dropped her purse on the floor before sifting through her mail. Bills. Receipts. Advertisements. Investment opportunities. And one handwritten envelope with the return address of Fitzpatrick.

Her own personal invitation to Toni Fitzpatrick's engagement party, which was slated for the weekend of February fourteenth, near Valentine's Day.

Wonderful. Another way to remember romance and the celebration of love. She tossed the invitation onto the counter and watched the raindrops sheet down the window over the sink. Would Ben be invited? If so, would he bother to attend a formal party? Even though he worked for Fitzpatrick, there was no love lost between Ben Powell and Thomas Fitzpatrick, the man who had a stranglehold on the town of Gold Creek.

Time would tell.

Ben slid the finished blueprints across the kitchen table. "Voilà."

While his crews were out hauling debris and preparing the site for Nadine's cabin, or scraping the peeling paint off the old Hunter house or checking the wiring, insulation and roofing at Fitzpatrick Logging, he'd put in hour after hour at the computer. Finally, after his rough draft was complete, he'd met with an architect-friend again, made sure that the building was as sound as it was eye appealing, then made the final revisions to his plans.

Nadine, her green eyes twinkling, slowly unrolled the plans. As she looked at the front elevation of her new cabin, she shook her head. "This is a little more elaborate than I had in mind."

"Hayden insisted on his input, as well."

She sighed, but smiled at the drawings as she flipped through the oversize pages. "Three bedrooms, *and* a loft, plus a den with sewing alcove. And what's this—four—no, three bathrooms."

"A concession to you."

"The original cabin only had one."

"Resale value."

Her lips compressed. "I'm not reselling. Not ever."

Ben laughed. "Why do you want it, Nadine? You're married now. You live in a damned mansion—" He swung his arm around the kitchen of the Monroe manor, trying to impress upon her the width and breadth of the house. "And you're rebuilding right across the lake? I hate to be the one to tell you this, sister, but it doesn't make a whole lotta sense."

She bristled slightly, her pencil wiggling in agitation between her fingers. "That cabin was the only security my boys had, and now, with Sam still out of work..." She frowned at the thought of her ex-husband who was still recovering from the burns that covered his hands and upper arms, burns that were the result of the fire he'd inadvertently started, the fire that had destroyed Nadine's house. "I want to make sure John and Bobby and whoever—" she said, patting her still-flat tummy, as if she were caressing the baby growing therein "—aren't robbed of their education."

"Hayden would never do that," Ben said, standing up for the brother-in-law he'd sworn to hate.

"I don't think so, either, but I hate to be dependent."

"The man's a multimillionaire, Nadine, and unless you signed some god-awful prenuptial agreement, I don't see how you're ever going to end up destitute!"

"I didn't sign anything."

"There you go."

Nadine's green eyes darkened with memories. "I just don't want what happened to Kevin and you and me to happen to the boys."

"It won't," Ben said and though there had been a time when he hadn't trusted Hayden Monroe, he knew that the man adored Nadine and the boys. He hated to admit it, but Monroe seemed to be one helluva good husband and stepfather. The kids, and Nadine, couldn't have asked for more. Though it galled Ben to concede that Hayden had proved himself to be a stellar kind of guy, he couldn't deny what was so damned obvious. "Besides, I heard somewhere that your little jewelry and clothing business is really picking up."

"I guess I'd better remind you that it's not a 'little business' or a hobby or something to fill my hours. I've got more orders than I can handle and have thought about hiring someone to help."

"Really?"

"Really." With a cat-that-ate-the-canary smile, Nadine studied the blueprints as Ben poured himself a cup of coffee from the pot simmering on the coffeemaker. She made a few notes with a red pencil, chewed on the inside of her lip and finally said, "You know, you really are brilliant. I can't find much wrong with these."

Ben nearly choked on his coffee. Praise from his kid sister was unusual. "Good."

"Just put in another dormer in the loft and add a ceiling fan, shore out the back porch two feet and change the bath tub to a shower for the boys."

"Anything else?"

"That's it for now."

"Thank God."

She started to roll up the plans, but he said, "Keep 'em. I've got copies. I'll make your changes, file one with the county, make sure the permits are all in order and then we'll start excavation, so—"

"I know. If there are any more changes, I should let you know yesterday."

"You got it." Ben swallowed the rest of his coffee and set his empty cup in the sink. He then moved to leave.

Nadine shooed her black-and-white shepherd off the rug near the front door. "Move, Hershel," she commanded and the dog cocked his ears without budging. She opened the door and finally Hershel got the message. He bounded outside to join the grizzled yellow lab who was standing guard near the rhododendrons. "Did you get an invitation to the big party?" Nadine asked.

"If you're talking about the Fitzpatrick extravaganza, the answer is yes, but I don't know that I have the stomach to go."

"Come on, Ben. Be a sport. He's practically family now," Nadine said with a gleam in her eyes. "Besides, you can take Carlie. I heard you were seeing her again."

"This damned town."

"Is it a secret?"

He studied his sister intently. "I just like to keep things private."

She laughed and waved as he climbed into the truck. "Then you shouldn't have moved back to Gold Creek."

"You're telling me," Ben grumbled, stepping on the throttle a little harder than he'd planned. Just the mention of Carlie set his teeth on edge. It was true, he'd been seeing her and he'd tried like hell to keep his hands off her. But it had been a losing proposition because it was driving him out of his mind.

He told himself that he was going straight home, but then he conjured up an excuse to stop by the Hunter house to see if the electrical crew had shown up.

As he walked up the front steps he caught sight of Mrs. Hunter peeking through her curtains. She met him in the vestibule, her eyes shining.

"Good news. I won't have to rent the studio to you."

"You must've heard I inherited a dog," he said with a wink.

"Oh, my, no. I love animals, but you haven't even finished your work around here and it looks like I might have a buyer for the house," she said, beaming brightly. She was wearing a pair of her deceased husband's overalls, a faded red flannel shirt and a smile that wouldn't quit.

"Looks like all this remodeling worked."

"Well, the deal isn't signed yet, but when Thomas Fitzpatrick says he's going to do something, he usually does."

"Fitzpatrick?" Ben said, his guts clenching. "He's the buyer?"

"If things go as planned." She picked up a pair of rubber boots she'd left by her door. "Wish me luck."

"You got it." Ben climbed the stairs and told himself it didn't matter who was buying the place. Mrs. Hunter wanted to sell the old house and Fitzpatrick had the money.

They were working on a deal. So what if Fitzpatrick's name was on everything in town? Who cared if he was going to be Carlie's new landlord?

Nonetheless his good mood was destroyed, and when he rapped on Carlie's door, he fidgeted, anxious to be away from the cloying grasp of Fitzpatrick. His feelings were irrational he realized. Just because Fitzpatrick had been part of the scheme with H. G. Monroe III that had forced the Powell family into near bankruptcy didn't mean that Ben should hold a grudge. Oh, hell, why not?

Carlie opened the door and smiled at the sight of him. "I didn't know you were coming over."

"I'm not. I thought we'd go out."

"Are you sure? I could cook—"

"I'll cook," he said, anxious to leave. He wondered if Fitzpatrick had a key. Surely not yet. Nonetheless he wanted Carlie out of there.

She was laughing, staring at him as if he'd said he was going to fly to Jupiter. "Ben Powell, chef extraordinaire?" she teased.

"You'll be surprised."

"It won't be any of that army stuff, will it? You know...what do they call it...something on shingles?" Her blue-green eyes twinkled and he was reminded of sunlight refracting on a tropical sea.

He laughed despite himself. "Believe me, you'll love it."

"Just let me get my jacket."

He followed her into the apartment and wondered why it seemed like home. He looked around at the smattering of antiques, modern pieces of art and the cork bulletin board with notes pinned haphazardly on it. And everywhere, on the walls, propped against the floor, stacked on an old bookcase, were her photographs. All different. They hadn't been here before. "What are these?"

"My work. I had them stored at the studio, but I decided I needed a few pieces around here. You know, to show off a little."

As she walked to the closet near the daybed, he looked through a stack of black-and-white pictures of Native

Americans in Alaska. A kayak with a single oarsman on a vast sea, whales breaching . . .

"Ready?" she asked.

"Not quite." He was fascinated with the pictures. "I don't know much about photography, but I like these."

"Do you?"

He saw the hint of her smile and his gut tightened. "Maybe we should go—"

The phone jangled and Carlie ignored it. "The machine'll pick up," she explained as she slid her arms into the sleeves of her jacket. After a few rings and a slight pause, a woman's shrill voice rang from the speaker.

"Carlie? Are you there? It's Constance. Come on, I know you're probably working in that damned darkroom or something. . . . Look, I know you're not all that interested in trying to reestablish yourself, but Cosmos Jeans is doing a retrospective, wants all the women who have posed for their 'out of this world' commercials. They're willing to pay and . . . if you want to launch that career again, this would be the perfect time. Well, think about it. You know my number. Can't wait to hear from you."

There was a loud click and Ben watched Carlie's face as it lost all of its animation. "Let's go before she calls back." Grabbing her purse, she opened the door.

"Your agent?" he asked.

"Owner of the agency I worked for." She locked the door behind them and hurried down the stairs.

"In New York?"

"She's there, but there are offices in L.A. and London and Paris."

"Big time," he said.

"I'm not going."

"Sounds like quite an opportunity." He couldn't hide a trace of mockery in his voice.

"It is. I just don't want it."

"You did once."

"A long time ago." She shoved open the door and stepped outside. The night was clear and cool and a soft breeze tugged at Carlie's hair. She didn't want to think about Constance, or New York, or the fact that she could really use the extra money modeling could provide. She was getting older; not too many more opportunities would come knocking on her door. And yet . . . she'd come back home because she was through with the fast lane.

Wasn't she?

As Ben started the truck, she stared out the window. He was suddenly silent, wrapped in his own thoughts as he drove into the heart of town. She didn't know what to expect from this night, but she didn't really care. She slid a glance at him from the corner of her eye. Despite the call from Constance, being with Ben gave the evening a tingle of excitement and she let herself think about falling in love with him again.

Don't! She couldn't let herself start thinking about anything so foolish as falling in love. Especially not with Ben.

"This is cheating," she said as she struggled with her chopsticks. They sat at a small table in the kitchen of his house. White cartons and sacks from a local Chinese restaurant littered the tabletop.

"Why?"

"I definitely heard you say 'I'll cook,' not 'I'll order out.' Big difference, Powell." She wagged a chopstick at his nose.

"Next time," he promised.

"I'll hold you to it." She started to shove her plate aside but his black shepherd, seated next to her, barked and wagged his tail, hoping for a tidbit. "He likes chop suey?" she asked.

"He likes anything but me."

The dog, as if on cue, placed his head in her lap. She ruffled him behind the ears and he yawned, displaying pink gums and sharp white teeth. "I think he knows a sucker when he sees one," she said, giving the beast a piece of ginger chicken.

Ben grinned. It was funny how comfortable he felt with Carlie in his home, almost as if she belonged. He'd expected her to wrinkle her nose in distaste at the furnishings in his austere house: a single leather couch that he'd bought secondhand, desk, table and chairs from garage sales. No warm, soft rug, no throw pillows, not an afghan in sight and not one picture on the walls.

But she didn't seem to mind and he was surprised. Although she'd grown up with humble roots, she'd always dreamed of escaping Gold Creek to the fame and glitter of Manhattan. She'd planned to model, had even considered acting and felt that she might end up in L.A., so it amused him to see her sit, jean-clad legs tucked beneath her on his couch. She swirled a glass of wine as he built a fire and he imagined how easily she could fit into his life, into his routine.

"So why'd you quit the army?" she asked, when he settled back on his heels and watched the mossy logs ignite. The fire crackled and spit.

"It was time."

"Because you were wounded."

He sighed and rubbed the wood dust from his palms. "I joined to get out of town, just like you took off for New York. Kevin was dead, my family was splitting up—I just needed time away. I wanted order and discipline and...adventure, I guess." His eyes darkened. "I liked it at first. I felt duty-bound and patriotic and felt that I was important, but... Oh, hell, I don't know, I just got older. I saw some of my friends get killed and it all seemed so useless. When I was wounded I was offered a discharge. I took it. Seemed like it was time for something else." He snorted. "Time to grow up, I suppose."

"And that something else was Gold Creek?"

"It's home, Carlie." He stood and reached for his beer on the mantel. "And you can't run away forever."

"Are you talking about yourself or giving me advice?"

"A little of both, I suppose." He drained the beer and walked over to her. She wasn't a tiny person, but she was thin, and curled up on the couch, her eyes wide and luminous, her hair gleaming black, he found her irresistible. He'd kept his hands off her for a couple of weeks, ever since their passion had exploded in her apartment, but now seeing her beautiful face tipped up to his, her lips parted in an inviting smile, he couldn't stop himself.

In two swift strides he closed the distance between them and took her into his arms. His mouth covered hers and he tasted the wine on her lips, heard the weak little moan from the back of her throat. Her skin smelled of lavender and felt like warm silk against his fingertips. Heat pulsed through his body and his mind shut off any protests. He didn't care about the past, didn't want to remember that he'd told himself for years he couldn't trust her, wouldn't think of the ramifications of making love to her. All he knew was the want that started hot and hard in his loins and swept upward through his body.

Carlie closed her eyes and concentrated on the feel of him. His lips, his hands, his tongue. Liquid fire swept through her veins as he began to unbutton her blouse. She knew she should stop, that making love to him was dangerous, but her heart persuaded her to take a chance. The smell of burning wood, the feel of his hands against her flesh, the musky flavor of the wine, the intoxicating feel of him shoved aside all her doubts.

She wound her arms around his neck, kissing him hungrily, her tongue anxiously mating with his. Her blouse parted and he nuzzled her neck, dipping low in the dusky hollow between her breasts, trailing his wet tongue over the silky lace of her bra.

Arching upward, she felt his hands span her waist, holding her against him, making her aware of the hardness swelling against his jeans.

"You make me crazy," he whispered as he breathed across her nipple.

She could barely speak and when she did, her voice was unrecognizable. "Please," she begged, "please, Ben, don't stop."

"Never." He shoved her blouse from her shoulders and stripped her of her bra, until the firelight played upon her naked torso and he stared down at her nipples. "So incredible," he murmured, running a work-roughened thumb across one dark peak. He lowered his head and sucked gently and she wound her fingers in the thick strands of his hair.

His fingers found the waistband of her jeans and dipped low over her buttocks.

Like lava, liquid fire swirled deep within Carlie and she found the buttons of his shirt. Her blood pounded in her ears as he stripped her of her clothes and he kicked off his jeans, pausing only long enough to reach into his pocket for a plastic-wrapped packet of protection.

"I've dreamed of being with you again," he admitted, holding himself above her, lowering his head to kiss her lips lightly, or brush his tongue across her nipples.

"So have I," she said over a suddenly thick throat.

"You're sure?"

"Absolutely," she cried.

His lips clamped over hers and after a moment's hesitation, he entered her. Not the high-speed, quick thrill of a teenager, but slowly and surely with long strokes that took her breath away.

Carlie clung to him, moved with his intimate rhythm and stared into the magnetic beauty of his hazel eyes. The pupils were dilated, his dark skin shiny with sweat as he moved more quickly, taking Carlie on a roller-coaster ride that soared upward, faster and faster.

"Carlie!" he cried, as if he'd found something he'd lost for so long a time. "Oh, Carlie."

In a flash of brilliance, the world exploded behind her eyes. Her body convulsed and he shuddered against her. The world seemed to tilt a little as his weight settled comfortably over her and she wrapped her arms around his muscular back. *I love you,* she thought miserably, knowing that loving him was her burden in life. *God forgive me, Ben, but I love you!*

She would never tell him, of course. But as she clung to him and the fire hissed softly, she realized that she would never love another man.

Chapter Ten

An affair. She rolled the thought around in her head and stretched, the back of her calves rustling the cotton sheets. She'd never believed in affairs; she preferred being single or the permanence of marriage.

Ben was already up. She heard him rattling around in the kitchen and smelled the rich scent of brewing coffee. Stretching, she relived their night of lovemaking that had taken place first, in the living room in front of the fire and later, in here, this tiny bedroom that was large enough for only a double bed and a chest of drawers. Sparse. Utilitarian. Perfect.

She looked out the window and saw ice collecting on the thin panes. Frost covered the grass in the yard and a wintry sun was just peaking over the eastern hills. She found Ben's dark blue terry-cloth bathrobe and wrapped it around her middle, cinched the waist and rolled up the sleeves. Barefoot, she padded into the living area.

"Good morning, Sleeping Beauty," he said.

He looked so good. His hair was still damp from the shower and a knowing smile played upon his thin lips. Yes, she could fall in love with him too easily. "I don't feel very beautiful."

"Take my word for it. Coffee?"

"How about a shower first?"

"All yours," he said, and she made her way to the bathroom.

She'd just ducked her head under the hot spray when she heard the door open and the curtain was thrown back. "I lied," he said, grinning devilishly as he stood stark naked on the tile floor. "The shower isn't all yours. You'll have to share." He stepped inside and took her into his arms and while the sharp needles of water sprayed her back and mist rose around them, he made love to her again.

He touched her water-slickened breasts, kissed her sleepy eyes and opened up that special part of her, touching her with strong fingers, forcing her to moan and gasp until at last he became one with her.

She clung to his slippery body as wave after wave of hot desire caused her to cry out. When he finally finished, he held her close, the water beginning to turn cold as it ran down their bodies.

He kissed her until her teeth began to chatter, then shoved the curtain back. "How about coffee now?" he asked, his eyes twinkling.

"Sounds like heaven."

Within minutes she'd towel-dried and dressed and was cradling a cup of coffee as she sat in front of the fire warming her feet. They ate toast and scrambled eggs and, since it was the weekend, didn't worry about work.

"Rory works Saturdays," she explained when he asked.

"Unfortunately I've got a seven-day-a-week job." But he didn't rush out the door. Instead, he rubbed a kink from his back and asked, "What about that call from the modeling agency?"

"What about it?"

"Aren't you tempted to go back, make a big splash, prove that you've still got what it takes?"

She shook her head. "I don't think so."

"But you're not sure?"

"I think I am, but I've thought that before." She stared deep into his eyes. "I don't have any plans to go back to New York, Ben, but I can't predict the future."

They sat together on the couch and the phone began to ring. Ben didn't bother answering, but listened to the messages as they were recorded. His foreman, Ralph Katcher, called and his sister, Nadine, left a message about a few last-minute changes to her plans, but Ben didn't move. They sat side by side on the couch, sipping coffee, talking and laughing and tossing a tennis ball to the dog.

Carlie told herself to stop dreaming, but she felt as if she'd finally quit running and come home. She let herself think that maybe they had a chance of a future together—if not marriage then a long-term affair.

The word that she'd avoided for so long didn't seem so wrong when she considered that the affair would be with Ben. *One day at a time, girl,* she cautioned herself. *Don't get ahead of yourself. Remember what you just told him. Who knows what the future may bring?*

The phone rang again and Ben nuzzled her ear. "Maybe we should get out of here. Go on a picnic."

"It's February."

"So what?"

"We'd freeze."

"I can think of ways to keep warm."

The answering machine picked up the call and after the tape of Ben's voice instructed the caller to leave a message, a woman's voice filled the room.

"Ben? It's Tracy—"

Carlie's heart slid to the floor and beside her, Ben tensed.

"I was hoping to catch you at home."

She sounded vastly disappointed.

"Anyway, I left a message yesterday.... Maybe you didn't get it, but I was hoping that we could do something together. Randy has been talking nonstop about you since the last time you came over and I could make us lunch...or whatever. He's, um, got Little League tryouts this morning at the park in just a few minutes.... Oh, well, don't worry about it.'' There was a weighty pause and Ben shifted restlessly on the couch. Tracy added, ''Randy misses you,'' before hanging up with a click that seemed to echo through the cozy little house.

Carlie glanced at Ben and noticed that the fun-loving glint in his eyes had disappeared. His mouth curved into a frown and he shoved an impatient hand through his hair.

''Tracy Niday,'' Carlie guessed.

''Damn.''

A deafening roar seemed to fill her ears. ''You're... seeing her?'' All Carlie's dreams shattered in that second when she saw the answer in his eyes. Her heart cracked. Good Lord, what had she expected? That he was in love with her? That because they'd made love, he wasn't involved with anyone else? Her world tilting wildly, she set her empty coffee cup on a table and stood. ''I...I think I'd better go,'' she whispered, hearing her voice as if from a distance. Bitter disappointment flooded through her.

Strong fingers clamped around her wrist. ''Let me explain.''

''You don't have to.''

''Of course I do.'' He pulled her down to sit next to him. ''I'm not dating Tracy, if that's what you're thinking. I only saw her a couple of times.''

Oh, Lord!

''She waited on me when I had lunch at the Buckeye and then she invited me over to dinner. That was a couple of weeks ago.''

''And you haven't seen her since?''

He rubbed his jaw, as if guilt were eating him up. ''No,'' he admitted, ''but I plan to.'' He looked at her and must have seen the disappointment in her eyes. ''For Randy. Kevin's boy. He...uh...he needs a man. You know, to toss a football, to talk about baseball with, to fix his bike, to—''

''To be a father,'' she said and hated the dead sound in her voice. *Randy is Ben's nephew. The poor kid doesn't have a dad. He just needs a man. But, why, oh, why does*

Tracy have to enter into it? She hated her jealousy. It made her feel so small. Tracy was a struggling single mother, for crying out loud, and yet Carlie felt this overwhelming need to hold on to Ben with all her might—to possess him! But he wasn't a man who could be possessed. That's why she loved him. Oh, God, she'd never admitted that horrible fact to herself before!

"I'm not Randy's father," Ben said as his gaze searched her face.

"But Kevin was," Carlie whispered and everything became clear to her. She could never have Ben, not while Tracy was interested in him. Maybe Tracy only wanted to see him for the boy's sake, but Carlie had a gut instinct, feminine intuition, that Tracy wanted Ben for herself. Carlie couldn't blame her for that. Didn't she feel the same?

"Yes, Kevin was."

"So you need to see him."

"I think so," he admitted, still scowling into the fire.

Carlie didn't have the heart to tell him to stay away from his nephew. She didn't doubt that the boy needed a father figure in his life and Ben was the most likely choice. She saw Ben as Tracy saw him: strong, good-looking, responsible and sexy. Fresh out of the army, starting a new business and a new life, he'd be the perfect catch.

Carlie's heart squeezed. "Look," she said, suddenly yanking her hand away from him as she scrambled to her feet, "I really have to go."

"You're angry."

"Just confused."

He stood and wrapped his arms around her, holding her close, as if afraid she might disappear. "I don't feel anything for Tracy, you know that. She just happens to be Randy's mother."

Her voice failed her for a moment and tears burned at the back of her eyes. "I understand," she whispered, though her voice threatened to crack.

"Do you?"

"Mmm. We're not teenagers any longer. A lot has happened. I have to share you."

He held her at arm's length and shook his head. "No way," he said before dragging her close again and kissing her long and hard. Tears, unbidden, streamed from Carlie's eyes. He didn't understand—not the way she did. He was naive enough to think that they could still be lovers while he had dinner at Tracy's and played ball with her son. Thoughts she'd never before experienced raced through her mind and she felt guilty for her need to have him to herself. She had to let Ben go. Kevin's boy needed him. Probably more than Carlie did.

Slowly she disentangled herself and started for the door before she heard the jangle of his keys. "I'll drive you," he said, "unless you were planning on hitchhiking back to town."

She managed a short, bittersweet laugh and Ben whistled to the dog. Attila raced to the door and as it was open, bounded outside to leap at the sides of the cab.

"He's crazy about taking a drive," Ben explained. "Hope you don't mind."

"Never," Carlie replied, hoping that her broken heart didn't show in her eyes. She scratched the dog behind his ears and held open the door for him. Attila wanted the window seat so he could stick his head through the opening and Carlie ended up pressed tightly against Ben. She stared through the windshield and felt cold inside though the sun was shining brightly enough for Ben to reach in the glove compartment for his dark glasses.

They passed the park and Ben glanced at the baseball field. "Randy's already here," he said with a frown. "I really should stop—" Without waiting for her response, he turned onto a side street near the baseball diamonds and guided the truck to a stop near the curb. "It'll only take a minute."

"It's okay," she said, forcing a smile.

"You sure?"

"Absolutely. Take your time. I'll wait."

Ben didn't look convinced, but pocketed his keys and climbed quickly out of the cab. Attila, ready for adventure, leapt to the ground and took off at a sprint. Hands

in his back pockets, Ben strode across the dewy grass to join
a huddle of men and boys, some of whom were already
tossing a ball around. Carlie's heart twisted as she watched
the sunlight gleam against his dark hair and his face break
into a smile as he spied his nephew.

Ben was irrevocably tied to Randy, whether he knew it or
not, and therefore tied to Tracy, as well. Carlie felt like a
selfish fool for the jealousy that balled in her stomach.
Randy needed him. More than she did.

Swallowing back a lump in her throat, she watched. Ben
stood out in the crowd of men wearing warm-up suits,
baseball hats and league jackets. In his faded jeans, rum-
pled leather jacket, T-shirt and aviator glasses, he looked
more like a stuntman for a Hollywood film than a father.

Carlie couldn't help but watch. A skinny kid with brown
hair and an Oakland A's cap ran up to Ben. Ben teased the
boy and yanked off his hat to rumple his hair. The kid
danced around him and made a big fuss over Attila, who
barked and jumped like a puppy. Carlie's heart cracked as
she realized this should be her son—she and Ben should
have had a child—a son or daughter—this very age.

Other kids raced over to check out the dog. Bundled in
sweatpants and sweatshirts, with major league caps on their
heads and huge fielding gloves on their hands, the boys
were laughing and talking and shoving each other, their
faces red, their eyes sparkling with anticipation.

One big lanky kid threw the dog a ball and the anxious
shepherd took off at a sprint. Excited voices and peals of
laughter floated on the morning breeze.

Carlie felt numb inside. This was where Ben belonged.
He glanced to the pickup and waved as he extracted himself from the group. She lifted her hand but he'd already
turned away and helped sign the boy up at a table where
mothers were sipping coffee while guarding application
forms.

One mom offered him coffee and a smile; another was all
business, pointing to the registration forms. Other boys had
already batted and pitched while judges in windbreakers

and baseball caps watched their performance from bleachers that needed a new coat of paint.

Tracy was there, too, wearing a baseball cap and hovering nearby and smiling up at Ben. It hit Carlie like a ton of bricks: *she* was the outsider, the one who didn't belong. That thought made her stomach clench into a painful ball. Why wouldn't she ever learn?

Ben said something to Tracy and she laughed. Then Randy handed his uncle a ball and they started playing catch, Ben squatting like a catcher, Randy winding up to pitch.

If only their own child had lived! Knowing that she had to leave before her raw emotions started to strangle her, Carlie hopped out of the truck and trudged across the wet grass. She would explain to Ben that she could walk back to the apartment. The hike was less than a mile and the exercise would do her some good. She could leave him here with his nephew—where he belonged—and she wouldn't have to torture herself any longer.

Randy was just getting ready to bat for the judges. Carlie was close enough to hear Ben talking to the boy.

"Remember—eye on the ball," Ben encouraged, his face as intense as if his own son were trying out. "Address the plate and don't let that pitcher scare you." Ben took off his glasses and gave the boy a wink.

"I won't."

"You can do it," Tracy encouraged, straightening the boy's sweatshirt. "You're the best, honey."

Was it her imagination, or did Carlie see Randy's back stiffen a little as he walked to the short line near the on-deck circle.

"He's just got to do well," Tracy confided in Ben. She was so nervous, she was chewing on her polished nails. "Jerry Tienman is here and he's the coach I want for Randy."

"Is he who Randy wants?"

"Of course. Tienman is the best coach in the league and last year, over half his team became all-stars...." Her voice drifted off as she noticed Carlie approaching. A web of tiny lines formed between her eyebrows.

"I didn't mean to interrupt," Carlie said, forcing a smile as she caught Ben's attention. "But I've got to go."

Ben glanced from Carlie to the plate. "This'll only be a few minutes."

"Randy would really be disappointed if you left," Tracy cut in, and Carlie felt like a heel.

"Really. You stay here. It's okay. I'll just cut through the park. It's only a few blocks."

Ben's lips tightened. "Just hang in here, okay?"

"Really—"

His eyes found hers and for a moment the crowd of boys, Tracy, the dog and all the action at the plate seemed to stop. "Please, just a couple of minutes."

"Sure," Carlie said, rather than cause a scene, and she knew in that instant that if she and Ben were to have any relationship at all, she would have to settle for coming in second. Whether he knew it or not, he was committed to his nephew. She saw it in his eyes.

Tracy's eyes narrowed a fraction before she turned and leaned against the wire backdrop. "Come on, slugger!" she yelled and again, Randy's back tightened.

The pitcher, a big, rangy boy, wound up and let loose. The ball streaked across the plate. Randy swung and fouled the ball over the backstop.

"That's good," Ben encouraged. "You got a piece of it."

"Come on, honey!"

Randy threw his mother a hard look over his shoulder. He twisted his feet, adjusting his stance, and stared back at the pitcher.

The boy wound up. Another pitch. This one, right down the middle, hit the catcher's glove with a thud. Randy hadn't moved, not even swung.

"Come on," Ben said under his breath.

"That one was good as gold," Tracy said, with more than a trace of irritation. "You can do it, Randy!"

The next pitch was high, clear over Randy's head, and he swung wildly.

"No!" Tracy yelled.

"Hey, lady, put a lid on it," one of the coaches said. "Let the kid do his thing."

"He's my son."

"So lighten up."

Tracy looked as if she wanted to tear into the guy, but Ben grabbed her arm. "He's right, Tracy."

Three more balls and three more misses. Carlie wished she could disappear.

"I can't believe it," Tracy said, shaking her head. "I don't know what's wrong! He's usually so good."

"He is good," Ben assured her. "His timing's just a little off."

"But we've been to the batting cages, I've worked with him. Oh, God, if he doesn't make Tienman's team, he'll be so disappointed."

"Will he?" Ben asked. "Or will you?"

"He will! He wants to be the best!"

"Next! Number eighty-seven!" the coach yelled and Randy threw off his batting helmet and dropped his bat. His face was contorted and he was swearing under his breath.

"Honey, what happened?" Tracy asked.

"I screwed up!" He kicked at a clod of dirt with the toe of his baseball shoe and battled the urge to break down and cry.

"You did fine," Ben said, clapping him on the back. "That pitcher was really on. His curveball—"

"—sucked! And so did I!"

"Don't talk that way, Randall," Tracy said, her face flushing with color. "Pull yourself together. You've got to pitch next."

"Don't want to."

"Oh, come on, honey. You know you love this."

"No, you love it!" He threw his mitt to the ground and stalked away, Tracy chasing after him, Attila romping as if it were all a game. Several kids watched him leave. "What a jerk," one boy said around a wad of bubble gum.

"Crybaby."

"He's just having a rough day," Ben told the kids.

"Yeah, so what's it to you?"

"He's my nephew."

"Well, then, your nephew is a jerk."

"Shut up, Billy!" a big, unshaven man said. "Warm up. You're after this guy."

Grumbling, Billy and his friends wandered away.

"I think I'd better stay," Ben said to Carlie, casting a look behind the bleachers where it looked as if Tracy were reading her son the riot act.

"I know," she said. The boy needed him. It was as simple as that.

"Tracy's got some crazy notion that Randy's got to be the best at everything he does."

Carlie managed a smile, though she felt like breaking down and crying. "You'll fix things, Ben. I'll walk home." When he started to protest, she placed her palm against his face. "Go on, I'll be fine. I'll see you later."

"At least take Attila with you. I'll pick him up in a little while." He whistled for the dog, kissed her lightly on the cheek then took off at a jog, catching up with Randy and tossing his arm around the boy's slim shoulders. Randy tried to pull away, but Ben kept up with him and Tracy managed to throw one look over her shoulder—a smug look of victory.

Carlie's blood began to boil, but she gritted her teeth as she started across the park. Attila bounded ahead, scaring birds and chasing runaway balls. Carlie barely noticed because she was thinking of Ben and their one night together. It would have to be their last. Just like before. She was too damned selfish to share him with Tracy and her son, and Ben belonged with the boy.

She'd just crossed Main when she heard a horn blast behind her. Ben's pickup cruised up to the curb and he leaned over the seat and shoved open the door. "The least I can do is drive you the rest of the way."

She didn't argue and both she and Attila climbed into the cab. "How'd Randy do?"

"He didn't."

"No?"

"No one, not even God himself, could have talked that kid into finishing tryouts. If you ask me, it was a case of flat-out rebellion. He's tired of his mom pushing him so hard."

"So what're you going to do about it?"

"Nothing I can do. This is Randy's call."

"What about Tracy?"

"She's fit to be tied," he admitted as he slowed for a corner, "but then she's got to remember that Randy's just a kid—no special hero and certainly not his father."

"She wants you to be his father."

"I can't, Carlie." Ben stared out the window. "I'll be his uncle. Hell, I'll be the best damned uncle in the world. He can call me anytime and I'll do whatever I can to help out. But I can't be the kid's dad."

He pulled into a parking spot beneath a spruce tree and walked her upstairs. "Can I see you tonight? As much as I detest the idea, I think I should put in an appearance at Toni Fitzpatrick's engagement party."

"I, um, I'll have to meet you there. I promised my mother I'd take her and Dad, and since she had to twist Dad's arm to go, I don't want to change plans."

He hesitated. "Hey, look, I'm sorry about Randy—"

"Don't be," she said. "Life's just a lot more complicated than it used to be."

He offered her a smile that lifted one side of his mouth. "Then I'll see you there."

"I'd . . . I'd like that."

He hesitated. "I think the whole damned town will be there. People at tryouts were talking about it. Even Tracy."

Carlie's muscles tightened. "She was invited?"

"Her father worked for Fitzpatrick for forty years. Seems as if she knows him and Toni."

Carlie felt a huge sense of disappointment, but Ben reached for her and drew her into the circle of his arms. "I guess I'll have to wait until tomorrow to be alone with you." His smile was sexy.

"Yes." She knew she should tell him no, but couldn't, not while he was touching her. Then she remembered. "Oh, no, that doesn't work, either. Believe it or not, I've got a dinner meeting with Thomas Fitzpatrick."

He didn't move, just stood there stunned, as if she'd slapped him. "A dinner date?" he repeated, his eyes slitting suspiciously.

"Yes. He asked me a few weeks ago and I turned him down, even canceling once, but he insists that we have to talk about the photographs for the company brochure—"

"Over dinner?"

"Hey, it wasn't my idea."

"But you went along with it."

"That's right, Ben, I did," she said, suddenly angry. All her coiled emotions released in a burst of fury. "Just like you might have lunch or dinner with a potential client. It's no big deal."

"With Fitzpatrick, everything's a big deal! Do you know that he's planning to buy this house?"

"This house?" she whispered, glancing around her apartment. "*This* house."

"Yep. All of a sudden it seems as if old Tom has an interest in the property." He clamped his hands under his arms. "I wondered if it had anything to do with you."

"Of course not!"

His skeptical look said he didn't believe her.

"What is this phobia you've got against the man?"

"He's slimy and two-faced and out for number one."

"I know that. Don't worry about me, Ben. I can take care of myself."

"Maybe I don't want that," he said, his eyes growing dark. "Maybe I want to take care of you."

Her throat closed for an instant and her anger melted away. It was so easy, so damned easy, to trust him. "I don't want someone to take care of me. I'm not a child. I make my own decisions, one of which is to go out to dinner with Fitzpatrick and hear what he has to say."

The skin tightened over his cheekbones and he looked as if he wanted to spit out a string of blue oaths, but he held his tongue, turned on his heel and headed down the stairs.

"Great," Carlie mumbled to herself. "Just great." She slammed the door behind her and wondered why she bothered with Ben. His moods were mercurial and now he wanted to control her.

You bother with Ben because you love him.

"Then you're a fool, Carlie Surrett," she told herself as she flopped down on the couch and wondered if she'd made a mistake returning to Gold Creek. Maybe she would have been better off staying away.

You can't run forever. And she wouldn't. Ben Powell or no Ben Powell.

Toni Fitzpatrick's engagement party was the social event of the year. Miniature lights twinkled from a forest of potted trees and red, white and silver ribbons looped from the chandeliers which were suspended above the main dining room at the Coleville Country Club. Silver balloons floated lazily to the two-storied ceiling. An ice sculpture of twin swans rose from a table laden with platters of fruit, caviar and hors d'oeuvres. Champagne bubbled from a three-tiered fountain and chefs stood at attention behind serving trays of roast beef, turkey and ham. Lobster, prawns and salmon were served at yet another table and a dessert cart offered chocolates, truffle cake and raspberry mousse.

"How's he gonna beat this?" Weldon asked as he, with his cane, hobbled across the upper balcony and stared down at the party below. A curved staircase swept from one floor to the next and a string quartet played love songs while waiters scurried back and forth to the kitchen. "When the girl gets married, I mean. How can he top this spread?"

"He'll find a way," Carlie predicted. She let her gaze wander through the bejeweled guests, searching for Ben.

"Always does," Thelma agreed as they used the elevator and rode down to the festivities.

"He'll have to rent the damned Ritz," Weldon grumbled. The elevator doors opened. Her father, moving stiffly

with his "damned walking stick" headed toward the open
bar.

"Should he drink?" Carlie asked.

"I don't know." Thelma threw up her hands. "But he's
been such a bear to live with since he gave up cigarettes and
chewing tobacco, I'm not going to be the one to tell him to
lay off the drinks. At least not tonight."

"All right. We'll let him cut loose a little," Carlie said
with a smile.

Even though she'd spent two hours in the beauty shop
and was wearing a shimmery new green dress, Thelma
looked tired. Her days of working at the soda counter and
evenings of taking care of her husband were starting to tell.
Between her shifts she'd had to run Weldon back and forth
to the hospital for physical therapy and even though Carlie
helped out when she could, the strain was beginning to
show on Thelma's pretty face.

"Come on. You, too. Have a glass of champagne,"
Carlie encouraged her mother. "I'm driving, so you can
have all the fun you want. Come on. All your friends are
here. It's a party."

"Fun—" her mother started to complain, but changed
her mind. "All right. Don't mind if I do." Her lips twitched
and she headed off to the champagne fountain.

Carlie saw people she'd known all her life and stopped to
speak to old classmates and friends, but she couldn't help
searching the crowd, hoping to find Ben. She allowed herself one fluted glass of champagne and mingled with the
other guests.

"Glad you could make it." Thomas Fitzpatrick's voice
was a gentle whisper behind her.

"Wouldn't miss the social event of the season," she said,
turning to face him. His wife, June, stood fifty feet away,
her inflexible back turned toward her husband as she chatted with a wasp-thin woman in purple and an elderly man.
The woman was a reporter for the *Gold Creek Clarion*. The
man with her owned the newspaper.

"Oh, this isn't the event of the season," Thomas said
proudly. "Just you wait until the wedding. *That* will be

something. Oh, here they come now." He touched Carlie lightly on her upper arm and pointed to the top of the stairs where Toni, in a shimmering silver dress, was speaking with a tall blond man of around thirty. An engagement ring with a huge, sparkling diamond graced Toni's hand.

"That's Phil," Thomas said as he gazed at his future son-in-law. "Phil Larkin, attorney, stockbroker and financial whiz kid."

"You like him?"

"Couldn't be more pleased if I'd hand-picked him myself, which, come to think of it, I did. Introduced the two of them last year. Phil's father—you remember Kent Larkin—was a state senator in the sixties, and Phil's ambitious. He could follow in Kent's footsteps."

"I suppose," she said, shifting to put a little distance between her body and his. Thomas dropped his hand from her arm as casually as if he hadn't known he was still touching her.

Thomas had always been interested in politics. Just before Roy was killed, Thomas had considered running for office himself. Now, if his future son-in-law's dreams were realized, Thomas would have an ear to the state legislature and a doorway open to push in his ideas. It all depended upon Phil and how much he wanted to please his soon-to-be father-in-law.

"When's the wedding?" Carlie asked, trying to make small talk.

"Around Christmas, if all goes as planned." His lips tightened a bit as he watched his daughter. Toni flung her blond curls over her shoulder rebelliously and with a pout, started down the stairs without Phil. He scurried to catch up to her, his face red in embarrassment. Toni didn't seem to care. She mingled with the crowd, smiled and seemed to ignore the man of her dreams.

A blast of February wind seeped inside and Carlie glanced behind her as one of the pairs of French doors opened. Ben, dressed in a black tuxedo, walked into the room and Carlie's heart kicked. His hair was slightly mussed from the wind, his cheeks dark, his expression thunderous. As if he knew exactly where she was, he glared in her direction, grabbed a drink off the tray near the door and took a long swallow. His gaze shifted for a second on her companion and his scowl deepened as he began threading his way through the crowd.

So he was jealous. Carlie didn't know whether to be angry or flattered. She started to excuse herself from Thomas and meet Ben, but Ben was intercepted by a petite woman with straight brown hair and a skin-tight white dress. *Tracy.* Carlie's face seemed suddenly tight. Thomas whispered something to her, but she missed it.

Tracy wound her arm through Ben's and beamed up at him.

Ben leaned over to whisper in Tracy's ear. She tossed back her head and laughed lightly, as if she adored him.

Carlie's heart seemed to turn to stone. She told herself to relax, Ben was only talking to Tracy. She had no rational reason to feel the jealousy that coiled around her insides. Besides, if anything, she should admire Tracy. She'd overcome the stigma of being an unwed parent and was struggling to raise her child and all Carlie could think about was the fact that she was already irrevocably tied to Ben. Somehow, some way, Carlie had to learn to deal with Tracy or else she had to accept the fact that she had no future with Ben.

Rather than watch Tracy beam raptly up at Ben another second, Carlie turned her attention back to Thomas. There was a change in his tone and she wondered if he noticed that she hadn't been listening. He touched her again, lightly on the hand and she managed a tight smile.

"Friend of yours?" he asked when she glanced back to find Ben still in conversation with Tracy.

"I've known Ben a long time," she hedged.

"I was talking about Tracy."

"Oh." She felt her cheeks grow warm. "I hardly know her."

"Good woman. Responsible. Takes care of her boy and holds down two jobs." There was genuine admiration in Thomas's voice.

"She's . . . industrious."

"Hmm. Like her father. One of my best employees. I've known Tracy since she was a little girl." He smiled again. "As I've known you." He sipped from his drink.

"I think I'd better go check on my mom and dad," Carlie said as an excuse to break free of Fitzpatrick when a group of men approached him.

As she walked past one of the huge pillars supporting the roof, a strong male hand clamped over her arm.

"Carlie." Ben's voice was a harsh whisper. She turned and found him glaring at her, the back of his neck a deep shade of red, his lips white and thin. "Having a good time?"

"Good enough," she replied, bristling a little at his anger.

"With Fitzpatrick?"

"He cornered me."

"And you ate it up."

"Are you crazy?" she demanded, keeping her voice low. "I was just being polite."

His eyes narrowed on her and, as if realizing that they might be overheard, he took her hand and led her quickly through a knot of men who had clustered near a baby grand piano positioned near the front doors. The men were in a heated discussion of taxes and politics and were raising their voices over the mellow notes of "I Will Always Love You" being played by the band.

Ben shoved on the handle, opening the door, and drew her outside where the chilly February wind cut through her dress and brushed her face.

The door clicked shut. "I don't know how many times I have to warn you about him!" he growled through clenched teeth.

"Get over it, Ben," she shot back. "I'm not a sixteen-year-old virgin who can be manipulated and taken advantage of."

His shoulder muscles bunched beneath his jacket. "Fitzpatrick wants something from you."

"Like what?"

"Take a guess." When she didn't answer, he said, "Fitzpatrick's looking for a mistress. You seem to be top on the list."

"Give me a break!" she said, but remembered the lingering touches and the dark glances that Thomas had cast in her direction.

"The man's had affairs all his life. You don't need to be a genius to figure that out. Jackson Moore is proof enough. And now Fitzpatrick's wife has filed for divorce, or at least that's the rumor going about the logging company, so guess what? Good ol' Tom is going to have his freedom."

"I'm not interested."

"He's a wealthy man, Carlie."

"I should slap you for that one."

"A powerful man."

"Oh, come on—"

"He could give you everything you'd ever want."

Stung, she turned on her heel. "I don't have to listen to these insults!" She tried to push past him and reached for the brass lever of the doors, but Ben grabbed her again. Before she could say anything, he yanked her roughly to him, slanted his lips over hers and kissed her with all the passion and anger that stormed through his blood. His lips were hot and hard and demanding, his body lean and firm.

She jerked away, anger still coursing through her blood. "Don't drag me out here, insult me and then think you can make it all better by kissing me!" she said.

"Nothing's better."

"You're damned right. I don't like being manhandled, Ben. Not by you. Not by anyone. So cut out the Neanderthal macho routine!"

His eyes flashed fire, but he released her. "Oh, hell, Carlie, I didn't mean to insult you." He drew in a deep breath of the wintry air. "I'm just warning you about Fitzpatrick."

"I don't need a mother."

"I'm not—"

"Or a baby-sitter."

"Carlie—"

"Shh. I don't even need an older brother, Ben. I can take care of myself."

"Can you?" His voice was suddenly low and sexy. "Maybe I don't want to think that you're so damned independent. Maybe I want to think that you need a man."

"Are you applying for the job?" she asked, her anger beginning to fade.

"I'd like to."

She stood on her tiptoes and brushed her lips gently across his. "I'm a big girl now."

His grin, a slash of white in the darkness, was wicked and sensual. "I've noticed." His lips found hers and his hands spanned her waist. "Let's ditch this party."

"Mmm, I can't," she said with genuine reluctance. "I promised Mom and Dad I'd drive them home."

"Later?"

She wanted to say yes, to beg him to meet her at her apartment, but she held her tongue. She remembered their argument about Tracy, about the past, about Thomas Fitzpatrick. "Soon," she promised, closing her eyes and drinking in the smell of him—of soap and champagne and some musky cologne.

His lips found hers again and her head began to swim. Her eyes closed and desire pumped through her blood. She wondered what the future would bring, but steadfastly shoved all her cloying doubts into a dark corner of her mind. She was caught in the wonder and magic of loving him.

Slowly she opened her eyes and saw, through the steamy glass of the French doors, a woman in white. Tracy Niday, her eyes squinting through the glass, her jaw set in renewed determination was staring at them. A chill, deep as the February night, passed through Carlie's bones.

Carlie drew back from Ben's embrace, but he groaned and pulled her close again, his lips hot and wet against her own. She fell willingly against him and when she looked back to the glass, Tracy had disappeared.

"We can't do this all night?"

"Not here."

"Come home with me."

"I will, but not tonight," she said, regret heavy in her voice.

"I'll hold you to it."

"You'd better."

Ben took Carlie's hand as they walked back into the dining room. Though Tracy was drinking champagne and flirting with several of the men collecting near the open bar, Carlie was certain that Tracy knew the exact moment they'd walked inside.

Telling herself she was being petty, Carlie turned her attention back to the party. She talked to some friends, avoided any more champagne and held Ben's hand. His eyes sparkled when he asked her to dance and she couldn't say no. Other couples, including Hayden and Nadine, swept around the floor. Nadine looked radiant. Her red hair was piled in loose curls on her head and her dress, black silk with rhinestones, caught in the light. The newlyweds laughed and talked as they danced, and when they passed Ben and Carlie, Nadine winked, as if at a private joke.

"What was that all about?" Carlie demanded.

"Just my sister's perverse sense of humor."

"Meaning—"

"Meaning nothing." He held Carlie tighter and gazed into her eyes. "Just dance with me, lady. Forget about everything else."

She did. Snuggled in the warmth of Ben's embrace, she listened to the music and the beating of his heart and the muted sounds of conversation and tinkling glass. It was all so perfect, so romantic...

"I never want to see you again!" Toni Fitzpatrick's voice rang through the dining room.

The band stopped playing, instrument by instrument. Conversation lapsed. Carlie and Ben froze on the dance floor and turned, with the rest of the crowd, toward the ice-sculpture and the couple standing next to it: Toni and Phil, for whom this lavish party was thrown.

So furious she was shaking, Toni yanked off her diamond ring and hurled it across the room. "Never!" she repeated amid gasps and whispers and shocked expressions.

"Toni, please—" Phil said, his face as red as the lobster tails being served on the opposite side of the room.

"Get out! Just get the hell out!" Toni screamed, then realizing where she was, ran up the stairs. Tears streamed from her eyes and Thomas, lithe as a jungle cat, took off after her.

"I'm sorry," Phil said to the crowd as a whole and June Fitzpatrick, who was suddenly white as a sheet, waved impatiently to the bandleader, who cleared his throat and began playing a love ballad. The rest of the band joined in, adding a soft harmony to the hushed speculation that buzzed through the guests.

"I wonder what that was all about," Carlie whispered as Phil collected the ring and hurried up the steps.

"Looks like Toni got cold feet." Ben took her into his arms again. "I'm not surprised. She's a rebel and Phil Larkin is too buttoned-down for her. A lawyer and stockbroker? Boring combination."

"Jackson's a lawyer."

"Jackson deals with interesting cases. I read where he just got some oil heiress off the hook. The D.A. backed off."

"Alexandra Stillwell," Carlie said, remembering an earlier conversation with Rachelle. "The D.A. had originally thought she'd killed her father. Turns out Jackson found evidence proving she couldn't have done it." She arched an eyebrow at him. "Sound familiar?"

"Too familiar."

Her mother found her. "Can you believe that?" Thelma asked, motioning to the stairs. "Walking out on your own engagement party? That Toni always was a wild one. I know, too. Saw her cutting school and hanging around the drugstore, smoking cigarettes when she should have been in class." Thelma clucked her tongue. "Look, I think your father's about all in—" She glanced at Ben and her spine stiffened slightly.

"The party's about over anyway," Carlie said. "Mom, you remember Ben."

"I've heard that Carlie's been seeing you again," she said, her words clipped with old resentment. "I'd like to tell you that I approve because I believe that bygones should be bygones, but I remember—"

"Mom, please," Carlie cut in, realizing too late that her mother's tongue had been loosened by the champagne.

Thelma's face clouded over. "I just don't want to see you hurt again," she said, and Ben shoved his hands in his pockets.

"Look, Mrs. Surrett," he said, his features sober, his gaze sincere as he met Thelma's. "I know I made some mistakes, some big ones where Carlie is concerned. I won't insult you with excuses. I can only tell you that I won't be making the same mistakes twice."

"I hope not," Thelma replied and walked to the elevator where her husband was waiting for her.

"I've got to go," Carlie said.

"Me, too." Ben squared his shoulders. "While I'm mending fences, I may as well fix them all." He walked with her to the elevator and met Weldon's harsh glare with his steady gaze. He looked like a captured soldier walking into an enemy headquarters, Carlie thought as she noticed the tension in all of Ben's muscles. He extended his hand to her father who, after a second's hesitation, clasped it. "Mr. Surrett."

"Powell." Weldon's mouth tightened.

After a few minutes of small talk as Ben inquired into Carlie's father's health, Weldon said, "You may as well know, I told Carlie she should stop seein' you. It's the same advice I gave her ten years ago, and I think it still stands."

"I hope to prove you wrong."

"You can't, boy," he said, shaking his head and motioning for his wife to hit the elevator call button. "It's not in your nature."

"I might surprise you."

"I hope so." The elevator landed and a bell chimed softly. As the doors whispered open, Thelma pushed her husband into the waiting car.

"I'll see you later," Carlie said to Ben.

"When?" Ben held on to Carlie's arm while her mother impatiently pressed the door Open button and waited.

"Call me."

Ben let her go and Carlie slipped into the waiting car. The doors began to close and Carlie watched as Ben walked toward the stairs only to be caught in midstride by Tracy Niday. The doors closed, blocking her view.

Carlie's heart squeezed.

"I saw him with her earlier," Thelma said as the elevator began moving upward.

Weldon agreed. "So did I. She'll always be a part of his life, honey." He reached for his daughter's hand. "Because of that boy of hers."

The elevator stopped on the main floor and Carlie was left with the sinking sensation that her father was right. As long as Randy needed a father, Tracy's sights would be set on Ben.

Chapter Eleven

Ben watched the backhoe gouging out huge chunks of mud from the excavation site. He'd been lucky. The weather had broken and it looked as if the concrete foundation for Nadine's cabin could be poured in the next couple of weeks.

All in all, things were going well. Work on the Hunter apartment house would be finished by the middle of March, this cabin would take him through part of the summer and the projects at the logging company would keep his subcontractors busy throughout the spring.

So why was he so restless? The answer was obvious. *Carlie.* The woman he didn't know whether to love or hate. When she'd first returned to Gold Creek, he'd been certain that she was a user, a gold digger, a callous woman who stepped on men's souls. Then, as the weeks had passed and they argued about the past he'd seen a new side to Carlie— a side that beguiled him and told him that he'd made a mistake about her in the past. Then he'd made love to her and that lovemaking had been as soul-wrenching and earth-shattering as it had been eleven years ago. He'd thought he'd lost his ability to become so involved in a woman, but he'd been wrong. He could feel that same exhilaration. But only with Carlie.

Damn it all anyway! He kicked a stone with the toe of his work boot and wondered what the hell he was going to do about her.

He should trust her, get over the past, start fresh. That's what he wanted to do, and last night, when he held her in his arms and kissed her on the veranda of the country club, it had been all he could do not to pull her into the shadows beyond the interior lights and make love to her over and over again. She was in his blood, in his mind, and... it seemed, in his heart.

He was about to make the same mistake with her as he had in the past. His destiny, it seemed.

So why was she having dinner with Thomas Fitzpatrick?

Because Fitzpatrick was interested in her, and had been from the moment she set foot back in Gold Creek. Ben had noticed the way Fitzpatrick had watched Carlie on the dance floor, his old eyes following her every move as he'd pretended interest in another conversation.

He clenched his jaw so hard that it began to ache. "Son of a bitch!"

"Ben! Hey, Ben!" Ralph Katcher slogged through the mud. "Lookin' good here, eh?" He stopped to stuff some tobacco behind his gum.

"Better," Ben allowed.

"Hell, yes, better. A damned sight better. You know, I think you might just end up a solid citizen of Gold Creek. End up on the board of the chamber of commerce. You and Thomas Fitzpatrick!"

"That'll be the day," he said. They shared a cup of coffee from his thermos, then Ben drove off to check the other jobs he'd contracted.

All the work looked good at the Hunter house. He hung out for a while, spending more time than necessary checking the finishing touches, hoping that Carlie would show up. When she didn't arrive, he headed out to the logging company offices and told himself over and over that Thomas Fitzpatrick's money was the same color as anyone else's. However, dealing with Fitzpatrick burned a hole in his gut. He'd never forgiven him for being part of the scheme that had fleeced his father out of his life savings— and he didn't trust him now. With Carlie.

It was probably just his imagination, but he'd seen how Thomas had looked at her at Nadine's wedding, read the unspoken messages in his eyes. Again, last night, in front of his family and all the guests at the engagement party, Thomas had made a beeline to Carlie and hovered around her. Later, as she and Ben had danced, Fitzpatrick had eyed them. Then there was the sudden interest in the apartment house where Carlie lived. Why would Fitzpatrick want the old building?

Fitzpatrick was also throwing a lot of work Carlie's way, which wasn't a big deal in and of itself, but the fact that there were so many other strings that tied Carlie to him made Ben sweat. There was also the business with her dad. Fitzpatrick was playing God on that one, teasing a sick old man with his pension and retirement benefits.

Ben didn't like it. It smelled bad. But his hands were tied. Carlie, damn her, insisted upon being her own woman and she'd have to learn about Fitzpatrick on her own.

His teeth gritted and he told himself to forget it, but a black mood settled over him.

He drove home, changed quickly and after feeding Attila and skimming a Frisbee through the air for fifteen minutes, he left the dog in the yard and climbed into his truck again. But he hesitated before switching on the ignition. He wasn't looking forward to the evening in front of him. Tracy had called him on the car phone and invited him over and Ben hadn't found the spite in him to refuse. She'd wheedled and explained that Randy would really like to see him again after the disaster of Little League tryouts, so Ben had bowed to his own guilt and agreed to take them both to a restaurant and a movie. Tracy hadn't been able to hide the smile in her voice and Ben felt trapped.

He picked them up at six and they drove to the outskirts of town where they stopped at the Burger Den for triple-decker cheeseburgers and spicy fries. Randy ordered a large root beer milk shake and though his mother teased him about breaking training, she let him have the drink anyway and Ben was relieved. He didn't want to get into another discussion about child rearing. Randy was her kid and she had the right to raise him as she saw fit, as long as she didn't harm the boy.

They laughed and talked and Ben wondered why he'd felt so ill at ease earlier. Tracy was her most charming and she smiled at him often, her brown eyes twinkling, her full lips stretching into a sexy grin.

But Ben couldn't stop thinking about Carlie. Throughout the evening, no matter what direction the conversation took, his mind wandered and he wondered where she was. Tonight she was supposed to be meeting Fitzpatrick for a business dinner. Just the thought of it curled Ben's insides.

"Is something wrong?" Tracy asked, snapping him back to the present.

"Nothing."

She stared pointedly at his half-eaten cheeseburger. "Nothing?"

"Nothing that matters." He grinned at Randy. "Hurry up, sport. The movie starts in twenty minutes."

The film was an action/adventure film that featured teenaged stars Randy recognized from television. Randy ate popcorn from a tub and watched raptly and Ben tried to show some interest in the thin plot, but his mind continued to wander to Carlie. Always to Carlie. He felt like a traitor being here with Kevin's family, and yet there was no way out of this particular emotional entanglement—at least no easy way. He slid a glance at Randy and the kid looked at him and smiled—Kevin's smile.

Tracy touched him on the arm and he nearly jumped out of his skin.

"Where are you?" she whispered.

"Here."

"More like a million miles away."

"Got a lot on my mind."

"The business?" she asked hopefully.

"That's a big part of it."

"And the rest?"

Even in the darkness he could see the worry and sadness in her eyes. "Nothing important," he lied and glanced at his watch.

When he dropped them off at their apartment, Randy grinned at Ben and thanked him for the "good time."

"My pleasure."

Randy glanced at his mom. "Aren't you coming in?" he asked Ben.

"Not now."

"But...you'll be back?"

Ben felt as if Randy had been coached, but smiled and ruffled the kid's hair anyway. "Sure I will."

"When?" Tracy asked.

"I'm not sure."

"We're free tomorrow," she said lightly though Ben thought he detected a hint of desperation in her voice.

"Tomorrow doesn't work for me."

She waited hopefully.

"I'll call." He felt like a heel as he read the skepticism that flickered in her eyes.

"Good. Now, Randy, you go on inside and I'll be there in a minute," she said. "I need to talk to Uncle Ben alone." She handed her son her keys and Ben tensed, watching as the boy slipped through the door.

"He's a good boy, Tracy," he said. "I guess I already told you that."

"He thinks a lot of you."

"Not too much, I hope."

She ran a finger along the truck's fender. "You're the best thing that's happened to Randy...and to me...in a long, long while."

"I don't think so."

"Oh, yes. He lights up like a Christmas tree around you, Ben, and I know why." Before he knew what she was doing, she placed her hands on his shoulders, stood on her tiptoes and brushed his lips seductively with her own. Ben tried to step away just as her tongue pressed against his teeth.

"Tracy, don't—" His fingers curled over her waist but not before she traced the edge of his lips with her tongue.

"Why not, Ben?" she asked petulantly, her smile taking on a feline curve. "We could be good together, you and I."

"I can't."

"Sure you can."

"I'm already involved with someone," he said, firmly shoving her away from him.

She looked stunned, but just for a second. She would have had to have been blind at the engagement party not to have seen him with Carlie. Besides, Carlie had been with him at Randy's Little League tryouts. Surely she understood.

"I . . . I . . . guess I made a fool of myself."

"No—"

"It's just that I've been so lonely," she said suddenly as if a dam of emotions had cracked and burst. She blinked against a rush of tears. "I've dated a lot of men, but they . . . Well, they never seemed to measure up to Kevin and then you come back to Gold Creek and you're so . . . Oh, damn, look, I'm sorry." She sniffed loudly. "But, please, don't blame Randy for this. He really does like you, and just because his mother had the uncanny ability to make an ass of herself . . ."

"You didn't," Ben said and reluctantly folded her into his arms. "It was a mistake. I should have told you."

"No, it's all right. Really. Just . . . just don't stop seeing Randy." She took in a deep breath and her gaze shifted away from his for just a second. "I've seen you with Carlie and I, um, hope that you don't end up getting hurt."

"You don't have to worry about that."

"But I do. I care about you, Ben," she said blinking rapidly as if she were going to break down and cry. "You see, I, uh, know some things about Carlie that you might not."

"I'm not interested in gossip," he said defensively, but he felt more than a little worry. The look on Tracy's face convinced him that whatever her little secret about Carlie was, it was ugly.

"It's not gossip."

"Really. I'm not interested." Tracy was staring at him and measuring his reaction. Ben felt as if a thick hemp rope had been cinched around his neck. She was smiling, but it wasn't a kind smile. He stepped away from her and turned toward the truck. Fast. Before he heard something he didn't want to know.

"It's kind of private," she said but added quickly, "but I thought you should know since it involves you."

The noose tightened another notch. He grabbed the handle of the door.

"Did you know that when Kevin died she was pregnant?"

Ben froze. He could barely breathe.

"That's impossible," he heard himself saying, remembering Carlie's desperate eyes when she'd told him she'd been a virgin when they'd first made love.

"I saw her medical chart. At the Coleville Women's Clinic," Tracy said as he turned and saw a glimmer of a smile flit through her eyes. She was enjoying this! "Yep. Carlie was definitely with child."

Ben whirled, grabbed her by the arms and gave her a quick little shake. His fingers dug into her flesh. "You're lying. I don't know why, but—"

"It's not a lie, Ben. Think about it! What would I have to gain by lying to you? I'm not a nurse or a doctor, but I can read a medical chart if it's spelled out to me, and she was pregnant."

"What happened?" he demanded, not releasing her.

"She lost the baby. Miscarried, I guess. Maybe had an abortion. As I said, I didn't have a lot of time and—"

"You lying bitch—!" He dropped her as if her skin burned his hands.

"Oh, no, honey, you've got the wrong woman. You should be saying things like that to Carlie. After all, you had the right to know about your kid."

"My kid?" he said, his voice barely a whisper. "My kid?"

"Sure." She lifted her shoulders. "Whose do you think it was?" she asked lightly, then blanched when she saw the answer in his eyes. "Oh, God, not Kevin's..."

He didn't wait to say goodbye, just spun on his heel, yanked open the truck door and jumped in behind the wheel. *His baby? His? Carlie was pregnant with his baby?* A thousand thoughts raced through his suddenly throbbing head. But she'd sworn she'd never been pregnant! Who was lying? Tracy or Carlie?

He shoved the truck into gear and took off with a squeal of tires. Tracy was left standing in the parking lot of her apartment building and from the corner of his eye Ben noticed a curtain move in Randy's bedroom. The kid had probably witnessed the entire scene between Ben and his mother. What would he think? Ben couldn't begin to guess. He slowed for the street, then gunned the engine. He couldn't feel responsible for Tracy and Randy...well, not too responsible. They'd gotten along all right without him for all of Randy's life; they certainly didn't need him now.

He drove to Carlie's house like a man possessed, but when he arrived, he had to wait. She was out with Thomas Fitzpatrick. Impatiently Ben jammed his own key into the lock and climbed the staircase to her apartment. It was time they had it out.

Carlie knew she'd made a vast mistake when Thomas insisted that they go to dinner in the company helicopter.

"You're not serious," she'd said, as he'd driven her to the offices of the logging company and the flat stretch of ground where a chopper sat, pilot ready, to speed them to a hotel in San Francisco.

"I'm very serious," he said and her heart sank as she stepped aboard and saw two bottles of champagne chilling in a bucket. Once they were airborne, he offered her champagne, but she declined. Ben had been right, she realized, and wished she could change plans that had been set for nearly a week.

The view from the craft was beautiful. A full moon added luster to the dark skies and the lights of the city brightened the horizon. They landed gently and Thomas helped her through the doors of the hotel and down to a private dining room that overlooked the Golden Gate Bridge.

The linen on the table was a rich mulberry color, the napkins snow white. A bud vase held a single rose. "What exactly do you want me to do?" she asked when he presumed to order for them both.

"I told you. The pictures for the company—I've seen the first proofs and they're very good—and then there's the matter of Toni's wedding, if it's still on. After last night, who knows?" He sighed heavily and shook his head.

"We didn't have to come all this way to discuss wedding photographs," she said, taking a sip of wine.

His blue eyes caught in the reflection. "Well, I have a confession to make," he admitted, looking somewhat sheepish. "I wanted to be alone with you."

"With me?"

"My wife's divorcing me," he said flatly.

"So—"

"So I thought I could spend an evening with a beautiful woman without feeling guilty."

"Mr. Fitzpatrick—"

"Thomas, please." He reached across the table and took her hand in his smooth fingers. She thought then how unlike Ben he was.

"Just as long as we understand each other, *Thomas,* I don't like being manipulated."

"Did I manipulate you?"

"Not if this is strictly a business meeting, and if it is, I see no reason to discuss your marriage."

"The divorce will be final within the month."

"I'm sorry," she said as the waiter brought hot rolls and delicate salads garnished with tiny sprigs of asparagus. The waiter disappeared.

"No reason to be sorry. It's probably for the best. We started drifting apart years ago...when Roy was killed. Everything came to a head a few months ago when Jackson found out I was his father." Thomas frowned thoughtfully as if rolling old reels of memories over in his mind and for a second Carlie felt a jab of sympathy for a man who had tried so desperately to control and exploit the destiny of others only to lose sight of his own happiness. "June couldn't handle that. The scandal, you know. Things have gone downhill since then. Last night wasn't completely unexpected. Toni's going through a lot right now. Just when she's hoping to get married, her parents are throwing in the matrimonial towel."

She didn't know what to say and picked at her salad.

"So, let's talk about you. You've grown up, Carlie. I have to admit that years ago I was angry with you."

"Because you wanted Jackson to be blamed for Roy's murder."

Thomas sighed. "I didn't *want* it, Carlie. I thought it was what had happened. I would have supplied money for the best lawyers in town to see that he got a lenient sentence, but I truly believed that he'd killed Roy, either accidentally or intentionally. Whether he was my son or not, he had to face justice."

"But he was innocent."

"Thankfully," Thomas said, though the lines around his eyes deepened and Carlie remembered the fact that Brian's wife, Laura, had accidentally killed Roy.

The waiter cleared the salad plates and returned with the main course: a brace of quail on a bed of wild rice. Carlie said little and ate even less. Coming here had been a mistake. She should have listened to Ben.

Ben. Just the thought of him made her heart turn over.

"I'm thinking of buying Mrs. Hunter's apartment house."

"Is that so?" she said, trying to sound surprised.

"I like to preserve some of the unique architecture of Gold Creek."

"It's a beautiful house."

"I thought maybe you'd like to manage it for me."

"Pardon me?"

He smiled then, a practiced, patrician smile that had no warmth. "If you would manage the units—there're five of them with the studio, isn't that right?"

"Yes."

"I could give you a break on the rent. Perhaps your folks would like to move into Mrs. Hunter's place."

"Wait a minute—" Things were moving much too quickly.

"I'm just trying to help your father. I've talked to the attorneys and the accountants and the financial advisers and think that there's a way your father can collect disability for a little while, retrain for office work, at which time he'll be retirement age and be able to collect his full pension and benefits."

Carlie waited for the catch. "Have...have you talked this over with him?"

"Just this afternoon."

"And?" She held her breath.

"He seemed pleased. Even considered moving into the apartment house to be closer to you."

"If I stay," she said, setting down her fork. "Look, Mr.—Thomas, I appreciate everything you're trying to do for my family and I know you probably think you're doing me a favor by making plans for me, but I can't accept your offer."

"You haven't even heard it yet."

"I've heard enough. I have to live my life my way."

"Of course." He looked slightly offended. "I was only trying to help."

"Thanks, but I don't think I need any."

His nostrils flared slightly and if the waiter hadn't come to remove their dishes, she was certain he would have said something not particularly kind. They finished dessert in relative silence and afterward he helped her with her coat and his fingers trailed along her arm. She shrugged him off, told herself that she was imagining things, but when he brushed his lips to her nape, she whirled on him. "I'm not interested, Mr. Fitzpatrick."

Fortunately, he didn't press the issue but the helicopter ride back to Gold Creek seemed to take forever. She didn't notice the moon or the stars or the lights of the city. When they finally touched down it was all she could do not to bolt from the chopper.

He helped her into his white Cadillac and she sat stiffly on the leather seats.

Ben had been right. She should never have accepted anything that seemed to remotely resemble a date with Fitzpatrick. She stared out the window, listening to the radio and was thankful Thomas didn't want to make small talk. All she wanted was to get home.

Home. How would she feel when the old house where she lived was owned by Thomas Fitzpatrick? One more way to be indebted to the man. Would she ever feel safe, knowing that he had a key to the house as well as her apartment?

She slid a glance in his direction. She wasn't afraid of him, at least not physically. But powerful men could exert their force in other, more subtle ways. Her father's job had already become an issue. Her work, now that she'd done a photographic layout for him, if he didn't like it, could suffer. He had the means and the power in a town the size of Gold Creek to ruin her reputation and to make her work dry up.

There was still the studio, of course. Loyal customers wouldn't be aware that Fitzpatrick was unhappy with her work, but the larger clients, the CEOs of corporations who might want a photographer could be swayed if the word was out that Fitzpatrick, Incorporated was unhappy with her work.

Too bad. She wasn't going to back down or be afraid of anyone, including Thomas Fitzpatrick. If she had to, she could call Constance about that modeling assignment with Cosmos Jeans.

At her apartment, he started to get out of the car, but Carlie said, "Don't bother. I've been thinking, and I've decided that it's probably not a good idea to work with you."

"But—"

"This evening proved one thing to me. I don't need you, Mr. Fitzpatrick, and I won't be manipulated into doing everything you want."

"I didn't mean to imply—"

"You did. You have, since I returned. I'm sorry your personal life is a mess, but there's nothing I can do about it and I'm tired of veiled threats or promises or whatever you want to call them, about my dad. Do what you have to do. Take it up with him. As for me, I'm through with you. This wasn't a business dinner tonight, it was a planned seduction."

She thought he'd argue, but he didn't. "If you're offended—"

"I am, Mr. Fitzpatrick, but if you want to know the truth, I'm more disgusted with myself than with you. I should have known better. Good night!" Before he could say anything, she slid out of the car, slammed the door and marched up the steps to her house. As far as she was concerned, Thomas Fitzpatrick was out of her life.

She'd call Constance in the morning and take the Cosmos job, and maybe she'd move back to New York once her father was well.

You'd be running away. From your family. From Fitzpatrick. From Ben. So what? It was her life. She wasn't forced to spend the rest of her years in Gold Creek.

As for Ben. He was better off without her! Her heart squeezed painfully, but she fought the urge to break down and cry. No more tears. She was in charge of her life now and she didn't have time for any more pain and broken promises.

Ben was waiting for her. Shoulder propped against the window, arms folded over his chest, eyes narrowed suspiciously, he waited, like a tiger ready to spring as she stepped into her apartment.

"What're you—"

"Close the door, Carlie," he commanded, his voice firm.

She kicked the door shut but didn't move. "What's this all about?"

"First of all, you just got a call."

She glanced to the answering machine and saw the red light blinking.

"Your friend Constance. Seems she thinks you might be going back to New York for a commercial."

So this was how it was going to be. She noticed his jaded gaze and the cynicism etched in the lines of his face. So he'd come spoiling for a fight. "You aren't here because you decided to be my answering service."

"No." He studied her face for a long moment. "Running back to the big city?"

"It's business. That's all."

His lips curved into a smile that was as cold as the bottom of the lake.

"What is it, Ben? What happened that made you think you should let yourself into *my* house and start making insinuations again? For your information—I don't need it. Not tonight. Not ever."

"There is another reason." The light in his eyes was deadly.

Carlie swallowed hard. "What?" she asked, though part of her didn't want to know. He was too cold, too calmly angry.

Shoving himself upright, he walked across the short space that separated them and stared down at her. His skin was tight, the muscles in his face so tense, they stretched rigidly across the angles of his face. "Tell me about the baby."

"What baby? I already told you—"

"You lied!" he said. "I want to know about *our* baby."

"Oh, God," she whispered, swallowing hard. *Our baby.* "How—how did you find out?"

"So it's true." The sound of his voice seemed to echo in the small room and through her heart.

She nodded, unable to trust her voice. The pain and disappointment in his eyes cut her to the quick.

"And you didn't tell me," he said. "Didn't you think I'd want to know? Didn't you think I had that right?"

"I did try! Over and over again!"

"Did you? Or did you get rid of it and hoped that I never found out."

"No!"

"You lying—"

"No! Oh, God, no!" she cried, anger mixed with her grief. "I wanted that baby more than I wanted anything in my life! And do you know why? Because that baby was a part of you. The only part I had left."

His eyes accused her of lying, but she didn't care. "I found out I was pregnant just before you left for the army. I tried to tell you, to phone you or write you or let you know, but you wouldn't take my calls and you sent my letters back unopened. I didn't know who to tell, who I could trust. Don't you remember, Ben? Kevin had just died and everything was such a mess."

She was shaking with the old memories, her heart turned to stone. "Then you were gone . . . and so was the baby."

He didn't move, just stood in silent judgment.

"So you did have an—"

"No! I miscarried!" She could feel his breath in two hot streams against her cheeks. "Damn it, Ben, I would have done anything, *anything* to keep that baby. To keep a part of you! But I failed," she said, her voice cracking. "I barely knew I was pregnant when you left, not much more than a suspicion. Then the doctor confirmed it and the next week . . . well, it was over."

"You should have let me know—"

"You wouldn't let me. And then it was too late."

A muscle worked in his jaw. "Was it too late the other night?"

"Yes!" she said vehemently. "After all the accusations you leveled at me when I first got back into town, I didn't think it would be such a good idea."

"So you were never going to tell me?"

"I hoped to, but not until I thought we both could handle it." Tears were hot against the back of her eyes. "I'm not sure that would have ever happened."

"Neither am I," he said, and without another word he stalked through the door and out of her life.

Chapter Twelve

Carlie stared down at the bustling street below. Cars, trucks and cabs jammed the intersection. Pedestrians, heads bent against the sleet, umbrellas vying for space, scurried along the sidewalk and spilled between parked vehicles. The noise of the city never quit. Horns blared, people yelled, engines thrummed, twenty stories below.

New York. So far removed from Gold Creek.

"Okay, that's it!" Constance said as she hung up the phone. A tiny woman with a big voice, she snapped the file on her desk shut with manicured hands and swiveled her chair to face Carlie. "The photographer is happy with the shots—well, as happy as Dino ever is—and it looks like the Cosmos campaign is rolling."

"Good," Carlie said, forcing some enthusiasm into her voice.

"So—can I start shopping you around again?"

Carlie had anticipated the question. Constance had been after her for years to resume her career. "I don't think so."

"For God's sake, why not? You're through with your soul-searching in Alaska, aren't you?"

"Yes."

"About time." Constance leaned back in her desk chair until the leather creaked. "So you're going back to that little town in California."

"I have to. Even if it's just to tie up a few loose ends...." she said, thinking of her father. Thinking of the studio in Coleville. Thinking of Ben.

"There's a man out there, isn't there?" Constance shook her head from side to side and didn't wait for an answer. "It's always a man."

"I just think it's time to stop wandering all over the planet."

"Sure you do, honey, sure you do."

The intercom buzzed and Constance picked up the phone. After a one-sided conversation, she set the receiver in the cradle and cast Carlie an I-told-you-so look. "That man who doesn't exist?" she said picking up the conversation as if they'd never been interrupted. "He's outside in the reception area, making a big scene, scaring poor Nina half out of her mind."

Ben? Ben was here? In New York City?

"You'd better go on out there because as angry as he is, he's still interesting. Nina mentioned something about signing him up as a male model."

"I wouldn't suggest it," Carlie said, grabbing her purse and throwing her coat over her arm. She hurried out the door and had started down the short corridor to the reception area, when she saw Ben, arguing with the petite strawberry-blond receptionist as he turned the corner.

Her heart caught at the sight of him.

Ben hesitated when he saw her, then continued down the hallway and took hold of her arm. "We're getting out of here."

"Wait a minute—"

"Now, Carlie."

She stopped dead in her tracks. "You can't push me around, Ben. Haven't you learned that yet? I don't know why you're here or what you want, but you can't come barging into my place of business, or my house for that matter, and start ordering me around like I'm some damned private in the army!''

By this time Nina and two leggy models sitting in the reception area were staring at them. The models had dropped their magazines and Nina was ignoring the phone that jangled incessantly.

Even Constance was watching from her office doorway.

"I just thought we could use some privacy."

"Why?"

His gaze slid to the other women in the room, then landed with full force on Carlie's face. "Because, damn it, I was going to ask you to marry me."

The women behind her gasped and even the phone stopped ringing for a few heart-stopping seconds. "What?"

"You heard me. Now, let's go."

"You . . . you want to get married?"

"Yeah. Right now, if we can."

"Oh, Ben, we can't—"

"Carlie, I'm sorry. For everything. I was wrong."

"But—"

"And I want to marry you."

By this time the phone had started up again but all eyes were still trained on her. She felt embarrassment wash up her neck. "But just last week—"

"I was a fool." He stared straight into her eyes. "A lot has happened since last week and the upshot is that I know that I don't want to spend the rest of my life without you."

"Are you out of your mind? I don't think—"

"Don't think," he whispered, grabbing her suddenly, his lips crashing down on hers, his arms surrounding her. He smelled of brandy and rain and musk and he held her as if he'd never let go. His kiss was filled with the same bone-melting passion that always existed between them, and when he finally let her go, she could barely breathe.

"Go on. Get out of here," Constance said from somewhere down the hall. "This man means business. And the rest of you, back to work."

Carlie hardly remembered the elevator ride down to the lobby of the office building. Somehow, with Ben's hand clamped on her elbow, he guided her outside and they braved the icy sleet and wind. Two blocks and around a corner, he held open the door to a crowded bar. They found a small table near the back and Ben ordered Irish coffees for them both.

"Okay," Carlie said, her heart still pumping, her ears still ringing with his proposal. "Start over. Why'd you come here?"

"For you."

"The last I heard you never wanted to see me again."

"I sorted some things out."

"Maybe you should sort them out for me," she said, trying to stay calm. She couldn't marry Ben. His temper was too mercurial, his mood swings too violent. True, she loved him, but that didn't mean she could live with him. Or did it?

"I was upset the last time I saw you," Ben admitted. "Tracy had told me about the baby—"

"Tracy?" Carlie whispered, aghast.

The waiter brought their drinks and disappeared.

"Seems she saw you at the Coleville Women's Clinic once and figured out about the baby."

"Oh, God," she whispered. "Look, Ben, I know I should have told you but there never seemed to be the right time."

"It's all right." He grabbed her hand and held it between his. "I, um, have done a lot of soul-searching the last week. I talked to Nadine and we found all Kevin's old letters up in a trunk she'd stored in the attic. I read them again, made a little more sense out of the past and realized that Kevin did kill himself over a woman, but the woman wasn't you. It was Tracy."

"You know this?"

"I had it out with her," he admitted, his face creasing into a frown. "She admitted that when she found out she was pregnant, he'd wanted her to get an abortion. She'd refused and pressured him to marry her. Also, he was having trouble at the mill, more trouble than we knew about. He was probably going to be fired or laid off. All that, along with the fact that he wasn't completely over you and I was seeing you, pushed him over the edge. He did kill himself, Carlie, but it wasn't our fault.''

"But what about Randy?" she asked, her throat closing.

"Randy will always be a part of my life. I told Tracy the same thing. If the kid needs me, I'll be there. Even when he doesn't think he needs me, I'll be in his face. The one thing that Tracy was right about was that the kid needs a father figure." He sipped his coffee. "And I'm going to be it."

Her heart swelled in her chest.

"But that doesn't mean I don't want kids—our kids. I do. Three of them."

"Three?"

"Well, four. That way two won't gang up on one."

"You've got it all figured out, don't you?" she whispered.

"Nope. Just a couple of ideas. I think we should figure it out together."

"You're serious about us getting married?" she said, still unbelieving.

With a half smile, he reached into the inside pocket of his jacket and withdrew a tiny box.

"What—?"

He handed her the box and she opened it. A single clear diamond winked up at her. "I'd like to say that I bought this eleven years ago and kept it all the time, 'cause I'd planned to go out and buy you a ring the night Kevin... Well, anyway, I didn't get around to it."

Her hands were shaking so he slipped the ring out of the velvet liner and slid it over her finger. "Will you marry me?" he asked and her throat was so full, she could barely answer.

"Of course I'll marry you, Ben. I've been waiting to hear you ask me for as long as I can remember...."

Epilogue

December

Carlie heard a soft cry and burrowed deeper under the covers before she was suddenly awake.

"Want me to get her?" Ben's voice was groggy.

"I'm up." She leaned over, kissed her husband and felt the milk in her breasts start to let down. "Coming," she whispered, nearly tripping over Attila who lay at the foot of the bed.

The cabin still smelled new, the scents of wood and paint lingering as Carlie picked up her baby and cuddled the warm little body to hers. She crept downstairs, turned on a switch that caused the tiny winking lights on the Christmas tree to sparkle to life.

In an old rocker, near the window, she held her daughter to her breast and smiled at the tiny face with sky-blue eyes and a cap of dark curls.

"Here you go," she whispered and kissed Mary on her downy head. From the window, she could look across the lake and see the mist rising over the water as dawn approached. She felt an incredible calm.

Nadine had insisted on giving them this cabin as a wedding present. Ben had declined of course, but worked out some deal with his sister so that they could afford to live here. Nadine, caught up with twin girls and preadolescent boys, had finally realized that she didn't need a second home.

It was satisfying, Carlie thought, smoothing one of Mary's downy curls with her finger. They were all parents now. Turner and Heather had a second little boy, the spitting image of his older brother, Adam, and Rachelle and Jackson were the proud parents of a son. A new generation for Gold Creek.

And though some couples had divorced, others had married. Ben's father, George, had married Ellen Tremont Little, and wonder of wonder, Thomas Fitzpatrick was squiring Tracy Niday around, though Carlie had little hope that their affair would blossom into anything other than what it was.

"Hey, you two, how about a walk?"

"Now? I'm in my robe," Carlie protested as she gazed up the stairs. Ben was dressed in jeans and his leather jacket and he was carrying a snowsuit for Mary and Carlie's long black coat. "It's freezing."

"We'll be fine."

Wondering what he was up to, Carlie finished feeding and changing her daughter, then put the infant into the heavy snowsuit. Ben and Attila were waiting outside on the porch. "I'll carry her," he said, taking the baby from his wife's arms and walking toward the lake.

The sun was rising over the mountains to the west and mist danced upon the smooth water. "What's going on?"

"Just honoring a time-honored tradition." At the shore, he bent down and scooped some water into his hand.

"You're not serious."

"Absolutely." He pulled a champagne glass from the pocket of his jacket, bent down and scooped some of the water from the lake, then held the glass to Carlie's lips. "I think we've been blessed by the God of the moon—"

"Sun," she corrected.

"Whatever. Drink. But not too much."

She sipped and then Ben took a swallow before dunking his finger and spilling a few tiny drops on his daughter's forehead.

"Hey—wait—"

"Christening her."

"I don't think Reverend Osgood would approve."

"I'm sure he wouldn't," Ben agreed, kissing his daughter on her cheek. "But we have a lot to be thankful for. This pipsqueak of a daughter, your father's new job at the Bait and Fish, the house—"

"Each other."

He smiled and sighed. "Each other." Slinging an arm around Carlie's shoulder, he held her close. Little Mary yawned and closed her eyes again.

Carlie rested her head against his shoulder and watched as the sun rose in the sky, turning the mist on the water's surface to a glorious white cloud—the ghosts of Whitefire Lake.

She closed her eyes and imagined she heard the sounds of native drums but realized it was only the steady, constant beating of Ben's heart.

* * * * *

Author's Note

A SHORT HISTORY OF
GOLD CREEK, CALIFORNIA

The Native American legend of Whitefire Lake was whispered to the white men who came from the East in search of gold in the mountains. Even in the missions, there was talk of the legend, though men of the Christian God professed to disbelieve any pagan myths.

None was less believing than Kelvin Fitzpatrick, a brawny Irishman who was rumored to have killed a man before he first thrust his pickax into the hills surrounding the lake. No body was ever found, and the claim jumper vanished, so murder couldn't be proved. But the rumors around Fitzpatrick didn't disappear.

He found the first gold in the hills on a morning when the lake was still shrouded in the white mist that was as beautiful as it was deceptive. Fitzpatrick staked his claim and drank lustily from the water. He'd found his home and his fortune in these hills.

He named the creek near his claim Gold Creek and decided to become the first founding father of a town by the same name. He took his pebbles southwest to the city of San Francisco, where he transformed gold to money and a scrubby forty-niner into what appeared to be a wealthy gentleman. With his money and looks, Kelvin wooed and married a socialite from the city, Marian Dubois.

News of Fitzpatrick's gold strike traveled fast, and soon Gold Creek had grown into a small shantytown. With the prospectors came the merchants, the gamblers, the saloon-keepers, the clergy and the whores. The Silver Horseshoe Saloon stood on the west end of town and the Presbyterian church was built on the east, and Gold Creek soon earned a reputation for fistfights, barroom brawls and hangings.

Kelvin's wealth increased and he fathered four children—all girls. Two were from Marian, the third from a town whore and the fourth by a Native American woman. All the children were disappointments as Kelvin Fitzpatrick needed an heir for his empire.

The community was growing from a boisterous mining camp to a full-fledged town, with Kelvin Fitzpatrick as Gold Creek's first mayor and most prominent citizen. The persecuted Native Americans with their legends and pagan ways were soon forced into servitude or thrown off their land. They made their way into the hills, away from the white man's town and the white man's troubles.

In 1860, when Kelvin was forty-three, his wife finally bore him a son, Rodwell Kelvin Fitzpatrick. Roddy, handsome and precocious, quickly became the apple of his father's eye. Though considered a "bad seed" and a hellion by most of the churchgoing citizens of Gold Creek, Roddy Fitzpatrick was the crown prince to the Fitzpatrick fortune, and when his father could no longer mine gold from the earth's crust, he discovered a new mode of wealth, and perhaps, more sacred: the forest.

Roddy Fitzpatrick started the first logging operation and opened the first sawmill. All competitors were quickly bought or forced out of business. But other men, bankers and smiths, carpenters and doctors, settled down to stay

and hopefully smooth out the rough edges of the town.
Men with names of Kendrick, Monroe and Powell made
Gold Creek their home and brought their wives in home-
spun and woolens, women who baked pies, planned fairs
and corralled their wayward Saturday night drinking men
into church each Sunday morning.

Roddy Fitzpatrick, who grew into a handsome but cruel
man, ran the family businesses when the older Fitzpatrick
retired. In a few short years, Roddy had gambled or
squandered most of the family fortune. Competitors had
finally gotten a toehold in the lumber-rich mountains surrounding Gold Creek and new businesses were sprouting
along the muddy streets of the town.

The railroad arrived, bringing with its coal-spewing engines much wealth and commerce. The railway station was
situated on the west end of town, not too far from the Silver Horseshoe Saloon, and a skeletal trestle bridged the
gorge of the creek. Ranchers and farmers brought their
produce into town for the market and more people stayed
on, settling in the growing community, though Gold Creek
was still known for the bullet holes above the bar in the saloon.

And still there was the rumor of some Indian curse that
occasionally was whispered by the older people of the town.

Roddy Fitzpatrick married a woman of breeding, a
woman who was as quick with a gun as she was to quote a
verse. Belinda Surrett became his wife and bore him three
sons.

Roddy, always a hothead and frustrated at his shrinking
empire, was involved in more than his share of brawls.
Knives flashed, guns smoked and threats and curses were
spit around wads of tobacco and shots of whiskey.

When a man tried to cheat him at cards, Roddy plunged
a knife into the blackguard's heart and killed him before a
packed house of gamblers, drinkers, barkeeps and whores.
After a night in jail, Roddy was set free with no charges
leveled against him by the sheriff, who was a fast friend of
the elder Fitzpatrick.

But Roddy's life was not to be the same. One night he idn't return home to his wife. She located Kelvin and they ormed a search party. Two days later, Roddy's body ashed up on the shores of Whitefire Lake. There was a ullet in his chest and his wallet was empty.

Some people thought he was killed by a thief; still oths decided Roddy had been shot by a jealous husband, but ome, those who still believed in the legend, knew that the iod of the Sun had taken Roddy's life to punish Kelvin itzpatrick by not only taking away his wealth, but the only hing Kelvin had loved: his son.

The older Fitzpatrick, hovering on the brink of bankuptcy, took his own life after learning that his son was ead. Kelvin's daughters, those legitimate, and those who vere born out of wedlock, each began their own lives.

The town survived the dwindling empire of the Fitzpaticks and new people arrived at the turn of the century. New ames were added to the town records. Industry and comnerce brought the flagging community into the twentieth entury, though the great earthquake of 1906 did much lamage. Many buildings toppled, but the Silver Horsehoe Saloon and the Presbyterian church and the railroad restle bridge survived.

Monroe Sawmill, a new company owned and operated by Hayden Garreth Monroe, bought some of the dwindling Fitzpatrick forests and mills, and during the twenties, thiries and forties, Gold Creek became a company town. The eople were spared destitution during the depression as the ompany kept the workers employed, even when they were orced to pay in company cash that could only be spent on oods at the company store. But no family employed by Monroe Sawmill went hungry; therefore, the community, vho had hated Fitzpatrick's empire, paid homage to Hayen Garreth Monroe, even when the forests dwindled, loging prices dropped and the mills were shut down.

In the early 1960s, the largest sawmill burned to the round. The police suspected arson. As the night sky rned orange by the flames licking toward the black heavns, and the volunteer firemen fought the blaze, the

townspeople stood and watched. Some thought the fire wa
a random act of violence, others believed that Hayde
Garreth Monroe III, grandson of the well-loved old man
had lost favor and developed more than his share of ene
mies when the company cash became worthless and the
townspeople, other than those who were already wealthy
began to go bankrupt. They thought the fire was persona
revenge. Names of those he'd harmed were murmured
Fitzpatrick came to mind, though by now, the families had
been bonded by marriage and the timber empire of the
Fitzpatricks had experienced another boom.

Some of the townspeople, the very old with long mem
ories, thought of the legend that had nearly been forgot
ten. Hayden Garreth Monroe III had drunk like a gluttor
from Whitefire Lake and he, too, would lose all that he held
dear—first his wealth and eventually his wife.

As time passed, other firms found toeholds in Gold
Creek, and in the seventies and eighties technology crep
over the hills. From the ashes of Kelvin Fitzpatrick's gold
and timber empire rose the new wealth of other families.

The Fitzpatricks still rule the town, and Thomas Fitz
patrick, patriarch of the family, intends one day to turn to
state politics. However, scandal has tarnished his name and
as his political aspiration turns to ashes and his once-envied
life crumbles, he will have to give way to new rulers—young
men who are willing to fight for what they want. Men like
Jackson Moore, Turner Brooks, Hayden Garreth Monroe
IV and Ben Powell. With strong women at their sides, these
men are destined to rule.

In Gold Creek, old names mingle and marry with new
but the town and its legend continue to exist. And, to this
day, the people of Gold Creek cannot shake the gold dus
of those California hills from their feet. Though they walk
many paths away from the shores of the lake, the men and
women of Gold Creek—the boys and the girls—can never
forget their hometown. Nor can they forget the legend and
curse of Whitefire Lake.

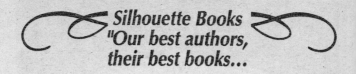

Silhouette Books
"Our best authors, their best books...

DIANA PALMER
Soldier of Fortune in February

ELIZABETH LOWELL
Dark Fire in February

LINDA LAEL MILLER
Ragged Rainbow in March

JOAN HOHL
California Copper in March

LINDA HOWARD
An Independent Wife in April

HEATHER GRAHAM POZZESSERE
Double Entendre in April

**When it comes to passion,
we wrote the book.**

BOBQ1

WHAT EVER HAPPENED TO...?

Have you been wondering when much-loved characters will finally get their own stories? Well, have we got a lineup for you! Silhouette Special Edition is proud to present a **Spin-off Spectacular!** Be sure to catch these exciting titles from some of your favorite authors.

HARDHEARTED (SE #859 January) That Special Woman!
Chantal Robichaux's baby is in jeopardy, and only tough cop Dylan Garvey—the baby's father—can help them in *Bay Matthews*'s tie-in to WORTH WAITING FOR (SE #825, July 1993).

SUMMERTIME (SE #860 January) *Curtiss Ann Matlock* introduces another of THE BREEN MEN when Oren Breen must convince the reluctant Lorena Venable that he's her man!

FAR TO GO (SE #862 January) One of the twins, Joe Walker, has his hands full when he's hired to protect the willful Lauren Caldwell in the latest from *Gina Ferris* and her FAMILY FOUND series.

SALLY JANE GOT MARRIED (SE #865 February) That Special Woman!
Sally Jane Haskins meets Cotter Graham, the man who will change her life, in *Celeste Hamilton*'s follow-up to her CHILD OF DREAMS (SE #827, July 1993).

HE'S MY SOLDIER BOY (SE #866 February) *Lisa Jackson*'s popular MAVERICKS series continues as returning soldier Ben Powell is determined to win back Carlie Surrett, the woman he never forgot....

Don't miss these wonderful titles, only for our readers—
only from Silhouette Special Edition!

SPIN3

CONVINCING ALEX

Those Wild Ukrainians

Look who Detective Alex Stanislaski has picked up....

When soap opera writer Bess McNee hit the streets in spandex pants and a clinging tube-top in order to research the role of a prostitute, she was looking for trouble—but not too much trouble.

Then she got busted by straight-laced Detective Alex Stanislaski and found a lot more than she'd bargained for. This man wasn't buying anything she said, and Bess realized she was going to have to be a *lot* more convincing....

If you enjoyed TAMING NATASHA (SE #583), LURING A LADY (SE #709) and FALLING FOR RACHEL (SE #810), then be sure to read CONVINCING ALEX, the delightful tale of another one of THOSE WILD UKRAINIANS finding love where it's least expected.

SSENR

Relive the romance...
Harlequin and Silhouette
are proud to present

A program of collections of three complete novels by the most requested
authors with the most requested themes. Be sure to look for one volume each
month with three complete novels by top name authors.

In January:	**WESTERN LOVING**	Susan Fox
		JoAnn Ross
		Barbara Kaye

Loving a cowboy is easy—taming him isn't!

In February:	**LOVER, COME BACK!**	Diana Palmer
		Lisa Jackson
		Patricia Gardner Evans

It was over so long ago—yet now they're calling, "Lover, Come Back!"

In March:	**TEMPERATURE RISING**	JoAnn Ross
		Tess Gerritsen
		Jacqueline Diamond

Falling in love—just what the doctor ordered!

Available at your favorite retail outlet.

REQ-G3

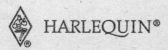